SUBWAY TO THE STARS

Book Two of the Subway Trilogy

Nathan B. Dodge

Cover designed by Laura Givens

Nathan B. Dodge
Visit my website at https://nathanbdodge.com/

Printed in the United States of America

First Printing: October 2021
1632, Inc.

eBook ISBN-13 978-1-956015-25-6
Trade Paperback ISBN-13 978-1-956015-26-3

CONTENTS

CHAPTER 1 BAD NEWS

We had not had a good evening. Kaley, aka Ms. Carol Sellers, had confessed her undying love for me some months ago, and declared she had every intention of marrying me. However, in the intervening months, my beloved had been pressured from pillar to post, always on the move, shuttling between the Jovian and Saturnian moons, Mars, Earth's moon, and even various Earth-based Subway portals, performing her main job, which was to serve as the world's greatest field technical expert for Subway Solar Systems.

I had been forced into an almost equally rigorous schedule, mainly trying to manage supplier relations as I attempted to get our many, mostly loyal, vendors to dramatically increase their production rates. Intersolar Command ("IC"), the US military unit which controlled military operations on off-world sites, was hounding us for every higher production, as they continued to increase the number of off-world portals as insurance against our still-possibly-active enemy, the Bugs.

No, I don't know the source of their new name, which sounds like a highly denigrating term, possibly even species-prejudiced, but after all, they sort of resembled oversized grub worms, and they did have a goal of eliminating all humans. After their possibly-accidental-but-probably-purposeful dial-in only last year to the lone Titan portal, plunging us into several months of war, the name had crept into the military, and then the civilian, lexicon. We thought we had eliminated the Bugs' presence in our solar system, but we were still getting phantom dial-ins to various portals, and the IC brain trust felt certain our new enemies were trying hard to forge a new portal to our solar system. As their home planet probably existed something between thousands and billions of lightyears from Earth—nobody knew for sure—that was more than likely their only possible pathway back into our solar system.

Entering our joint office—well, it's two offices connected by a double-wide door which is always open—I heard no clickety-click of Bobby pounding on his keyboard. Surprised, I cast about the area and found him leaning back on the small sofa in my office which sat against the back wall. His eyes were closed but one of his hands, scratching his nose, indicated that he was hard at work, grinding on some problem of interest.

Kaley and I were not holding hands. We weren't at war by any means, but there was a bit of frost in the air, relations-wise but not weather-wise, as on this bright March Thursday, the temp had started out in the sixties and might reach the low eighties. Such is the weather in Dallas in early spring—I had seen twenties in March, and I had seen nineties as well. March is a fickle month in Texas.

I had been pushing again, urging Kaley to set a date for our wedding. Unfortunately, Kaley moved slowly, at least when it came to romance. Yes, she didn't mind fooling around a bit, and she'd spent a couple of nights at my house recently. Despite the fact that she loved me, she was dragging her feet. I had not yet been able to pinpoint the reasons for her gun-shy behavior.

Hearing steps, Bobby sat up, shook his head, and focused on us. "You're late." He seemed to sniff the air. "Also, you've been arguing. What gives?"

Kaley shot a guilty glance at me, saying, "What are you talking about? We are *not* late."

"Yes, you are, by at least ten minutes. You're usually prompt. And you come in holding hands, and give each other such sweet, little 'I love you' looks that I almost have to hurl. But not today. Kaley's mad and you, my old friend Scotty, are a little steamed also."

"You're right," I told him as Kaley whirled on me. I didn't let her say anything. "No use trying to fool Bobby," I told her. "He knows what he knows."

Her eyes widened, but she stayed quiet. Probably because she knew if she said anything, she might regret it later. She turned back to Bobby. "Okay, Dr. Genius, sir, we've been arguing. You know the subject, I'm sure. You want to be our marriage counselor?"

Bobby, yawned, stretched his chocolate brown arms nearly to the ceiling, and lifted his towering, six-foot, nine-inch frame off the sofa. Bobby is a genius, gold-plated and certified, with an IQ that might be off the charts, except he won't take intelligence tests. He's one of the three driving forces behind Solar Subway Systems, which we refer to as "Triple-S" or "S-Cubed." I'm the second, making up for my lack of intelligence, at least compared to Bobby, with lots of drive and a good feel for the business of making and selling wormhole generators. Kaley is the third, not only my sweetie-pie but also the best field engineer/system debugger in the known universe.

"He wants to get married ASAP, but you're still having trouble believing he's in love with an old lady like you, so you're cautious—and scared," Bobby summarized.

"Now wait a minute—I'm no longer a teenager, but I—"

Bobby cut her off. "You worry about being so much older than Scotty, and although his affection leans more toward worship than love, you cannot believe it, and you're too scared to take the plunge. Boy, if I ever found a guy that would love me ten percent as much as Scotty loves you, I'd have him at the altar in ten minutes."

Bobby had uttered the one hundred percent truth, but my true love was beginning to look more than just irritated. I stepped in to deflect her anger. "It's okay, Bobby. I push too hard, and Kaley likes to think things over. You know as well as I do, we love each other, but it's been hard since the Bugs invaded. We're just now beginning to get back to normal."

Bobby hugged Kaley. With his arms around her, squeezing her pretty hard, she practically disappeared, and she is by no means a small person, standing about five-nine. "Sorry, love," he told her. "I just want you both to be happy."

Kaley squeezed back, leaning up to kiss his bowed cheek. "Yeah, I know it, you big doofus. It's just, after a lot of together time with Scotty, I feel a bit smothered, even though Scotty isn't a possessive guy. We'll work it out."

I started to second that, even though I was beginning to wonder if Kaley was too scared to take the leap. I was saved by the bell—my desk phone rang, and I peeled off across my office to answer it.

"Hays."

"Scotty? Kinsey McKissack."

Admiral—now vice admiral—Kinsey McKissack was one of the top ten officers in the United States Intersolar Command. Maybe the top five. The third star had been added to his epaulets because he now directed the USIC, the combination of US Army, Navy, and Air Force units that controlled our military presence across the solar system. IC, headquartered in Fort Worth, sat across the runway from Lockheed, the manufacturer that made the SF-77 space fighter, used by almost every country on Earth. IC included not only major installations on Mercury, Mars, and the moon, but also on the Jovian satellites Ganymede and Io, and Saturn moons Rhea and Titan, the base IC had re-established since the first invasion of the Bugs.

Our business with IC consisted of providing an increasing number of portal units, which allowed temporary wormholes to be created between bases on the various celestial bodies (and between many locations on Earth), allowing instantaneous travel between any two portals. Thinking back, I couldn't recall speaking to McKissack since we had been able to rid ourselves of the Bugs a few months ago.

"Good to talk to you, Admiral," I told him. "Hope you aren't having any problems with Triple-S products."

He harrumphed. "It's Kinsey, Scotty—and no, we don't have any problems, at least with S-Cubed. But we do have a problem. Could you and your team"—by which he meant me, Bobby, and Kaley—"come over here for a quick meeting?"

Anything for our best customer. "You get one of your portals to dial us up and we can be there ASAP," I told him.

He barked one of his frequent, sharp laughs. "We're dialing now."

So, it must be important. "See you in ten," I told him and disconnected.

Turning to my office-mates, I said, "That was McKissack. He needs us in his office five minutes ago."

That got me a couple of wide-eyed glances, but Bobby stood automatically. "Our best customer needs us, all he has to do is say so."

Kaley glanced toward me. "Do I need my travel bag?" She and I kept small cases in our offices for emergency trips to the outworld portal sites.

"It sounded urgent, but I think it's a local meeting, at least right now."

She nodded, causing her old-fashioned but very sexy, at least to me, bubble-do to bob back and forth. She grabbed one of my hands and one of Bobby's, and began to skip out, dragging us along, and singing "We're off to see the wizard." Bobby rolled his eyes but we submitted to the dragging.

Our lab portal had established connection with the IC base when we arrived, while Corey, one of our newer techs, stood by. He was slender, rather tall, and had hair so blond it verged on white, with a high tenor voice that told us, "A naval officer poked his head through and said some admiral or other was waiting for you."

Kaley laughed and said, "We make even the important people wait." He goggled, not sure if she were kidding or not, and frankly, neither was I. I refused to skip through the portal—Kaley had done it before—and shortly we stood outside McKissack's office. His aide, a rather short and serious naval lieutenant, who had brought us from the portal room and furnished our badges, directed us to McKissack's inner sanctum.

He came around his desk to shake hands, a gesture which indicated his regard for us as a unit. We had been able, perhaps with more luck than we deserved, to extricate IC (and the world) from a couple of dire situations. I hoped this summons didn't indicate another such problem. My hope was quickly dashed.

We took the three chairs before his desk as he resumed his seat. McKissack, tall, graying, and ramrod-straight, was a fair, measured, logical-thinking hard ass. He believed in straight-from-the-shoulder communication which came across as stern. I had no doubt within the inner workings of the military, he could be as Machiavellian as the next flag officer, but person to person, he was tough but fair. I liked him a lot.

"I ordered coffee," he said, "This is off the record, and classified. I don't have a lot of info, but I wanted to discuss the situation with the three of you to get ideas. How much do you know about the Shadow Network?"

I turned to stare at Bobby and Kaley, who stared back, Kaley vacant-eyed and Bobby with slitted lids.

"I don't know what you're talking about," Kaley said.

I'd heard the term, but as it was one of those concepts like the "dark web," or the "underground railroad," I had to admit I knew very little.

Bobby, on the other hand, knew quite a bit. I could tell by his expression. Never assume what a genius knows because he will always surprise you. There is absolutely nothing in the known universe that Bobby cannot become an expert on after thirty minutes of research.

He addressed Kaley. "The Shadow Network is a mythical entity. Some people think it doesn't exist. It's hardly talked about because few people know much about it. If it exists, it's a pirate portal network, probably started in Russia as a way to avoid having to pay for Triple-S services. There may be connections to China, the southeast Asian countries, one or more mid-eastern countries, and perhaps a bootleg group in Japan.

"These pirates—assuming that 'they' really exist—have apparently stolen plans for our portals and controllers and begun to build rogue portals that connect to some of the national networks of those countries. It was a way to create part of their portal networks at cut rates."

McKissack's expression had turned bemused, but he should have known better, as I said. Bobby didn't necessarily know everything, but he knew most things. The admiral repeated my thoughts. "Should have known you'd heard about it. You're right. Up to now, we couldn't even be sure such a portal network existed, but now we know."

"How so?" I asked.

He surveyed us. "Two days ago, one of our surveillance satellites picked up a Bug fighter buzzing over northeastern Siberia. Positive identification. So, where the hell did it come from?"

"Ah," Bobby said, sitting back. Kaley's eyes narrowed in sync with mine and I knew we were catching up.

"The thing is," Bobby continued, "the corners of the world in which the Shadow Network exists are sort of like the wild west a couple hundred years ago. No regulation, no rules, equipment cobbled together with bailing wire and chewing gum. Such portals can barely operate anyway, I would expect, let alone do what our network does to protect itself from Bug dial-ins. So, even though it's a piece of crap, it could get taken over and give the Bugs a new door to our solar system. Worst of all, for God's sake, it's right here in our own backyard."

"Mmm." McKissack cleared his throat, looked us over again, and said. "Quick on the uptake as usual. Yeah, you nailed it. The Bugs are keeping a low profile—the fighter was spotted at night, more than likely because they don't know about our wide satellite surveillance, or don't know how effective it is. Nail on the head, Dr. Taylor. It's appears to be a small beachhead, with a few of the enemy at present, but they're right in our backyard, as you said. We've contacted the Russians, but so far, no response. We have to move fast or we could be overrun quickly. I don't have to remind you how fast the Bugs can move."

"Not sure what we can do," I said. My mind was racing. Given that the Bugs had a base in Asia plus their speed in pushing an invasion, they could already be spreading out.

"On the military front, nothing," McKissack said. "I know you're always working on new portal technology. If you have any cooked up, we could use it now. We're trying to get more info. We're repositioning a number of satellites over Asia, searching for any traces of activity. Russia and China aren't happy about it, but because they know they might be in deep ca-ca, there's been no formal protest. They—or at least Russia—allowed the pirate sites to multiply, knowing it saved them a bunch of rubles."

"Their pirate portals have limited utility," Bobby observed. "They can connect to each other, and maybe a few portals in our network in those specific countries. Thing is, they would be forced to choose the rare times when no portal connect is scheduled for a few seconds. They still have to receive our sync signals and schedule around legitimate portal connections."

McKissack nodded. "True. However, they appear to be operating between the cracks of our formal system. Our problem is, with no control, or a lot less control over their portal network, and without the ironclad security systems we have, the Russians haven't been able to nip this problem in the bud. I think they're scared shitless and hoping we can help clean up their mess. Our sources seem sure countries like Russia that allowed the rogue portals either shut them down or are in the process of doing so but it's too late to stop the bugs from gaining a foothold."

I exchanged glances with my colleagues. "We need to think about this," I told McKissack. "I know you'll continue to monitor satellite surveillance to track any Bug movements you detect. We'll analyze this new threat and get back to you as soon as we have some answers."

I assumed I appeared as dour as McKissack and my colleagues. We stood, shook hands, and went back to headquarters.

CHAPTER 2 JUST THINKIN'

Back in my office, Bobby and Kaley commandeered the sofa near the window, while I sat in the somewhat worn but incredibly comfortable chair at my desk. Bobby leaned back, eyes closed, doing what I referred to as "grinding." That is, he was working hard on a problem, presumably concerning the Russian rogue portal, but I wasn't sure. The answer seemed simple to me—that is, the Russian government had to find the rogue portal (or portals) and destroy them, preferably ASAP.

But Bobby was really concentrating, meaning something about the issue had either caught his attention or had led to some other important concern. Either way, he had a major problem in his mental hands and he was giving it his full attention.

Kaley didn't say anything, but her eyes were fixed on me. That meant she had something else she wanted to discuss, out of the range of Bobby, either because she didn't want him to hear or she didn't want to disturb his grinding.

I stood. "I need coffee."

She came off the sofa in a flash. "Me too. Bobby?"

He didn't bother to open his eyes. "Black. Big. Hurry."

Our break room has a couple of Keurig units with various pods, as well as a commercial brewer that will make anything from espressos to lattes to extra strong coffees in carafes. I set the maker to do a full carafe of my favorite brand, loaded the beans, and initiated the grind/brew/fill cycle. Then I gave my true love the eye back.

"What gives?"

She made a sort of embarrassed shrug, but her voice came across clear and strong. "I do not want you, under any circumstances, going to Russia with IC forces to check out those pirate portals. Promise me."

I pooh-poohed her concern. "No problem. There isn't the chance of a snowball in hell the Russian leaders would ask for IC help. Ask for military help from another nation—admit you can't handle it yourself? No way."

"Okay, I'll accept that. Then I ask that you not go to any other country at IC's request to help hunt for Bug portals. Promise me."

I turned to check the brew process, then shifted back to her. "Hell, Kaley, you know I can't promise that! God knows how fast the Bugs could spread if they could make a beachhead here on Earth—and it looks like they have. What if they got a start in Japan? Or Australia? Or maybe in south or central America? Then what? You, Bobby, and I are the 'Big Three' in terms of field representation for Triple-S. Like it or not, our portals are the source of the problem. Period.

"They're a great boon to humanity, a way to make travel on Earth and throughout the solar system as easy as walking to the corner drugstore. But despite their advantages, humankind wouldn't have the Bugs as a problem if we hadn't invented the portals. With this newest problem, I wouldn't be surprised to see calls to cut off all portal travel—maybe ban portals completely. If we are to have a prayer of keeping a portal business going, all of us—you, Bobby, me, the rest of our employees—are going to have to do the bidding of IC to ensure we can reap the bonuses of portal travel without the problems."

Quite a speech for me. I ducked my head to the brewer, saw it was nearly full, snagged our cups, and prepared to pour.

As we walked back to the office, me with two cups, her with one, I remarked, "I'd listen to your requests more carefully if they were from my wife and not my reluctant girlfriend."

"Reluctant? I haven't been reluctant to be your girlfriend!"

"You've been reluctant to get married."

She didn't say anything for a moment. Just before we got to the office, she said, "That's a pretty low blow."

Bobby was still grinding, but he opened his eyes and sat up when he heard our footsteps. I handed over his cup, crossing to my chair, as Kaley sat beside him. I already regretted my nasty remark. It wasn't true—I'd listen carefully to anything Kaley said, one hundred percent of the time. I'd said it to turn the screws, dredging up our earlier argument, to get in the last word.

Kaley sat beside Bobby, drinking coffee and blinking. Not a good sign—she was either about to cry, not likely in Kaley's case, or cloud up and rain over us both, and it would be my fault.

Bobby had been too busy grinding to notice Kaley's unease. Now he said, "I've been thinkin'."

Kaley swallowed and said out of the side of her mouth, "What a surprise."

That stopped him. Wide eyed, he gave her a more detailed survey. "What's eating you? Some of our customers acting in their usual unpredictable way?"

Kaley continued to blink, so I stepped in before her cup (of resentment) ranneth over. "My fault. We argued and I was rather nasty."

Bobby refocused on me, a thorough inspection. "You? You're never nasty, well, not often."

I glanced at Kaley—still blinking—and back to Bobby. "You ever heard that old ballad, 'You Only Hurt the One You Love'?"

"No."

Of course not—it was hit from the 1940's, from a black singing group, the Mills Brothers, but it wouldn't have been anything that a teenager of either race would have heard twenty years ago. "Forget it, obscure reference. I said something nasty to the woman I love, continuing an earlier argument."

I turned to Kaley. "Please forgive me—my remark was nasty and stupid and beside the point. It's not like we aren't together a lot every week. I'm just anxious to get married, and you're not, and we are about as married as we can be without being married, so please forget I said it and I promise not to bring it up for at least a week. And by the way, I love you."

She blinked twice more, came over, and kissed me. She held on and I did too. "Just when I think you're a total jackass, you haul off and surprise me and say something really sweet," she said softly.

Bobby took a couple of large coffee sips, set his cup on the small table on his side of the sofa, and said, "Glad that's cleared up. Now, back to my point."

Arms still around me, she said, "Which is?"

"The more I think about it, the more convinced I am we can use a single portal to create a wormhole."

Kaley and I sat, her beside Bobby, me in my comfy chair.

"Wait," Kaley said. "Haven't we always known we can create a wormhole with a single portal? Isn't it what Ray, Wendy, and Grant did about twenty years ago when they discovered the wormhole effect?"

Bobby nodded. He had donned his patient, forbearing expression—that is, the facial map that said he would be happy to explain the obvious facts to us mere mortals, to whom they were *not* obvious. Just about any fact is obvious to him with a little thought. For the rest of us, a slow, detailed explanation is all that will help, and when that happens, I'm glad Bobby is a friend. Because, if he isn't your friend, and you ask a lot of stupid questions, he can be more than a bit snarky.

"Sure, sure," he conceded. "The thing Scotty and I have always come back to is when you connect two portals in the normal way, you always know the originating point and the destination, because it's the location of the two portals that are involved. In the case of a single portal, we know where the originating portal is, but where will the destination be?

"That was always the sticking point, but even though it will require some exploration and testing of such a portal maker, I think we can fix the destination portal location problem. It will require careful experimentation and tedious calibration, but with hard work, I believe we can make a single portal system that will open a wormhole to a desired destination. Within limits, of course. You won't be able to get the location down to the last millimeter, but maybe within, say, a few kilometers."

We stared at him. He loved to say new, outrageous things to prove he had licked a former technical barrier.

"Qualify 'within a few kilometers'," I told him. "Right now, portal-to-portal, we can go from exact spot to exact spot. Opening a portal in an approximate location might not only be dangerous to travelers but to whoever happens to be in the path of the wormhole."

He nodded. "I concede that, but for exploring the known universe, especially since we have yet to come up with faster-than-light travel, it might be the only way to go. It could be an easy method to explore new worlds. Think about it. You open a wormhole to a new, unexplored planet with room for the human race to expand, you send through a portal team in the same way our enemies, the Bugs have done, build a portal, and then you have easy access to the new world."

His idea was intriguing, although I still wasn't sure how easy it would be to direct a wormhole's far end to a desired destination with no portal but the originating end. If Bobby thought thus-and-so was possible, it more than likely was.

As I chewed over his summary, Kaley said, "Well, it sounds cool if you can make it work. We'll have to be careful so we don't accidentally dial in the Bugs' world. That could be a big problem all over—"

My desk phone ringing interrupted her. The display announced Admiral McKissack. Again.

I answered. "What's the word, Kinsey?"

He grunted. "It's not good. One of the areas in Russia near a pirate portal site has gone dark. Russian military is sending in troops prepared to shoot first and ask questions later. It's a smaller town near the Siberian border. I fear that the inhabitants are either dead, or soon will be due to the shitstorm that's about to rain down on their heads."

Just great. The operators of the illegal portal had not only brought the wrath of the Bugs down on those in the city, they'd guaranteed the Russian response would be large and lethal. Innocent bystanders were about to pay the price for Russia's lax control of their portal network.

"Any help we can provide?"

"Not really. The portal authority is about to kill the whole system as the Russians confront the threat and do their best to wipe out the Bugs' suspected installation and a helluva lot of the surrounding population. It's a friggin' mess. I expect a substantial part of Russian leadership will get booted out of the Kremlin because of this gaffe."

"When do you expect word of the result?"

"In hours. Some of our military leadership have been exchanging info. The other side is being fairly cooperative, as they realize they've created this disaster. I expect we'll need your help in the future, so that is why I'm keeping you in the loop."

He hung up, and I turned to the rest of our SSS leadership. "The Russians have identified the location of a possible Bug base, and they're going after it. I pity the Russian citizens who live nearby. Kinsey will keep us posted."

We stared at each other, faces wide with shock and concern. I suspect their thoughts mirrored mine: *Will these Goddam Bug problems ever go away?*

CHAPTER 3 ENEMY DIAL-INS

A weird rest of the day.

We had coffee, discussed the single-portal possibilities, had more coffee, and went out for a late lunch. Returning, Margie, our admin, had left a message from Admiral McKissack. Settling in our office, Bobby and Kaley again on the sofa and me reclining at about forty-five degrees in my chair, I returned the call.

I was told to hold and McKissack got on in about two minutes.

"Sorry to have to call again. I hope it's not a bother."

"Kinsey," I replied, "no call from our biggest customer is ever a bother. You have some news?"

His voice was neither bouncy nor upbeat. "Not good, I'm afraid. The Russian military discovered the Bug base and attacked. The Bugs had accumulated a solid thirty or so fighters—well camouflaged, I might add—and the Bugs did not go quietly. They had a small portal and were in the process of building one the size that they erected on Titan last year. Russia sent in hundreds of soldiers with guns blazing, air support, and even tanks. Obliterated the whole Goddamn site, killed all the Bugs. There were something like four or five hundred civilian deaths.

"Apparently the Russian military killed a fair number of those civilians, but the Bugs had already polished off half or more of the total population. There was substantial collateral damage, a lot of the dead were due to the Bug takeover of the rogue portal site.

"That's what little good news we have, and it's a mixed bag. Here's the bad news: Two more Russian sites have gone dark. A pirate site in southeast Asia is not responding. It sounds as though we have any number of Bug breakthroughs at the pirated portal sites. The bastards are getting what they deserve, but Earth is going to suffer as well."

Bobby spoke up. "Admiral, you need double or triple your current number of surveillance satellites to search for traces of Bug encroachment."

"You don't have to tell me. A military contingent of SF-Seventy-Sevens is launching with over two hundred small scanning satellites to cover the harder-to-inspect, more remote areas. You suspect the Bugs are spreading out, searching for obscure places to build additional portals." A statement, not a question.

"Yes, sir. They aren't going to build one in Times Square or Central Park. They'll try the Siberian plains, the outback in Australia, the African or South American jungles. We need top surveillance. Can you send me the feeds of those satellites, directly to S-Cubed headquarters?"

McKissack harrumphed. "Bobby, those feeds are extremely sensitive. Hell, *I'm* not supposed to see some of them without permission."

"I need them all. I hope I don't have to spout that old saw about permission and forgiveness."

McKissack paused and then gave Bobby a hearty har-har. "What the hell can you do with hundreds of feeds? You're smart and fast, but I'm not sure you're that fast."

"I've got video analysis software I developed, and it's really fast. Just forward me the feeds."

McKissack countered. "What about sending us the software? We got lots of computers and computer geeks that can use it."

Bobby was getting antsy with all the delays.

"Kinsey," I chimed in, "just send us the feeds. Bobby's software is like alpha-test modules. He's coded them, and they're lightyears beyond anything you have, but it's only been wrung out to the extent Bobby needed to get it operational. It's rough around the edges and requires the dexterity of a concert violinist to keep it running. We send it to your guys, they might screw up your whole operating system trying to install it.

"Our new computer system can handle a couple hundred data feeds running at a hundred megabits per second. The quickest way to spot new colonies is to give Bobby what he needs and stay the hell out of his way. That's what I do."

"As I uncover anything, I will vector it directly to you—or whoever you designate," Bobby added. "It's faster this way."

McKissack digested our statements. "All right. The data is encrypted, so you'll need decoders and keys for each channel."

"No problem," Bobby assured him. "Just transmit the keys to my office computer. We're cleared to receive encrypted messages. I'll get started."

He paused as though he were about to break the connection, then added, "One more thing, Admiral. Could you have your world-wide surveillance services forward any odd or unusual observed occurrence across the globe for the next few days?"

McKissack paused, then asked, "What sort of occurrences?"

"Just... oddities," Bobby said. "Odd sounds. Odd lights. UFO reports. Especially reports of military or civilian pilots on unusual observations. Any report that doesn't have a readily-explainable answer to an observed phenomenon."

More silence. "You're assuming a possible odd report could be a possible Bug presence."

Bobby nodded, though McKissack wouldn't see it.. "Absolutely. Have your team on the lookout as well. That's how we'll uncover Bug activity and Bug presence."

Bobby and McKissack batted a few comments and questions back and forth, then McKissack rang off. Bobby laid his head back on the sofa as I commented, "You're afraid there are multiple Bug groups already spreading across the world?"

He grimaced. "I am scared. Terrified, actually. We not only killed off the Titan Bug base last year, we hit them in their home system. Of course, we'll never know for sure which of their bases we hit, or how much total damage we did, but I'm willing to bet we dealt them a heavy blow. Not fatal, but a dangerous.

"Think about it. We transferred an active nuclear device directly to one of their major home bases. It probably damaged not only the military base, but any civilian population center nearby. What if we knocked off not only the largest military base but also a city of several million Bugs? And by the way, I think that's likely.

"In that case, they are full bore to get their revenge, and are pulling out all the stops. Revenge can be a major motivator, right?"

I thought he nailed it. "Yeah. The only good that can come of this is we get the pirate portals knocked off the air."

He shook his head, eyes still closed. "Yeah, but for how long? If we manage to solve the problem, I'll bet before too many months, we'll have to contend with illegals again."

Kaley leaned back beside him, also closing her eyes. She muttered, "We'd better change our field service agreements. If a customer has a problem, if it's due to a shadow network portal the customer knowingly allows to use their part of our network, there ought to be severe penalties, including having their network shut down."

"I'll vote for that," Bobby said.

"Probably be hard to prove," I reminded them. "The governments involved can always say they had no idea the pirates were piggy-backing on their network. Sure, you'd bet they had to know, but if they maintain they're innocent, what can we do?"

"Cut them out of the network.," Bobby said. "Any portal can identify a dial-in portal. If it's from, say Lower Slobbovia, and the country has a known pirate association, simply cut the connection. We can isolate the Shadow Network, if we want to."

"But we may force them to develop their own portal technology and install a full portal network," I told him. "Pretty soon we have a big competitor, and you know many of the Asian countries don't honor out-of-country patents. There's a million ways to avoid doing business with us if they want to."

"Most of Europe, the Americas, and Australia have interlocking patent laws," Kaley said. "The ultimate blockade for us might be to appeal to those countries to lock out non-complying portals. They might do it."

"Not a chance." I said before glancing at Bobby. "Am I right? It would inconvenience their travel too much."

He pondered a moment, then said, "It's beside the point anyway. The problem is no longer the Shadow Network. The problem is the Bugs."

Bobby's phone buzzed, an intercom call from our admin, Margie. Since she thinks Kaley is her real boss, it must be an urgent message to Bobby, and since he currently sat on my sofa, I buzzed her back on my phone. After a moment, she picked up.

"He's in my office," I told her. "What?"

"A high-speed link containing a bunch of video just showed up on one of our terabit digital lines. About a minute later, IC called to say it's what Bobby requested."

"He'll be thrilled," I said. "What internal channel?"

"Seven. There was a message from an Admiral McKissack that asked Bobby to call back when he solved the problem."

That was McKissack attempting a bit of humor, which I appreciated. "I'll relay that to our resident genius." I hung up and turned to Bobby. "Incoming data on Seven—I think it's a combination of all the data lines multiplexed together."

He was up in a second, headed for his workstation. I joined Kaley on the couch and kissed her.

"That was nice," she said sleepily. "If we were home, I might seduce you."

"We can go home."

"Of course, we can't, you big silly. Bobby's going to need our help."

"No chance. He may want us to stay and cheer him on but need us, he doesn't. Besides, even in times of stress, I reserve the right to make salacious suggestions, even if I know they won't go anywhere."

So we sat and held hands, as Bobby began his analysis. Demonstrating that nothing much bothered us anymore, due to all the crises we had faced over the last year, both of us dozed off. We were awakened by Bobby's cry of triumph. "Got you, you sumbitches!"

Shaking my head, I managed to stand up, Kaley beat me up, so I followed her into his office and stood behind his computer screen. What greeted our eyes was a smudged, black-gray pastiche of early Andy Warhol art, looking ever so much like a pair of dirty slippers sitting on clouds. Except—in the upper left-hand corner, a faint triangle of gray had been outlined by a bright dotted line—Bobby's detector outlining a discovery.

A Bug fighter. No doubt.

I breathed out a sigh, "You found one. Where?"

"The inner jungles of Brazil, say a hundred miles from Manaus. East of where the Rio Negro flows into the Amazon. That's an area of wicked jungle. There are small tribes and clans of people in those forests, even though its near Manaus, which has something like a couple million population. The Bugs, who don't give a shit about any other intelligent life, could wipe out the local population and hide a portal site easily. I mean, imagine a rainforest with an area half the size of the whole damn USA—it would be the proverbial needle in a haystack."

I stared. Oh, I knew the Amazon rainforest was one of the wonders of the world, but his metaphor drove home the problem of finding such a hidden installation. "At least we know where you spotted the Bug fighter."

"It's still only a clue to the location of the Bug beachhead. I mean, yeah, it's better than having no idea at all, but that fighter could be a hundred kilometers from its home base. And you can bet the Bugs only come out at night—ha, ha, that's almost funny. But true."

My mind was reeling. Bobby had missed—no, not really missed, as he probably realized it—just not stated the scariest point. The new Bug location was in an area roughly half the circumference of the Earth distant from the Bug site the Russians had obliterated. Another thought struck me, so ironic I almost laughed: It appeared the Earth was infested with Bugs.

"We gotta call McKissack. No doubt his guys are working on those video feeds as well, but they may have missed your catch. That was a pretty subtle form to identify as a Bug fighter."

I didn't wait, simply crossed to my phone and dialed McKissack's number, prepared to cringe at his reaction.

CHAPTER 4 A NEW PROJECT TEAM ASSIGNMENT

McKissack was cordial but terse, so we could tell he was covered up with work. When Bobby outlined his discovery, McKissack he swore and asked for the analyzed data. Bobby told him it had already been sent to the analysts. McKissack terminated the call, still terse.

Bobby shrugged and forgot the Bugs' threat for the present. "I want to get the Project Team together ASAP to discuss my thesis and begin exploration," he announced.

The urgency of his voice and apparent intention surprised me, but Kaley didn't blink. "Good idea. When?"

He countered with his own question. "How fast can we get them together?"

"Everybody's busy," I said, "but I can't think of anything that has a higher priority. Get Margie to make some quick calls ."

The so-called "Project Team" had originated days after our first portal connection between Earth and the moon. On that first attempt, we hadn't connected to the moon portal, but opened a transit to *somewhere*, the destination unidentified. We'd never figured out the location of that "where," but it had become clear to us those first few days it was a destination outside our neighborhood. Way, way outside. My own sneaking suspicion was we might have dialed into the Bugs' network, though I would never admit it .

Due to my prodding, we'd chartered a team to investigate the weird connection, see if it could be duplicated, and nail down a way to either (a) do such a thing again, or (b) *never* do such a thing again. The membership of the team had varied over the nearly six years since that first attempt, including faculty members of The University of Texas at Dallas, SSS, and occasionally invited participants, including some from other universities, members of the IC staff, or a wild card member, such as someone from our suppliers.

The current membership consisted of Bobby, Kaley, me, a married couple, Professors Wendy Simmons and Raymond Dougal, two of the discoverers of the wormhole effect), and Professor Frances Koenig from the UTD Physics Department, who was leaving on sabbatical abroad, so this was probably the only time we would see her for a while. Thuan Nguyen, one of our technical experts, was the other permanent member of the team from SSS.

Captain Martinez, the Ganymede base commander, currently made up the IC staff membership, but he didn't make it to many meetings, as he was more or less a billion and a half kilometers away, give or take a few hundred mil. As he stayed pretty busy most of the time, I thought it best to give him a pass. Kaley begged off, as she had dozens of active service calls in progress. Even with her chief assistant plus a couple of lesser assistants, they were swamped. The rest could could make it, so we agreed to meet at five P.M. at UT Dallas, which meant Bobby, Thuan, and I had to travel across downtown.

Bobby and I both kept working until about three, then picked up Thuan and started across the city, a doubtful maneuver during rush hour. We barely made it, slipping my elderly Toyota SUV into a parking place reserved for us near the new engineering building. We had to hurry to a ground-floor conference room which Wendy's admin had reserved.

Everyone else was seated. Bobby and I chose chairs nearest the conference room door. To my right were Wendy, Ray, and Professor Koenig, and to Bobby's left, Thuan took a chair.

"Does this have anything to do with possible Bug sightings in Asia?" Wendy asked. I knew she had good sources within IC, but they were clearly more high-level than I thought.

"Yes." Bobby dispensed with the question and said, "But not directly why we're here. The deal is, I want the team to look into something else for the present. We need immediate activity, so I can promise additional funding for graduate students plus as much time as you can spare."

Dr. Koenig spoke up. I always thought of both her name and accent as Scandinavian, but on looking it up, I'd been surprised to learn the names had German roots, from "Konig," German for king. "That could work out well. I have two new doctoral-level students who need support. Professor Simmons will guide their work while I'm away."

Bobby grinned. "Sounds good. I want you to explore setting up a wormhole with a single portal."

Our university friends—and Thuan—sat back to look that over.

Eventually, Wendy ventured, "Not sure I get it. I mean, we *know* a single portal can create a wormhole. It's how we discovered the wormhole effect—get a heavy enough cross field, add a dollop of vacuum fluctuations, and voila!—you create a portal. Trouble is, the portal creator has no idea where the other end of the portal lies. It's a crapshoot. It wasn't until you guys added another door and figured out how to connect the two that we got a repeatable phenomenon that could lead to travel."

"True." Bobby let his gaze take in the group. "So far. Here's the deal—I've been doing a bit of mathematical doodling," Bobby could doodle mathematically with the best of them, "and I'm convinced we can create a wormhole with a single portal that can repeatedly and reliably be tied to a predictable location."

"Ah..." Professor Koenig said. "Having done a bit of 'doodling' also, I see where you are going, but the equations are daunting, and the effort is as well."

Naturally it was, because she wasn't a genius like my pal. Smart, yes, smarter than even me, though I hated to admit it. Not smarter than Bobby, however. There was only one of him.

"You're right." he grinned. "You're gonna need a lot of time on the campus megacomputer, but we can buy that. Even with my doodling, I'm not close yet. I don't have the time I need to continue the effort solo. We want the team to take over, make it a formal effort. I can guarantee at least a million dollars of S-Cubed funding at once."

Actually, he couldn't. Only Virgil Oliva, our CEO, could do that. What the hell, Bobby was worth enough that he could pull such a sum out of his checking account if need be—and besides, Virgil would back Bobby up. Essentially, Bobby was speaking with Virgil's voice.

Koenig, Wendy, and Ray perked up. Wendy and Ray had plenty of bucks as well, as each had a small share of SSS, but faculty are always on the lookout for graduate student support. As a result, they were clearly thrilled.

"I haven't looked at the math," Wendy commented, "but if Franny says it's tough, I'll accept that." Her remark gave me Professor Koenig's nickname as well as showing Wendy's respect for Koenig's opinion.

"I can provide a limited amount of help," Bobby told the faculty members. "But I need you guys to wade in this minute. Scotty and I have other fish to fry, so we won't have much time." Thuan, American born of

Vietnamese descent, was one of our best technical experts, nodded his black-haired head, his intense dark eyes not even blinking.

Talk about no time. My phone buzzed and I checked it reflexively. It was Guy Smith, my personal attorney as well as his company's rep to our firm. He would never call unless it was urgent, I told the others, "Sorry, company issue," and fled outside.

In the hallway, I answered. "What's up?"

His big voice answered, as level as ever. "Because if it weren't important, I wouldn't bother to call but send you email."

"Yeah, that's pretty much it. So, what's the deal? The angels want to do a second stock issue to reap more benefits on their investment?"

"Well, yes, of course, they always do. But not why I'm calling."

"Hit me," I said, not realizing it was exactly what he was about to do.

"You may recall at one time, you were married to one Glynnis MacFarlane."

Glynnis. My ex-wife, whom Guy had successfully helped me divorce barely six months ago. Weird, I thought, shocked he had called me about her, I hadn't thought about Glynnis in several blessed months.

"What? She's getting re-married and wants to invite me to the wedding? If so, she's doing better than I am at getting to the altar."

He paused for a moment. "I wondered why I hadn't received an invitation to your wedding to Ms. Sellers. What, she got cold feet? Finally decided you were a bad risk?"

That was his attempt at humor, bad and ill-conceived as it was. Of course, he didn't know a wedding was the big point of contention between Kaley and me. "Ha, ha. No, we've just been out saving the solar system and Triple-S network, slaving about twenty hours a day, so we haven't had time for frivolity like getting married."

"Sorry, I know you're both national heroes now. No, Glynnis is not getting remarried. I only hear rumors, but my take is a couple of relationships at her firm turned out badly, and she has not been happy about that. Especially since a couple of the partners, upset at her, uh, dalliance with certain other partners, nearly got her forced out of the firm a few weeks ago. Or so the grapevine would have it."

Which I hadn't heard. Glynnis and I had not parted on especially good terms, but we'd been married for three years. I don't care how badly such a relationship ends, at one time, I had cared for her.

"Sorry to hear it," I said. "You'll remember, at the final conference, I wished her well. I meant it."

"I know you did, Scotty. You're one of the good guys, which is why I called. I though you ought to know Glynnis is in the hospital, in pretty bad shape."

Quite a shock. I remembered Glynnis as one of the most fervent healthy lifestyle and exercise advocates I had ever known. She took supplements and loads of vitamins and ate a diet of fresh vegetables, nuts, and moderate amounts of meat. I would've bet Glynnis would live to be a hundred, though thankfully, not with me.

"Odd," I commented. "G paid a lot more attention to her diet and exercise plan than she ever paid to me."

"Hmm. Didn't know she was a big fan of the clean life. Figured she got most of her exercise, well, you know..."

She'd gotten a lot of that kind of exercise far away from me but I did know what he meant.

"Then, what? I asked. "Some sort of illness? Surely not cancer or heart trouble."

"No, nothing like that."

He paused. I could tell he was working up to something.

"Uh, here's the thing, Scotty. I hate to be the one to bring bad news. Some people might argue I shouldn't have bothered you, but since she's your ex, I thought you'd want to know."

"And I do." I was getting tired of Guy dragging his feet. "What the hell is it? A jealous wife put a bullet in her?"

Yeah, my attempt at dark humor wasn't any better than his.

"She tried to commit suicide. She's in Methodist Hospital in Dallas. They sedated her for a while, but since she's come to, she's been asking for you."

CHAPTER 5 GLYNNIS

I did *not* want to see Glynnis. Not now, not ever again. Glynnis had been flawlessly beautiful, glamorous, and enchanting at one time. But that was at one time.

"Why the fuck," I said, "are you calling me about this? We're not married, I haven't seen her in six months, and I don't want to see her now."

Silence. After a long pause, leaning toward perilously awkward, he said quietly, "Maybe I shouldn't have, but she is asking for you, and her personal attorney called and asked me to pass it on."

"The operative word is 'asked,'" I said, still upset. "I don't want to hear anything about it, Guy! I want my life Glynnis-free."

"Okay, sorry." He hung up.

Goddamit. I'd have to dial him up later and apologize. It certainly wasn't his fault that I had been stupid enough to marry Glynnis in the first place. And, he had been asked to call.

What to do? First thing was to re-enter the meeting.

Bobby was saying, "...I concede reliably finding an end-point to a wormhole with only one portal will be challenging. However, with careful study and calibration, I believe we can develop the ability to navigate across light-year distances accurately. I gotta say, a big second reason to do this is to provide us with a tool, maybe even a weapon.

"I want to be able to use a single-end wormhole generator to act as a lever to snatch control of portals used by the Bugs right here on Earth. It's damn certain Bugs have multiple portals on Earth. If so, eradicating insect infestation just became our main concern. Right?"

The other attendees nodded. I gestured to Bobby, who had heard the door open and looked at me. "Something has come up," I told the assembled group. "I need to leave. Bobby, grab a taxi to get you and Thuan back to the office."

"Anything serious?" he asked as the others focused their attention on me.

I felt that I lied convincingly. "You know the drill. If it isn't a customer griping, it's a vendor."

He eyed me critically. I could tell he suspected something was up but didn't want to launch a discussion in an open forum. "No problem. You're not indispensable, you know."

The assemblage laughed, I waved, and set out to visit Glynnis.

Realizing I had forgotten the hospital where Glynnis currently resided, I had to call Guy once I got into my car.

"Sorry I was such a jackass," I started out. "You were asked to call and you did. I decided to shoot the messenger."

He paused. "I was a little surprised at your reaction. Sure you don't have a bit of affection left for your former?"

Probably I did. You don't stay married for three years, assuming there was the slightest shred of affection at the beginning, and not have some elements of left-over emotion for your previous life partner. The act of love with Glynnis had been an enormous emotional and physical high, especially at first, and those memories don't end when you sign a few forms. Yes, Glynnis had made me miserable and angry, especially at the end, but there had been some good times. I loved Kaley far more than I ever loved Glynnis, but as Guy guessed, traces of earlier affection no doubt lingered whether I liked it or not.

"I'm not a psychiatrist," I replied, "but perhaps there are. However, I love Kaley about a thousand percent more, and if things ever quiet down, we will get married. I am going to go see Glynnis, however. I forgot the hospital."

"Methodist Central, Dallas. So go, wish her well, and you can get her out of your life again."

"The sooner, the better." I disconnected and continued south, across the Trinity river on IH 35E, to Colorado Boulevard, and west to the hospital. After parking in one of the high-rise parking structures, I entered the building.

The original Methodist Hospital was built long before I came into the world, the original unit opening to service on Christmas Eve, 1927. Since then, it had grown into a massive complex with sister sites around the metroplex. Glynnis was listed on the fifth floor of one of the older buildings. Exiting the elevator, I moved down one long hallway and turned left, stopped at a station that existed as a hub to three more hallways. A small, dark, female sat behind the front desk, her appearance Hawaiian, perhaps Filipino.

She answered my inquiry. Yes, Glynnis' room was down the right hallway and she could have visitors. What was my connection?

I didn't think it was any of of her damned business, but I answered politely that I was her former husband, and she'd asked if I could drop by. Ms. Nosy-but-efficient nodded and let me move on. Moving down the directed hallway, I came upon room 527. It was a single, dimly lit from the windows, as the bedside light was off.

I entered, assuming she slept. No, after a moment, she said, "Scotty, I'm so glad you could come."

She reached out to turn on the lights. I'm afraid I couldn't totally mask my dismay.

Her appearance resembled, to be as kind as possible, a scarecrow. She'd lost something like fifteen pounds, and I couldn't imagine she now tipped the scales at even a hundred. While too young to display crepe-paper skin, her flesh hung loosely on her arms and neck. Her eyes were sunken, the sockets dark, and I'd have sworn she was fifty years old if I hadn't known better.

"I know," she said, "I look terrible. It's been rough. I discovered my choices in life were all awful and suddenly, I just didn't care anymore."

"Chrissake, Glynnis," I muttered. "It's not like your life is over. You're young, you're a huge success in business, and let's face it, you can get just about any man you want. You may need a few sessions with a shrink to get your focus back, but believe me, you'll be fine."

"Fine. An interesting word. My problem is the only time I was really fine, I was married to you. I wasn't a very good wife, I know it. I could be again, I know I could. If you'd give me a chance."

I sighed. "Glynnis, I'll admit our first years of marriage were fine." Which was a lie. By the end of the first year, I knew I'd made a terrible mistake. "But you know I'm engaged to Kaley ."

She gave me a once-over. Oddly, the scheming look that usually appeared on her face when we talked that last year or two was missing. "Scotty, I know I let you down. And I was the one who filed for divorce. But if you love Kaley so much, why aren't you married yet?"

She saw the surprise on my face, I'm sure. "Yes, I've kept up with you, to a degree. Not constantly, but I know you and Kaley aren't married. I just wondered if you still had some love left for me."

I surveyed her weakened, slim form. "Glynnis, I'll always have some affection for you. For God's sake, no matter how bad things finally turned out, we had some good times. If you'd have come to me a year ago and said, 'Things aren't going well, let's seek some counseling help,' I'd have gone with you. Instead, you locked me out of our home and filed the divorce petition. You clipped the line between us. It's gone. I love Kaley and that's that."

"If you won't give me a chance, I'll try again to end my life. The next time, I'll be better prepared, and I'll succeed. It'll be on your conscience."

I was surprised her words carried no heat. She simply spoke the truth as she saw it: she still loved me and unless I came back, she'd finish the job she'd started .

Glynnis appeared small, vulnerable, and quite ill, her body defenseless and weak. Despite the bitter schism she had precipitated, I couldn't work up any anger at her matter-of-fact blackmail attempt, threatening to try to kill herself again.

I replied more gently than I would have thought possible. "Glynnis, it won't be on my conscience, not at all. You're right, down deep, I still have a reservoir of feelings for you. But understand, I *love* Kaley, far more than either you or I ever loved each other.

"See a psychiatrist, get good counseling, get your life together. You're smart, beautiful, and an excellent executive in your business. I'm sure any number of men could make you happy, far happier than I could. I want you to be happy, I really do. But the one to make you happy is not me. Not anymore."

She stared up at me , her eyes surveying me, as I had looked over her. "I won't argue about it, Scotty. You're a good man, a far better husband to me than I ever was a wife to you. I do believe you. You've grown beyond me, now that I managed to cut the cord that bound us together. You're so right. It's my fault."

I spied a tear leaking out of her left eye. Then she said, "Would you do me a favor?"

I suspected she was about to ask for something either maudlin or distasteful. I didn't want to make any sort of open-ended promise.

"Glynnis, I might, but I can't give a carte-blanche promise when I don't know what you're asking for." She nodded. "I understand. It's not anything unpleasant, at least at one time, it wouldn't have been unpleasant."

"What?"

"I'd just like a kiss. Just one, to remember you by, whether I live another fifty years or five days." Shock strangled my reply.

"I know, I know—you're engaged to Kaley. I accept that. I'm not asking for any funny stuff. Just a simple kiss, a goodbye. I didn't get one of those when we signed the divorce papers."

For a moment, I remained stock still.

After a moment, she said, "Please?"

I gave up. It would be the best way to grease my exit. I bent over the bed to touch my lips to hers. Up close, the aroma of her favorite fragrance lingered. The soft touch of her mouth held all the promise of passion and pleasure it always had. I froze in position, prolonging the moment far longer than I wanted.

I pushed back. She smiled.

"Thank you," she said. "I see that we still have that connection, if only a bit."

Shaken, I straightened. "Take care of yourself, Glynnis. Get the help you need, go back to being the powerhouse you've always been. I have to go."

"I love you, Scotty. I'm really sorry I figured it out too late."

I turned and left. Perhaps I should have stopped at the nursing station, said something to the nurse who still sat at the desk. But I didn't. I fled the building as if pursued by evil spirits.

CHAPTER 6 NOT JUST A RUMOR

Seating myself at my desk, I saw that Bobby not yet returned from the university, when the desk phone rang. I picked up with a tepid "Hello," and heard McKissack.

"Scotty, glad I got you. Wanted to keep you in the loop."

"It's where I want to be, Kinsey. I assume the news is bad since you are delivering it in person."

He grunted. "Hmm. I suppose that's a good guess but I hate to be so predictable. Yes, not good, not at all. Matter of fact, the news is shitty ."

"If you called to tell me the stock market is down, you're wasting your time. I checked my portfolio this morning, which left me depressed."

My feeble attempt at humor got a chuckle, so his overall mood must be scraping bottom. "No, I wasn't going to bring you up-to-date on the stock market. Figured you were keeping tabs. I'm just damn glad what little I have invested is in bonds.

"My news is worse, sorry to say. Russia has appealed to the UN and privately to us for help. They discovered a well-hidden site that sports a few hundred well-concealed fighters. Not well enough concealed, it turns out. We've been sending the Russian military our scan data, so they can assist in the visual analysis, since we're spread thin analyzing scans from all over the Earth.

"They climbed on the band wagon. Rumor has it they have something like two hundred experts covering the various over-Russia scans and they need that many. I don't know how many terabytes we're vectoring their way, but it's a bundle—Russia is like China, it covers a lot of territory."

"Is this site near Siberia where they sighted the first Bug base?"

"Oh, hell no, it's a lot farther north, deep into Siberia. They're evacuating as many inhabitants as possible, although I don't have a clue how heavily populated the area is."

I felt equally clueless. My overall impression of Siberia: a cold and dreary land most of the year, with endless stretches of snow and/or tundra, given the season. It didn't have any population centers like New York or Los Angeles, or even Moscow.

"What do they propose?"

"They aren't saying, but IC Command is damned worried. We're afraid if they don't act quickly, those fighters are going to disperse to half a dozen, or even half a hundred, new bases. Which will make them harder than ever to stop. We've volunteered to send troops or support them with a wing of SF Seventy-sevens. No answer yet."

"I'm surprised they called ," I said.

"Me, too. They're about to lose control of the situation. The CNO told them that in our opinion, they have less than forty-eight hours to act."

I agreed with the CNO, except my deadline was twenty-four hours. In just six months, our military, though not perhaps IC, had forgotten how fast Bugs moved.

"I wish I could help," I told him. "It seems the current situation calls for a military solution."

"Agreed. We may need your help. Be prepared to leap into action at a moment's notice."

I didn't mention our new project team undertaking. First, I didn't want to get his hopes up. Second, I felt he was still suspicious about our project team, a chartered activity now for a full six years, suspecting it was funded by magically-siphoned-off money from one of our contracts. It wasn't, but it was near impossible for someone in his position to imagine that one of their vendors would spend company profits to push additional research.

After a moment's thought, I said, "You think there's any chance Russia, with or without our help, can contain this threat?"

"No chance. It's already too Goddamned late to help. My bet is some of those fighters they've been watching have flown the coop already."

—And if they really had managed to accumulate a hundred or more fighters on one site, the Bugs were far and away intelligent enough to realize a huge group of hardware increased the chance of discovery. They'd disperse ships and crews as fast as they could.

I was sweating. The last thing IC wanted to happen was a Bug beachhead on Earth—and lo and behold, the Bugs had made one.

"I shouldn't think this or at least say it out loud," I said, "but I hope every one of the people who built that first pirate portal died in the Bug takeover."

"Me, too. We should be ashamed."

"Keep us up-to-date," I said. "Not that you don't have enough to do right now but have some low-level flunky give us a call when you know more."

"Ha. All the low-level flunkies who report to me are commanders or captains." True; when he had gotten his third star, he inherited a lot of high-level helpers .

"Sorry, I forgot how important you are now. Haven't you got an aide or admin assistant or somebody who can call?"

"Nah, I keep them busy twenty-four-seven. I'd rather call you anyway. It's one of the few times I can say what the hell I want and know you won't repeat it."

He killed the connection and I sat for a moment, thinking that not only IC and SSS, but all humanity, were now in deep doo-doo. Bobby wandered in.

"You look serious," he commented. "What's going on?"

I prepared to bring him up to speed.

CHAPTER 7 DRASTIC MEASURES

I let him summarize the part of the meeting I missed. There was little to learn, as they had discussed some avenues to explore, but nothing of interest with respect to specific hints at concrete solutions. Then I summarized my visit to the hospital.

After I finished with the Glynnis episode, he muttered, "Jesus. Even divorced, she's still a pain in your ass. Will she ever just go away?"

"My thoughts exactly. I didn't really want to, but I felt I pretty much had to visit her. Now, my duty is done and I hope she can get back on track and leave me the hell alone. By the way, where's Kaley? She's not in the building."

"No idea," Bobby said. He crossed to his desk, picked up the intercom phone, and dialed Margie. I couldn't hear the conversation. "There was a major problem with the Rhea jumbo portal so Kaley sent Bets to look it over. Bets called early in the afternoon, asked Kaley to drop everything and head to Rhea. She didn't give Margie any ETA for her return. Margie saw Kaley before she went to the portal room and Kaley was carrying her bag, so the assumption is she might not be back until at least tomorrow."

If the problem required both Bets and Kaley, it had to be major, as Rhea could not do without their big portal. I glanced at him.

"Think we, or one of us, ought to run up there?"

Bobby laughed. "Are you kidding? Do something to indicate we don't have total confidence in Ms. Queen of Field Service or her princess? Not a friggin' chance."

"If I showed up, she wouldn't think that. She'd know I wanted to help."

"Maybe. Tell you one thing—*I* ain't goin'."

"Okay, okay, I get the point. I'll call to get her best estimate of a return time."

The good thing about having dozens of portals now, many of which are connected simultaneously, all over the Earth and to Mars, the moon, Mercury, and a fistful of Jovian and Saturnian moons, was the communication routes we had almost everywhere. Given that most of the portals were connected just about one hundred percent of the time, and since radio waves went right through a portal with no problems at all, we had a com path, not only to every place on Earth but to most of the other solar system portal sites.

I dialed Rhea. After a moment, one of the IC non-coms answered, and soon I had Kaley on the line.

"I'm busy," she said, which told me right at the moment, she did not want to be bothered by her sweetie-pie, i.e., me.

"I need to know your schedule, if you're coming back to the office or if you need to make more calls."

"We're about wrapped up here. Nasty problem, bad FlucGen circuit plus a power supply that was shaky, the first one of those in more than a year. I'll come back later today, but given Bet's workload, I may have to go out tomorrow. We got maybe twenty active calls and our tech staff can't handle them all, so I've got to hit several Earth sites."

"You want me to wait here?"

Usually she'd say something like "How lovely, you miss me." This evening, she was all business. "No. Go home, get some sleep. I'll go to my place tonight and see you tomorrow."

"Okay. I have a personal issue I need to discuss with you. Try to make time tomorrow."

She hesitated. "Anything important?"

"Yeah, but too complicated to get into on the phone. See you tomorrow. Just save me some time."

I left it at that and we disconnected.

Bobby stared at me. "Now you've worried her. You shouldn't have mentioned it or told her the problem."

"I know. I seem to be pissing off just about everybody today. On the other hand, she was so damn brusque, it was like she broadcast, 'Don't bother me now.' So I slipped in a zinger to get her attention."

"Holy potatoes," he muttered, "You, laid back, easy going Scotty, are getting nastier and nastier in your old age."

"What can I say? Maybe I've always been a closet asshole, and the last year with Glynnis brought me 'out.'"

Bobby directed his attention to his terminal screen with a snort, while I lay back in my chair and contemplated my navel, at least metaphorically. I had a bunch of tasks lined up, and didn't want to do any of them. I felt so frustrated that I considered calling our regular chartered air service and flying up to my cabin in Estes Park for a few days.

The phone rang. Saved by the bell—no need to think, just answer the call.

McKissack. "Scotty, I know it's getting late, but can you and your tech chief run over here for a quick meeting?"

Basically, since Intersolar Command was far and away our best customer, the admiral had only to snap his fingers. I did appreciate his polite request.

"Of course. I assume you mean right away."

"I do. Sorry to call this late."

"And the topic would be...?"

"Sorry, this isn't an encrypted line. It's fairly secure, but in this case, not secure enough. Just say 'important' and leave it at that."

"Right away, Admiral. Clear one of your small portals."

"Already dialing up your lab portal. Say, five minutes?"

So, he wasn't kidding. The topic sailed far above urgent. I answered, "Have the coffee pot on, please."

"Already making a full carafe."

I hung up, whistled at Bobby, and said, "McKissack. He wants us at his place now, and don't spare the horses."

He blinked, stood, and said, "I gotta pee." Which, given his size and bladder capacity, was not often.

"Meet me in the lab," I said, and headed there myself.

In Fort Worth, at the main IC hangar, they were expecting us, and a salty-looking captain, for God's sake, led us over. I didn't know him, but in the navy, you don't generally get to be a full Captain unless you are on the admiral path, so I supposed he belonged to McKissack's inner circle and was doing the admiral a favor. The reason for the high-level tour guide became obvious, as McKissack had called a meeting in a room that lay off the beaten path in the IC facility.

As we entered, the captain followed us in and took a seat, McKissack stood at his chair, holding his coffee cup, and I suspected he had just filled it.

"Grab some caffeine," he directed us. "You'll need it."

He was right—outside, darkness had fallen an hour ago. In addition to coffee there was a doughnut platter set up on a back table which made sense, as it was past dinner time. Bobby glommed onto a fistful plus coffee, sitting beside me across from the admiral. Aside from the gray-haired

Captain, "Jennifer," on the nameplate over his breast pocket, a one-star sat adjacent to McKissack, rather young for an admiral, olive-skinned, and dark haired, plus another captain at the end of the table, and assorted commanders and lieutenant commanders scattered around the rest of the circumference.

McKissack spoke, "In case any of you have not met them, this is Doctor Charles Hays, who goes by Scotty, and Doctor Robert Taylor, or Bobby, if you will. They are two thirds of the brain trust of Subway Solar Systems, our portal provider." He directed his stare to me. "Where's Kaley?"

"Out saving your ass, sir," I said, deciding to add a bit of humor to meeting, perhaps a bad choice of words. "Bad problem on the Rhea jumbo needed her personal attention."

He had the courtesy to smile. "Thank God for her." He addressed the general assemblage. "Doctors Hays and Taylor hold the highest clearances, so you can be candid in your comments." Back to Bobby and me. "Everyone else has heard this. Earlier today, Russia went nuclear with that problem in Siberia. There is now a quite large crater at the former Bug base."

Russia had decided not to wait. I shook my head. With probably little warning to the surrounding populace, they had decided on the ultimate "fix" for their problem.

"How much collateral damage?" I asked.

"They aren't saying. My bet is in the tens of thousands, although some of the dead will be due to the Bugs' intrusion."

"How successful were they?" Bobby asked.

McKissack stared into the seamed face of the captain who had brought us over. The good captain cleared his throat, his voice as gravelly as his face was craggy. "They claim they eliminated all the enemy craft, which is total bullshit. We know for a fact dozens, probably as many as a hundred, enemy fighters left the Siberian site earlier. Even as the Russians attacked, more got away.

"The blast got some spacecraft in the air, but a number got away. I'd say a large number are on the way to the South American site that Doctor Taylor identified. We're still looking for it, no luck so far. Others headed in various directions. Hell, there are probably a dozen new Bug bases being built all over the blasted world. For all we know, they could even be headed off-world."

Which was enough to make my blood icy. I exchanged glances with Bobby.

"Enemy fighters neutralized?" I asked the captain.

"Not enough," he growled. "Maybe five hundred."

We had a hundred or more enemy fighters spreading out, probably to every continent on Earth—and, as the captain said, maybe to the out-worlds. I could understand the Bugs' intent. Start lots of sites, each one with a small portal, and try to get one large portal constructed and operational to their home planet. Fly in a few hundred thousand fighters. If they could, we were finished. They increased their chances by starting up multiple sites and hoping we missed one.

"How's your scanning working out?" Bobby asked. I knew he sent some of his most advanced visual analysis software to IC, even though it was highly fragile.

One of the lieutenant commanders spoke . "Slow, although your software helps. Problem is, we're uploading a hundred terabytes of data a day. I mean, we have *petabytes* of info, and even with all the supercomputers we can scrounge up supporting the effort, we're falling farther and farther behind."

The one-star I didn't know spoke up. "How many verified sightings so far?"

The second full commander, seated on the other side of McKissack spoke. "There are two validated sightings of Bug ships in Canada, one in Montana, five in Australia, and three in Siberia. Suspected but not verified sightings in China and southeast Asia. Two successes today, you don't know about," that addressed to McKissack, "A Bug nest in Australia, and another in Canada identified and destroyed, both small and out of the way. God only knows how many more will pop up."

A lengthy discussion followed, the attendees offering status of ongoing exploratory efforts . One fact surprised me. A group of our SF-77 space-based fighter craft were placing additional spy satellites in orbit at breakneck speed. By the end of the week, we would have more than fourteen hundred new eyes in the sky, in addition to the host that already existed. At least, IC was determined to make it a lot harder for the Bugs to hide.

During in a lull, I asked, "Admiral McKissack, what can Triple S do to help you in this new conflict?"

He considered, glanced around the table. "Keep us supplied with portals as needed. Second, I expect this is not possible, at least for the present, but I have to ask. Is there any chance you could identify a method to locate enemy portals as they are activated? If we could find them as they come on line and neutralize them, it would make our job a helluva lot easier."

A number of nods followed his question. I was at a loss , but Bobby rescued me. "You're right, Admiral. At this moment, we can't help you, other than to improve that visual analysis software I sent you. We're working on things that might eventually help. Can't give you an ETA." At least Bobby hadn't volunteered a solution by tomorrow. He added, "But it's possible such a capability might be available in the future."

The admiral thanked him and we continued to meet for another half hour but everything had been said. We headed back to the IC headquarters portal. All the way back to our offices, all I could think was, *We're within an eyelash of losing Earth to the Bugs again, just when we thought we'd whipped them.*

Kaley hadn't returned. I headed home, mulling once again, on my Glynnis encounter. There, I planned to down a rather large helping of Jack Black and water, and probably sulk for a while.

CHAPTER 8 TAKING A FLYER

As I had hit the sheets at about nine PM, I was up early the next morning to exercise, shower, and meet Bobby at one of our favorite spots for breakfast, Billie Lou's. I doubt there had ever been a Billie Lou. It had been run by Alex and his wife for a long time, though the female spousal unit, a tiny woman with a loud voice and a knack for baking heavenly pastries and pies, had retired. Alex, eighty-plus but looking thirty years younger, stood behind the counter in the mornings. Slender, olive-skinned, slicked-back black hair without a trace of gray and a white apron over jeans, he was one of my favorite people, a no-nonsense guy with a wry sense of humor.

"My favorite customers," he said in his croaky voice, without a grin, as we took stools at the long bar to the right of the longer room. The place sported tables to the left, all but one occupied and serviced by two frantic waitresses. The stools were taken except at the back, where we sat.

"We're the favorites because Bobby leaves outlandish tips," I said.

"Of course, that's the only way I rate customers. What'll it be?"

Bobby ordered his favorite breakfast, migas, with a double side of bacon. I'd been trying to eat healthier at Kaley's request, aka constant nagging. Today, my mood dark for a host of reasons, I had an "Everything

Omelet," with three kinds of cheese plus bacon, sausage, chorizo, ham, and assorted vegetables, heavy on the onion. Plus, a Belgian Waffle with a lot of butter. My breakfast made me look as though I had a death wish. Maybe this morning I did.

We didn't say much as we ate, but when I asked Alex for coffee, Bobby brought up the work topics I had been shoving under the rug. "With the Bugs spreading out all over hell and half of Georgia, I want to amp up the effort to yank portals away from the bad guys and get access to attack them."

"You know we always have the problem that if they suspect a takeover, they can kill power and shut off the wormhole."

"I'm working on that too. What if we could take over a wormhole and then sustain it from one end only?"

"So that's why you've been pushing the search for single-ended wormholes."

"Sure, one of the reasons. My main reason is exploration, but I got to thinking if, in addition to exploration, we could take over a regular portal and sustain it from our end, we'd have any Bug portal just where we want it. We'd have to be prepared to wrench control, blast the bad guys, and send in soldiers to complete the takeover or destruction of the portal. It would make finding and destroying Bug sites a lot easier."

It would, I thought . "I like it. How quickly can the team come up with a portal design ?"

He grinned. "Maybe quick like a bunny. Wendy called me yesterday with a suggestion for a circuit change, and it makes such good sense I've been exploring it. Just before you walked in this morning, the solution hit me."

By which he meant he'd been at it, heavily grinding, all morning and part of last night. Not good for his sleep, but good in another way—Bobby was never happier than when he was enmeshed in problem solving.

Out of curiosity, I asked, "You gonna run this by Wendy and Ray later?"

"Yeah, as soon as we get to work. It's a simple solution really, less static voltage and more vacuum fluctuations. I'm a little jealous. I should have seen it, but Wendy got it first. She's a real genius."

A significant complement, coming from a guy who *is* a real genius. And maybe she was—I'd known Wendy since she taught me undergraduate courses, and she was very smart. As was her husband and fellow professor, Ray Dougal. Come right down to it, we had a helluva brain trust on that project committee, and I was glad we did.

We both wanted another cuppa, but took them to go. Bobby wanted to get to work and I hoped to see Kaley this morning. I needed to talk about Glynnis, and it might as well be Kaley, as her sensible advice always helped on any problem. Bobby had experienced enough romantic drama in his life over the last year so I didn't want to overburden him. As we each had our own car, we continued to work separately. Bobby was clearly doing some last-minute grinding, which made me hope he put his Porsche SUV in auto-drive. I tried to puzzle out how best to try out the team's new idea .

I went from the underground parking straight to Kaley's office, and lo and behold, she sat at her desk, chewing on a pen and consulting the large desk monitor. She met me for a long, therapeutic kiss at mid-office. We held that pose for about, I don't know, three minutes or so.

She pushed back. " Are you glad to see me or is that a mouse in your pocket?"

"Hah. No, not thinking of sex, simply affection. Where have you been?"

"Too many places to name, even for a single day. I slept exactly one and a half hours in the last twenty-four so I'm heading home pretty soon."

Since she hadn't mentioned Glynnis, nobody had told her, and come to think of it, other than Bobby, probably nobody knew. Guy had called me, I had only mentioned it to Bobby, and he never blabbed anything to anybody. Kaley didn't look tired, her bubble-do making an attractive halo around her face. I didn't see how she did it. I'd followed her around Earth and the solar system a few times for days on end. After three weeks, it was time for me to either go to bed for a month or simply die. Kaley, on the other hand, could keep to such a schedule for months and so could her faithful second-in-command, Bets.

I couldn't bring myself to burden her with out-of-work problems, since she needed sleep, whether she realized it or not. "Well, thanks for the morning dessert to my breakfast, but you need to get on your way. Bobby's got a wild hair up his nose about a new way to attack the Bugs, so I'll help him explore it. Anything you need from me?"

She leaned forward to peck my lips again. "Other than a little romance in my life, no. Okay, I will go home for a nap or three, then see you later, or tomorrow maybe. If you and Bobby head off into the wild blue yonder, leave word where you're going."

"Yeah, like you do."

"Sorry, we went so many places yesterday I just left a list with Margie. She apologized and said she'd been so busy, she forgot to drop that list off to you."

"Huh. A likely story." I pecked back and left her to her field service reports.

I wasn't sure she'd get away immediately, because she must have about a hundred incident reports to complete. She had to get her summary down before she turned them over to Margie to finish.

Bobby sat at his desk, grinding. His hands were on the keyboard before him, but his mind was in genius-space, wherever that is, putting the final touches on what must surely be a recommendation to IC. I crossed to his desk, waited, and after a moment, he surfaced.

"You need to call McKissack and introduce the topic. I want to use Ganymede for our test vehicle, the small portal, and we need permission."

"Yeah. Ganymede won't be so busy now, with all the Earth traffic, but I doubt if he's going to be overjoyed to loan out Ganymede Alpha portal for an extended period."

Bobby pondered a minute, then said, not regretful at all, "We saved his ass, and he owes us, and it's time to collect. Remind him if you have to."

Well. Bobby is a nice, friendly person, actually a bit shy and retiring. Today, he was on the hunt for new solutions, and anybody who got in the way might get run over. I've compared him to a tracking dog. Today, he assumed full arf-arf mode. "I'll give him a yell. When I make my request, you'll hear the yowl directly from Ganymede."

"It's not a request."

I left the hound to his solution-tracking and went to the lab to see if we could set up a direct link to Ganymede ASAP. Turned out a lull in traffic allowed the Portal Authority to schedule a time slice and in ten minutes, I was connected to Ganymede Alpha.

Instead of calling, I walked through, asked for Captain Martinez, a good friend. Five minutes later, he was standing beside me at the portal. We shook hands.

Short, a bit pudgy, but heavily muscled, Martinez seemed far more relaxed than when I'd last seen him, months ago, in the act of ending the previous Bug incursion. "Must be important for you to run up here," he commented, as I tried to get circulation back into my hand. "How are you? It's been a while."

"That it has. I need a favor, and since it's a big one, I thought I'd better ask in person."

He shrugged. "Anything. You and your crew helped save our collective ass not long ago. How is my favorite field tech, Kaley?"

"As bright, clever, capable and busy as ever. We're engaged."

His brow elevated. "Aha. It seemed to me there was something between you guys, even though you wouldn't admit it. Hang onto her. She is a jewel."

"You won't get an argument from me. If we ever get time for a wedding ceremony, you want an invite?"

"You're kidding, right? You don't invite me and that will be the end of favors forever. So, how can I help?"

I explained, stressing our exercises, should he approve them, would be strictly research, with no assurance we'd have a good outcome. He pooh-poohed my reservations. "Hey, there's a lot we don't know about wormhole creation and use of portals. If you can make progress, it could help us beat back those oversize grubworms. With the problems on Earth, you know traffic out here has lessened, so our Alpha portal seems to be a good fit. What's your timeline?"

"I think within forty-eight hours."

Half an hour later, I was back on Earth, and within twenty-four hours, Kaley and I and most of the special project team traveled to Ganymede.

CHAPTER 9 A SWING—AND A MISS

There was the matter of petitioning the Portal Authority to allow us to steal time slices from the portal connect schedule. That would assure our trial would be when no connects were scheduled and no portals, with one exception, were connected. It took time, but we had McKissack working on it, and he came through as usual. An IC request to the authority, especially with the Bug problem at its present level, got high priority.

Three project team members joined Kaley and me, Professors Wendy Simmons Raymond Dougal, a husband and wife team, and our own Thuan Nguyen. I was there to oversee the activity per Bobby's instruction and to run interference with IC and/or the world Portal Authority if needed. I checked and we had about an hour to set up, at which point our first time slice would be open, meaning every single portal, both on Earth and on the out-worlds, would shut down.

Kaley and I still hadn't discussed Glynnis's antics, my visit, nor the kiss. That would come before the day was out.

Wendy charmed the on-site team like Kaley did. Faye Bailey, our lead tech, began a conversation which soon involved Kaley and Dave, another tech. Normally, techs work their way out of a job, return to headquarters when IC personnel learn their jobs and take over portal operations. In the case of Ganymede and the two Saturn moons, our techs had stayed on site much longer. There had been problems with the equipment both due to sabotage and also to the efforts of our insectile enemies. I hoped Faye and Dave would be on their way home in a couple of months. I was glad to have them now, as we would be pulling off some weird exercises with the Alpha portal.

I tried not to converse too much with Wendy, although I was fond of her. That was the problem. She and Ray were married and I had Kaley. In the distant past, still at the university, I had held an enormous crush on Professor Simmons. Of course, she was married then, but it didn't prevent me from making her the girl of my dreams.

Until Glynnis entered my life and dazzled me with her beauty and seductive ways, I had thought way too much about Professor Dougal's wife. Nothing terribly racy. My thoughts had been pure and virtuous. I built a high mental pedestal and installed Wendy atop it, whiling away my days thinking about her and visiting her during office hours.

Wendy had been sweet, sympathetic, and forbearing, and the crush had worn off. I had to admit that maybe I did have a thing for older women. Wendy was just a bit older than Kaley. With the center of my affection standing nearby, I was happy to note that at last, I had affection for Wendy, but I loved Kaley.

Kaley and I joined the team at the portal, and Wendy, who would lead the first exercises, took over to direct the settings for our primary attempt. I listened as she explained the situation to Faye and Dave.

"You can tell from the cross field settings and the FlucGen levels we are trying a whole new setup for this particular try. When all operational portals are shut down, the only active tunnels will be those initiated by the Bugs. There may be one or two active tunnels due to pirate portals, but they're just as heinous, and if we catch one of those, it's just as good a deal.

"Understand, we are not setting up to perform an invasion right now. If we do catch a pirate or Bug portal, we disengage and declare our technique a success. We turn the exercise over to IC, let them not only take over portals, but invade them and pacify the portal initiators, whether a pirate group or Bugs. Clear?"

Everybody nodded.

Now we had to wait. The Ganymede Beta site, about twelve kilometers away, was connected to IC headquarters. It would get the word to terminate, as would every other portal in the solar system that subscribed to Portal Authority Control. That means, all but the pirates and the Bugs. As its operators turned the Beta portal off, they would send us a message as our cue to fire up and see what happened, if anything.

The minutes dragged. I signaled Kaley and we went for coffee, asking others if they wanted any. We got four takers, including Faye, Wendy, and two of the naval non-coms. No problem. We loaded up a cardboard box with cups, and returned to distribute the drinks.

About halfway through my cup, I realized that I had forgotten to add cream but was so edgy I hadn't even noticed at first. I was debating about returning to the coffee table when the signal came through on the local com line. Wendy, lounging at the edge of the small portal with Kaley, straightened, gestured to Faye and the two IC operators, and they started to bring up Ganymede Alpha portal.

I had attended the event mainly to run interference by calls to IC if any impediments stood in the team's path. As there were no outside problems, my role was reduced to onlooker. Kaley backed up our techs and the naval portal operators, standing with Faye as the exercises started, while Wendy ran the show. Even Ray had little to say other than join me and Thuan as the unofficial cheering section as our portal came up.

Wendy and the operators brought up the Alpha portal five times in a row with no sign of a tie to anything. We had an hour, and that only consumed about twenty minutes, so Wendy varied the cross field and FlucGen parameters. Twice more the team initiated the system. Twice more, we got no reaction at all.

After some discussion between Thuan, Ray, and Wendy, the portal was brought up with slightly lower cross field voltage and currents, but with the FlucGen near maximum, far above the normal operating parameters. As the operators started the initialization, I asked why.

"From long ago," Wendy said with a smile. "Long before your time, Scotty. The first few times we saw the phenomenon, we had no idea what was going on. It became clear quickly that without vacuum fluctuations, we never got anything. When we figured out the routine to get a portal to form dependably, a high level of fluctuations always helped."

She gave me a grin. "I'll admit, a stab in the dark, but with solid reasons to try."

The portal came up, power stabilized, and abruptly darkened, flickered, and then cleared, to reveal nothing out of the usual.

"Rats," Wendy said. That was about the worst epithet I'd ever heard her use. She signaled for the power to be cut.

Time was running out, so she had the operators dial the IC jumbo in Fort Worth to give them the all clear. As had been the case before, in the frequent times when we had used IC's clout to shut down the entire portal network, we had to let the Portal Authority have several hours to catch up on traffic.

Jay, as I referred to Martinez, had lunch prepared for us in the small mess hall, though it was about mid-afternoon GMT, which was Ganymede standard time as well. Kaley and I sat near Thuan, Wendy, and Ray, discussing options for our next time window. We had one more slot today, then we would have to regroup and let both Earth and solar system operations get back, more or less, to normal.

Ray seemed upbeat. "It looked like we almost had something once," he said. We'd seen the slight blink in the portal view once, but I think he wanted to keep everyone optimistic.

"Maybe so," Wendy seemed reserved but pessimistic and I had to side with her.

"This may be the beginning of a long haul," I said, trying to hit the middle ground. I wanted to be as cheery as Ray but realistic. "We're on the right track. Bobby thinks so and he's rarely wrong. It may take time and a good deal of experimentation before we hit the jackpot."

Kaley sided with Wendy and me, hopeful, but not overly buoyant. "There are a lot of variables. If any team can do it, it's us. I think we may have to do some careful calibration, especially the cross field values, not just the FlucGen."

Wendy nodded, Ray chewed on the lack of support for his rosy outlook, and nobody said much for the rest of the meal.

Time seemed to drag but after a few centuries, our next slot came up. Wendy seemed to heed Kaley's comment, keeping FlucGen signals high, and varying both static voltage and the magnetic field levels. Near the end of the hour, we started to get flickers more often, when the magnetic fields were higher, so Wendy ordered voltages down and magnetic fields higher still, keeping FlucGen high to cram more attempts into the hour.

On the next-to-last try, the portal darkened, filled with the familiar dark swirl of fog, and for a fraction of a second, I thought I perceived a scene , possibly a lab-like setting, including a wall and a row of instruments. Then it vanished and the dark swirl dispersed, leaving us frustrated, and me swearing under my breath.

The last try, using the same operational parameters, netted nothing, as though the portal we'd accessed had been killed. A frantic call to IC for more time struck out, as pressure from the Portal Authority was too strong, with the travel backlog building across the world.

We gave up. Near the portal, we stared at each other in disgust. Thuan said it all. "We're missing something. We need to regroup and consider what we've seen so far."

Kaley underscored his words. "I agree. Ray, Wendy, we need to take a step back, and try again."

I seconded that. We closed down, thanked Jay for his hospitality and the use of Ganymede Alpha portal, and went back to Earth.

At home, I corralled Kaley long to discuss the Glynnis situation. Over a healthy evening aperitif, I related the whole story—Guy's call, my trip, meeting Glynnis, and the final kiss.

When I had finished, she said, "A kiss, huh?"

I felt guilty. "I should have turned her down, but she looked so ill, and frail, and pitiful, I gave in. I'm sorry."

She managed a grin. "Don't be such a doofus, you doofus—I'm just giving you a hard time. It's the sort of thing G would do, milk the scene for all she could, and do anything possible to lure you back.

"You aren't such a dumbass as to go for that. I get it, all guys are horndogs and she was trying to use her wiles to snare you. Basically, she was just taking advantage of the fact you're such a nice guy. Don't worry about it. I think it was a bit dopey to get taken in, but don't worry, there's nothing to forgive. You're out from under her spell. I've known that for a long time."

We were seated on a sofa in the den. She stood. "Now let's go to bed, and I'll make certain any leftover longings are put to rest." She held out her hand.

As promised, she did just that.

CHAPTER 10
RETALIATION

After a night's love and sleep at home, and with Kaley again gallivanting over the known solar system, I entered our joint office to find it deserted. Assuming Bobby had chosen to sleep in for once to catch up on his rest, I made a call to Margie, about Kaley's schedule. As she usually did, Kaley had left a schedule showing two Earth calls followed by a jaunt to Mars, and also a note saying she hoped to see me this evening. Of course, it was Sunday, and you'd think some people would take off. If she'd had time to stay home, Kaley would have collared me and dragged me to church. As it was, all of us were far too busy to take day off, so Sunday was just another work day.

As I hung up, our CEO, Virgil Oliva, stuck his head in my office.

"Busy?"

"Never too busy for you," I told him, and he took one of the uncomfortable chairs before my desk. That was on purpose. I never wanted anyone to spend more than the minimum time in my office. If Kaley or Bobby visited, there was the sofa. As he sat, I asked, "Problem?"

He shook his head. "Not at all. We have one supplier issue and you like to take those if you can, but I thought I'd check. I can take it if IC has designs on your time."

Of medium height, olive-skinned, with dark hair and unerring style, he was attired as impeccably as usual in a dark gray suit sporting a subtle houndstooth pattern, with a light gray shirt and a gray-and-maroon striped tie, plus Gucci loafers. I think all his suits are ordered directly from Kilgour on Savile Row. His request was typical Virgil. Glad to do more, but not wanting to encroach on my area of responsibility.

"They do," I assured him, "and I'd be glad for you to handle that. I was about to call McKissack. Our trials on Ganymede were a bust, although knowing Bobby, he'll soon have the problems solved."

"That's what else I had to tell you," he continued. "McKissack called early, so Margie shifted him to me. He needs your help. Sounded unhappy but wouldn't say more. Your clearance is a good bit higher than mine."

Mine was as high as it went. IC had seen to that shortly after the first Bug incursion . "I'll call him," I assured him. "We're pretty damn sure Bugs are present in northern Russia or Siberia, and possibly in South America, and other places. Bobby thinks there could be more secret locations. I thought we were clear of the buggers, but they're back, in force."

He stood. Virgil is discreet, effective, and understated, just like his suits. "I'll get on it. If there is any way I can help..."

"Not sure there's any way *I* can help," I said. "But if there is, you'll know as soon as I do."

He made his exit and I called McKissack on his private line. An aide answered and told me to hang on. I didn't have to wait long.

His voice sounded breathy, so he'd probably hurried over from his current meeting. "Scotty? Sorry to call you on a Sunday, especially if I woke you."

"You didn't. I'm in the office, only missed your call about three minutes. What's the word? Good news or bad news?"

He paused to gather his thoughts. "Hell if I know. It's news, one way or the other. Our Russian friends found the other Bug nest, but it was heavily defended. They dropped another nuke. Collateral damage will probably amount to around twenty thousand or more casualties, but they got the nest, leaving a big crater. It's visible via our satellites."

"Sounds bad for the locals."

"Yeah, maybe for the not-so-locals as well. Our experts estimate some four to five thousand square kilometers in southern Siberia is a wasteland. The leadership decided it was better to sacrifice the locals and protect the homeland."

"That was the last known Bug site in Russia. Does the leadership think they're clean?"

"Yeah. I'd want to consult with you and your colleagues before I agreed."

I didn't blame him. I was in no way sure Bobby would agree Russia had rid itself of the last Bug nest.

"Thanks for the report. Anything else, or were you just keeping us up to date?"

"You know me better than that. I need a favor."

A favor. Not something McKissack usually asked for. He hardly ever asked for anything, as a matter of fact—he gave directives. It must be pretty touchy.

"Your wish is my... Well, you know."

"Okay. We have a bit of a an unusual situation in South America. Bobby spotted that Bug fighter a few days ago, and so far, the Brazilian authorities haven't found a trace."

"Yeah. That jungle is so dense they could hunt forever and not find it."

"Right. They need some help. Here's the deal. They don't particularly want to ask the US military or IC itself to do surveillance on their soil. They asked us to ask S-Cubed to assist in scanning the area near Manaus."

"I don't see the difference."

"You guys are a civilian entity, as is the Portal Authority. If you help organize and supervise the surveillance, you're just a vendor of hardware to Brazil who is volunteering to help look for the Bugs. You're not the US military. They have a good number of SF Seventy-sevens, so you'll be using a modern aircraft-spacecraft to surveil. I told them you insisted on using your own pilots, so they expect you to bring one. The pilot will actually be IC personnel but won't wear a uniform so that should keep them happy."

I thought that over. "You know me—always ready to help out. In this case, I'm not sure how my presence ensures success more than one of their people, or a Portal Authority person."

"Agreed. It's a matter of form. If a civilian helps out, nobody gets their feathers ruffled."

Politics. I know such odd maneuvers keep nations from straining for each other's throats, but sometimes I want to scream, "Forget the Goddam maneuvering and just do what makes sense!" In this case, it was too late. I felt sure McKissack had committed me to the assignment, so better not say anything, just man up and get to work.

"How do I get there?" I asked.

"As I'm sure you know, there's a jumbo at the Manaus airport. Transit over here to headquarters and we'll get you connected in minutes. We can set you up in a flight suit."

"They expect me there yesterday, right?"

He chuckled. "Day before, but they'll be happy if you'll just come."

"Dial into our lab portal," I told him. "I'll see you in about ten minutes."

Stopping only to tell Margie the situation, I passed by the restroom and went to the lab, where the portal had connected with Fort Worth. Putting Bobby and the project team out of my mind for the next few hours, I crossed to the IC base to await a connection to Manaus.

CHAPTER 11 EXPLORING THE EMERALD FOREST

The Naval Air pilot who accompanied me was dressed as a civilian. Admiral McKissack had no desire to let the pilot of any other government chauffer around one of the key engineering personnel of Triple-S. I flattered myself he worried about sending me out into the field as he had when I'd gotten involved in a firefight with the Bugs. I gave him credit for concern, and frankly, I preferred one for whom English was not a second language.

She was a lieutenant commander, had nearly twenty years in military service, trained new pilots on SF-77's, and was one of the toughest hard-asses I ever met. I liked her. She showed up via portal in the Manaus military airport within twenty minutes of my arrival, said a terse hello, and turned to the base commander beside me. A full air force colonel, he impressed me as an equal hard-ass, and I had no trouble decoding his lack of enthusiasm that a US pilot, even one supposedly not in the military, would take the place of one of his sharpshooters.

LC Alice DeGolyer didn't give a shit what Colonel Joao Silva thought. She just wanted a ride ASAP. "Where's my bird, Colonel?"

I noticed she acted quite casual, not saluting, as though she wasn't in the military, and not offering to shake hands. She sensed his hostility and returned it in spades.

Silva sized her up. "You are an SF-77 pilot?"

She sized back. "What, you think somebody's got to sport a pair of balls to fly a Seventy-Seven?"

He sized some more. "You are not a military pilot?"

"I'm a test pilot," she said shortly, and for all I knew, she was. "I flew the first test flight ever flown in a Seventy-Seven and I've logged more hours than any pilot in the world on 'em. Want to go up with me for a check flight?"

No, he didn't. "I did not mean to imply a female pilot could not handle our craft. When do you wish to begin?"

"How about now? "

I had barely shaken hands with the colonel, so I thought I'd better step in. I reached out a hand to shake hers. "Charles Hays, Ms. DeGolyer. I agree, we need to get up and begin our search. I've got new satellite data, and we can use it to direct us initially. Colonel, I agree with my pilot. The sooner the better."

He eyed m , understanding I wanted to be the peacemaker. "Of course. The ship is being readied in the hangar." He turned and led us toward a large door.

We'd alighted via their portal, in a small, gray room with the support equipment. The colonel led us into a cavernous hangar containing more than twenty 77's, repair stations, and hundreds of personnel. We could barely hear each other over the cacophony of cargo trams, riveters, engines being tested into special exhaust pipes, and a buzz of conversation. We followed the colonel to the left, along a group of the fighters, and to a ship that sat alone, buttoned up so to speak.

As we came beside it, a maintenance officer and a couple of non-coms joined us. The colonel spoke in Portuguese and they answered. I caught a word or two but couldn't follow. The general direction of the conversation consisted of the colonel's questions about the ship's readiness and the crew's assurance it was in A-one shape.

He turned to us. "Fully prepared. As soon as you are aboard, a tug will take you out of the hangar."

I thanked him and the crew. My pilot ignored our Brazilian hosts. We donned the flight suits IC had provided and climbed the ladder to the open cockpit door. I climbed to the second of three seats in a row, one for the navigator. She took the pilot's seat. As I buckled my helmet and strapped in, she came across the com link.

"They told me you were a pilot. You checked out on Seventy-Sevens?"

I wasn't. I had flown second seat a few times in my reserve days, but 77's hadn't been around then. This was my first '77 flight as a part of the crew. I'd become very familiar with them in the first Bug War. "Nah. F-X-Twos and Threes, but no formal checkout in a Seventy-seven. If something happened to you, I could land it if the runway was long and the autopilot was in good shape."

She barked a harsh laugh. "Hell, nowadays, the auto pretty well flies them anyway. Glad to know I've got backup."

The pushback tractor began to drag us out to the line. Alice continued the checklist and I repeated her notes, just to keep in the loop. In minutes, we were moving down the taxiway to the end of the runway. A voice spoke in English over the tower com, and we were cleared to launch. In seconds, we were streaking up and toward the east, the last sighting of the Bug fighter.

In Dallas, it was late morning, but in Manaus, noon had passed. Beneath us, the great emerald forest spread in every direction. The

Amazon River, already monstrous even though nearly a thousand miles from the Atlantic Ocean, flowed east after meeting the Negro River, on whose banks the city sat.

"You got the data about the sightings?" Alice asked.

"Loading now." I'd loaded the info on memory cubes and now transferred it to the 77's control computer.

She consulted the map data. "That's close, maybe forty miles east. What altitude makes sense for this sort of scan?"

Bobby had made a suggestion. "Three thousand meters or so. Is the metal detector installed and working?"

"It's set up as an auxiliary pod. It's on, and says 'ready' on the data screen. Let's assume it works."

"Fair enough. When we get ten kilometers out, start recording. Mainly use your eyes, look for motion. I don't think they'll come out until after dark. Consider this an orientation scan."

We started to climb. At the ten-kilometer point, she started the scanner recorder, and I peered toward the northeast, where Bobby's visual analysis had pinpointed the Bug fighter.

We spent two hours scanning, with no results.

Alice brought us in for refueling. We waited until dark, then took off again. Our fighter had effective stealth coatings. The higher up we got, the longer view we had. I ordered us up to six thousand meters. We crisscrossed the area of about twenty-five hundred square kilometers ten times, with no luck. Nearing midnight, we got a call from the military tower. A US satellite directly above us had spotted a "possible enemy spacecraft" over the area we had just patrolled.

Alice swore and I did a bit of the same.

"Didn't see a Goddam thing," she said.

"Me, either. It's so dark, we're really relying on the metal detector, let's face it."

"You got that right. What now, Scotty?" She had decided to call me by my nickname, claiming that in her case, there wasn't one.

I considered. I had done this whole exercise as a favor to McKissack. I'd had no big hopes to start with, and I still had none. "Pack it in, Alice. I don't think there's the chance of a snowball in hell of us finding anything. I'd hang around if I thought the Bugs might attack and give themselves away. Let's face it, they gotta stay out of sight until they can build up forces or get one of their giant portals operational."

Silent for a moment, she said, "Hate to give up, but in this case, I think you're right."

She banked to port, and we headed back to Manaus.

CHAPTER 12 GLYNNIS AGAIN

I got back to my office about midnight. Margie had posted a note on my desk: "Call Virgil. Regardless of the hour. Kaley is still on Mars." She had attached Virgil's phone number in case I needed it. I sat in my desk chair and called.

He was still up. "Sorry to keep you up even longer."

"Likewise. What's the problem?"

He hesitated, not long enough to become awkward, but for sufficient seconds my concern increased. "Not a company problem. Guy called." He knew our company lawyer, Guy Smith, my personal lawyer.

He didn't have to say anything else. "Glynnis."

"Yes. The way he spoke, I don't think he wanted to talk to you at all. He wanted me to act as an intermediary."

I felt my sense of well-being at returning to the office plummet. "She tried to commit suicide. Again. Or pretended to."

Another snatch of silence. "I don't understand how you would pretend to commit suicide, but she did try again, and nearly succeeded. She's in critical condition at Parkland hospital trauma center but is expected to survive."

"And asking for me."

"I don't know about that. Guy told me her lawyer called to notify him. The lawyer made no request."

"I apologize for his bothering you. I suppose I needed to be told, but since I blew up the last time he called, he has no desire to talk to me. I'm going to take him out to lunch and apologize. He's a good friend and didn't deserve my reaction last time."

"Hmm. Probably a useful idea. I don't know if this requires anythin on your part but I thought you ought to know."

I sighed, probably audible to Virgil. " Yes, I needed to know, but not sure what to do."

"Maybe nothing. She broke the trust in your marriage and you divorced her."

I felt, as a concerned former spouse, that perhaps I ought to visit. This was a woman I had feelings for in the past, with whom I had shared a bed. One part of me felt torn. Another part ranted, *Won't I ever be free of this woman?*

"I'll decide tomorrow," I answered. " Get to sleep. You need to catch a few zees."

"Get some sleep yourself."

The connection went dead, and I sat back in the desk chair, activating recline, pondering my course of action. I needed to talk to Kaley, but she was still on Mars. I had no idea if she would be asleep. Mars, like all the off-world bases, had been standardized to Greenwich Mean Time, so it was five AM there. I decided to wait. She might get back anyway.

Returning home, I had a large dollop of Jack Black with a splash and my usual half-teaspoon of sugar. I slept until about six-thirty. As further rest was out of the question, I did thirty minutes in my home gym, showered, and entered the office before eight. I had to walk by Kaley's seldom-used office, and there she sat, behind her desk, summarizing her calls off-world.

"You're back." I rushed across her office as she rose to meet me. We hugged and I held onto her until she finally pushed away.

She guessed the problem. "It must be bad. It must be Glynnis. Another suicide attempt?"

"Yes. She did a better job this time. She's in Parkland ICU. I've been trying to figure out if I should go see her."

Kaley's brow creased. "Figure out? Of course, you should see her. She was a pain in the ass, and she probably cheated on you for most of your marriage, but she was your wife, and you loved her once."

Loved. I thought about that. "Not sure I ever loved her. I've told you that. We were good together at first and we had fun. That faded. I don't hate her. I'm not sure I want to help nurse her through her personal crisis. I'll hear a pitiful plea for us to reunite Not going to happen. Period. If she wasn't successful this time, maybe she will be next time."

Kaley got this horrified expression on her face. "Scotty, what an awful thing to say! I know you wouldn't wish death on anyone."

"Not really," I had to confess. "It's just that I don't handle painful encounters very well."

Kaley hugged me again. "Go see her," she whispered. "I've got two visits to make but I'll be home this evening."

We kissed again, and she left her office as I did. I felt pleased to see that she did not take her overnight bag with her, a good sign.

Parkland Hospital is the Dallas county hospital. Like most big hospitals, it's not just one building. It's basically a whole city , a gargantuan collection of structures, including Children's Medical Center, that extends for blocks in several directions. I found Glynnis had been moved from ICU with a room of her own. Delayed at the office by pressing issues, it was almost noon when I found Glynnis sitting up in bed.

"Scotty!" Glynnis smiled and seemed genuinely pleased I had come. She appeared more rested and in better condition, than the last time. Her skin held some color, and although still perilously slender, her eyes were not so sunken and her face appeared a bit rounder and better nourished.

I took her hand—a good, neutral way to show concern. She smelled of her usual perfume and soap.

"I heard you were in the ICU here," I said.

She brushed the comment away with her left hand as I let go. "They just put me there as a precaution. I wasn't trying to die, Scotty. I just can't sleep, so I take pills, and a bit of wine, and I took too much of both. When the cleaning lady found me, she called nine-one-one."

. Perhaps Glynnis was beginning to cope a bit, although sleeping medicine and wine didn't seem like a good combination to me. "I glad it wasn't on purpose," I said. "Have you gotten counseling?"

" My shrink costs me more than a nice BMW but she's not doing much good. She won't prescribe any strong sleeping medication at all."

"I'm glad you're in counseling. It's bound to help ."

She looked up, giving me a measured appraisal. "What would help the most is if you came back to me, Scotty. With you beside me in bed, I'd sleep easily every night. Especially if we, you know, had a little exercise first."

"Glynnis, you know I can't. I love Kaley. I love her a lot. What you and I had was good for a while, but it wasn't love."

"But we were so good in the bedroom."

"Glynnis, you were good in the bedroom. It was a performance, and I will admit, you dazzled me. But sex isn't love. Love is how you feel about your partner when you *aren't* in the bedroom. What I have with Kaley is love. Look, I would always like for us to be friends but my relationship is with another woman, not you. You have to deal with that.

"Keep going to counseling. Find a nice guy at work, someone with whom you share interests. You can do it. You can have a great life that doesn't include me. That's best for both of us."

Her face had fallen as I spoke. It hadn't gotten hard and hateful, as it had in the past. She surprised me by appearing stoic and perhaps thoughtful. I hoped she had begun to discover there might be a path to a good life without yours truly. I made up my mind: if she ended up in the hospital again, either on purpose or accidently, I wouldn't drop by again.

"Sorry, I have to run. You've probably heard we've got trouble with the Bugs I just got back from South America and may have to go back."

She nodded. "I understand. Keep safe, Scotty. I don't want to lose you. Or for Kaley to lose you ." She neither smiled nor frowned, her face perfectly neutral.

I left to return to the office. I had no idea what would become of Glynnis and I found I really didn't care .

CHAPTER 13 BACK TO GANYMEDE

I entered the office to find Bobby on his phone, not pounding on his keyboard, his usual activity. Only hearing his end, it became obvious Ray Dougal was at the other end of the line.

"...by the end of today," Bobby said. "I'll have to call McKissack but I'm sure Ganymede is available with a few hours' notice. It'll put the Portal Authority out of joint but they'll get over it. Can you and Wendy be ready to go later today?"

Ray apparently said yes, so Bobby finished, "I'll grab Thuan and we can be ready in a couple hours, if we get permission."

He hung up and turned to me. "You heard that. Want to call McKissack?"

"Sure. You think you got it this time?"

"It's a gold-plated cinch. Wendy really came through. We're pretty sure about what went wrong last time, so making those changes, I think we're good to go.

"One problem. If we connect, we're going to confront a Bug base that's live and dangerous. We need to have the military ready with beam weapons primed and aimed at the portal, and a contingent of soldiers ready to defend us. It will take IC some time to set up."

"Not if it means eliminating a Bug portal," I said. I picked up the phone and called McKissack's private number.

In less than two minutes, he came on. Another minute to sketch the situation, and he promised that, with the defensive weaponry on Ganymede due to the former conflict with the Bugs and given the swiftness with which IC could commandeer troops, Ganymede would be ready by oh-seven-hundred, Dallas time.

I hung up and told Bobby, "We need to be on Ganymede in four hours."

I left a message for Kaley, then joined Ray and Wendy, Thuan, and Bobby at the portal. We walked through to Ganymede Beta to be greeted by Captain Martinez.

We needed the IC Beta base this time, as it had the jumbo portal, and if you're going to attack and invade a site, you need room for weapons, troops, and maneuvering. I was shocked to see a full US Marine platoon camped on the far side of the hangar, the normal group of SR-77's moved to the outside surface of Jupiter's largest moon.

In addition, four, count 'em, four, beam weapons were installed, all aimed at the innards of the portal. If we were able to take over a Bug site, the insects were going to get a nasty surprise.

"You guys ready for a party?" Jay asked.

"We're gonna give the Bugs all the fun they can handle," Bobby told him.

We gathered around the jumbo. In addition to the naval portal operators, our tech, Faye, had come from Alpha, so we made a good crowd. "Gonna pull it off this time?" Martinez asked.

"Absolutely," Bobby said.

"One thing bothers me," the captain said. "Suppose you yank control away from the Bugs and take over their portal. Can't they just cut their power and kill the wormhole?"

Bobby grew a wide grin. "Not this time, Jay. We've been experimenting, to come up with a method to create a wormhole with a single portal. We can create one but the problem is it's not repeatable, so we don't always go to the same place. A side benefit of our work is we've discovered how to yank control of a portal and then sustain the wormhole from only our end. Get it? Once we get control, *they can't kill the wormhole.*"

Martinez gaped. "Holy crap."

"Yeah. Now the bad news. Since we'll keep the portal open regardless, we need to have a helluva lot of firepower on this end, because although that lets us attack them, they can counterattack. We better be sure if we take over the wormhole, we can blast anything in proximity to their portal before they have a chance to react."

Martinez thought it over, looking toward the Marine contingent and the weaponry aimed at the portal. "We're okay, but you need to brief the Marine attack leader."

We explained upcoming events to the platoon commander, a first lieutenant, and his platoon sergeant, ten years older than his leader, with a face that said he had seen it all. Both nodded, focused and stoic, and returned to give their platoon instructions. As for us, the captain had all those in the hangar gather to the far side of the portal, except for the operators. Again, we had to wait for all portal systems to be idle. We were transmitted the okay, Martinez gave us the nod, and the operators started the sequence, bringing up our portal with some of the oddest cross field values and FlucGen settings I could remember.

Nothing happened on the first try, Bobby yelled instructions to Faye and the operators, and they adjusted the instrumentation. He whispered to me, "They set the static voltage too low, so we increased about ten percent. I'll bet we're go this time."

The operators began the routine of magnetic field, static voltage, then the vacuum fluctuation input, set to a high level.

I stood so far to the side, per Jay's instructions, I could barely see the portal interior , but I could tell when the interior darkened, pulsed, and lightened to reveal a vague outline. I was too far off-center to decipher it.

The cannon commander yelled, "Fire!"

The cannons blazed beams of death as we bystanders ducked behind concrete barriers , similar to those we had used on the Titan base last year. The barrage didn't last long. The officer called out, "Cease fire!" A rocket launcher sent a rocket bomb through the opening, as a blast shield of thick stainless steel popped into place. Everybody threw themselves flat on the floor.

A monstrous explosion sounded, flinging smoke, dust, and debris back through the portal, although we were well protected. The platoon leader yelled and the Marine contingent charged through the opening.

I had no idea what weapons the Bugs could bring to bear but our guys mainly carried seven millimeter machine pistols, a few having beam rifles. I heard very little through the portal, unable to determine if the sound became too attenuated to carry into our hangar or if there weren't any survivors to confront.

I heard the thump-thump of heavy boots and the harsh voice of the sergeant called out, "All clear!" We scrambled to our feet, following Captain Martinez . The sergeant saluted.

"Sir, the enemy is pacified. No survivors—we finished them off or they killed themselves. Resistance was minimal."

Bobby asked, "Any pieces of their equipment saved, sergeant?"

The sergeant gave Bobby a curious stare. Bobby is a solid nine inches over six feet, but didn't answer until Martinez told him, "Tell him whatever he wants, Sergeant."

"Yes, sir." He turned back to Bobby. "We did find electronics. Some of it was damaged by the bomb."

I interrupted. "Sergeant, any idea of the location of the Bug base?" Because we had no idea, having wrenched control of it to our bidding, whatever its location.

"No sir, except it's pretty warm and surrounded by heavy jungle. Equatorial Africa or maybe South America."

"Can you see the sun?"

"No, sir, it's nighttime."

Bobby chimed in. "What about the sky?"

The sergeant nodded. "Yeah, we can see a patch. The Bugs made a clearing for the portal they were building. Not finished, but it's big."

The portal we had taken must be similar to the one we destroyed last year. "The portal, how large?"

He considered. "The bomb took it out. Maybe the size of one of our larger portals."

So, not as big as the Titan portal, but jumbo-sized. The Bugs didn't build small portals. I addressed Captain Martinez. "Could we take a look?"

Jay considered, appearing doubtful. The sergeant said, "Sir, permission to speak."

"Granted."

The sergeant looked me over. "You're ex-military." Despite my astonishment at the people in IC who'd made that statement before, some of the discipline and organization had rubbed off. I nodded at him. "Six years in IC."

His eyes narrowed. "Thought so. Sir, that jungle is a dangerous place. We've already killed poisonous spiders the size of dinner plates, and one snake that would tip the scales at three hundred pounds. We'll bring any equipment we find through the portal, assuming it's not too badly damaged. Do you need samples of the Bugs themselves?"

I shook my head. "Had plenty of contact with those bastards, Sergeant. Yeah, bring back anything that might help us. If that patch of sky is large enough, try to get a reading on constellations. "

He went back through the portal. Bobby, Wendy, Ray, and Thuan migrated to the coffee pots where a naval E-1 manned the booth. I stood in line , took coffee, discovered there was no sugar or cream available, and took it, glad to get a jolt.

Suddenly, the sounds of battle echoed through the portal. The deck officer, who had been reduced to observer after the assault began, yelled commands. We hit the deck behind the barriers . Nothing came through the portal, either debris, or personnel, and the sounds quickly died out. After a long pause, the sergeant yelled from the mouth of the portal, "All clear."

We stood, as the Marine contingent dragged pieces of alien equipment, metal boxes that might be instruments from a fighter, and articles that could fall under the umbrella of "junk." Martinez crossed to talk to the sergeant and I followed, as the platoon leader, Lieutenant Travis, appeared.

"Some of those Bugs not as dead as you thought?" Martinez asked.

Travis, who appeared to be about fifteen years old, replied. His eyes made him about ten years older. Those eyes told me, like the sergeant, he'd seen a few things in his time. "We'd blasted a couple Bug fighters when we came through," he supplied. " Another Bug ship came in to land, detected our presence, and opened fire. We took it out."

Very matter-of-fact, which I had to admire.

"No survivors?"

"No, sir." The lieutenant turned to look back through the portal. "It crashed a ways off, but we saw a flash of red, and heard it go up. We can check, but I doubt if much is left."

Martinez agreed. As we had talked, platoon members retrieved pieces and parts, and now, a corporal spoke to the sergeant in a whisper. The sergeant addressed his commander. "That's about it, sir. We took a gander at the sky but did not recognize any familiar stars or constellations. Request permission to withdraw."

I had no idea how familiar our doughty Marines were with the sky but took his comment at face value. For all we knew, they could have been staring up at the night sky as seen from Brazil or South Africa, although the light of day now fell on most of Africa.

Martinez spoke up. "One more task, Corporal." He turned to the platoon leader and its sergeant. "Lieutenant, to your right and across the hangar is a GBU-57C blockbuster bomb. It had a delay fuse and is mounted on a small tram car. Get it positioned, withdraw, trigger it, and we'll close the portal. We have Brazilian Air Force planes in the area where we suspect the base is located with five US satellites overhead. When that baby goes off, we'll have the proof we need."

That got a grin from both officer and sergeant. "Sounds to me like they'll get to see a show. That bomb is one big baby." It was—the largest non-nuclear weapon in our nation's inventory, the successor to the GBU-43B used in earlier wars.

Operators trundled the bomb over and prepared to take it through. About ten meters long, roughly a meter in diameter, and with a yield of more than five tons of TNT, it would make a big hole, hopefully visible from above. I was betting the Brazilian fighters would spot both the explosion and the resulting hole. I also hoped none of the more primitive tribes were in the area.

Martinez told the lieutenant and us as well. "A quick scan from above by the Brazilian aircraft has verified there are no villages in the immediate area. We're going to kill flora and fauna, but I see no way to avoid it, to make sure we destroy every vestige of the Bug site."

The lieutenant and his sergeant passed back through the portal and the bomb carrier puttered up the ramp and onto the Bug site. Soldiers filed back, and soon only the lieutenant remained by the portal. Martinez handed him the remote control, explaining how it worked.

"Lift this cover, toggle the red switch, and wait for the confirmation of countdown. Give me the nod and we kill the portal."

"Yes, sir." The lieutenant took the controller as though it were the bomb itself. He turned, lifted the cover, aimed the controller, and toggled the bright red switch. A tiny screen on the lit up, showing the number 20 and then beginning to count down.

..19, 18, 17...

The lieutenant said, "Countdown confirmed." He needn't have bothered. The portal operators were already attending the portal management center, and in an instant, the portal fogged, swirled, and faded to show the far wall of the hangar.

I finished my now-cold coffee and shuddered at the awful taste. We all stood around like statues, waiting, some holding our breaths. The Alpha site portal was dialed into Forth Worth, had been as soon as we took over the Bug portal. In less than a minute, the com phone next to the jumbo control cabinets buzzed, an operators grabbed it, and listened. He turned to us with a grin.

"Captain, Brazilian spotters aloft report a very large explosion at roughly the site we had suggested." That was the site where Bobby spotted the Bug fighter days ago. "Smoke and debris are still clearing, but they say there is no doubt everything within a square kilometer has been reduced to rubble."

We let out a cheer. Bobby jumped in the air, while Wendy and Ray hugged each other. I found myself wishing Kaley was around.

Had we gotten the last major Bug installation? I hoped so.

CHAPTER 14 WANNA BET?

No, we hadn't. The Bug infestation seemed infinite and forever.

I arrived home about two thirty. Kaley wasn't in evidence, and a call to her house bore no fruit. I checked my messages and found two from her, one from Mars and the other from Earth's moon. A minor failure on Moon Delta meant she had to stay overnight, as no parts were immediately available, and could I light a fire under both our local suppliers and IC in Fort Worth to find the part, a circuit board used in the FlucGen system?

Yes, of course. I compromised my sleep schedule. Awakening at six, I called Virgil, who would always be up by then, and asked him to work the problem. Yes, he would. I caved into the sack to sleep three more hours, arising to exercise, shower, and grab coffee and a sandwich at the local Starbucks on the way to the office.

Virgil had solved the problem, working with Thuan, who came in early as well. Thuan was Kaley's male equivalent in stamina. He could get by on about four hours sleep, although I knew he snuck into one of the two sleep rooms we maintained for power naps on occasion.

Where was Kaley? Neither Virgil nor Margie had a clue. She'd finished up the moon problem with Virgil's help, then told Margie she had to make a stop in Paris. A call to Paris revealed she had completed the visit and left, destination unknown. I gave up and got ready to leave. Rain fell briskly, not the heavy thunderstorms we get in north Texas in early spring, but a cold, heavy rain, more usual in late winter. Throwing on a waterproof jacket with a liner, I headed out, glad the office was only minutes away.

As I arrived , the sky was lowering and dark, the rain coming down with determination that promised a wet and dreary day. I stepped into the joint office about eleven AM to find Bobby in residence with the bad news.

He didn't even bother with a hearty good morning. Given the conditions outside, I couldn't blame him.

"Got word from IC a Bug fighter was spotted over central China. A possible sighting in northern Canada, near the eastern shore of Hudson Bay. Reports of South American sightings, but I'm hoping those are earlier sightings that are just catching up with us and they concerned the base we destroyed last night."

The news didn't improve my disposition. "Oh, goody. I was hoping we'd solved that problem for good."

He sipped from a Starbucks cup. "I believe we got the biggest Bug installation, one that was about to fire up its portal. I think it's as we suspected. When they took over that pirate Russian site, the Bugs dispersed small teams, say four to ten fighters each, and spread them out so far as they could. It's a damn good plan, making our job a thousand times harder."

"Agreed," I muttered. I had no idea how many teams the Bugs sent through before Russia blasted the original pirate base. Ten? Fifty? A hundred? However many, their plan had been masterful. We had to be alert and utilize those extra satellites we had planted. The Bugs could be anywhere.

"One more thing," Bobby added after another gulp of caffeine. "My caller from IC, some lieutenant on McKissack's staff, wants us over there today at one PM for a pow-wow with the brass about any take-aways from last night's exercise."

So, McKissack and the rest were just as concerned as we were about unidentified sites. I wasn't sanguine about how we could provide IC substantial assistance, but I assumed word had filtered back to McKissack, via Martinez, about how we'd taken control of the site and maintained the wormhole while the Marines attacked.

McKissack would want us to provide the same magic for other suspected sites. We might be able to take control, one after the other, just as Bobby and the project team had last night. On the other hand, it had not become clear to me that grabbing a Bug site would always be effortless.

I motioned Bobby over to my sofa and sat in my recliner. "Last night was a dazzling *tour de force*, all due to the team's discoveries. How repeatable is it?"

He frowned. "Pretty solid, I think. If we can continue to get time slices when the world turns off all portals, I'm convinced we can grab some of them. Maybe all. I'd request one hour, every twenty-four to try again, starting today and using Ganymede as the attack base. We'll have to be more careful. Last night, I was convinced, and I think you were too, the Bug site was near Manaus in Brazil. We have no idea where some might be located, so we can't just take control, blast everything in view with laser cannons, and slip through a blockbuster to detonate. We could find a site near a population center in, say, Canada, Australia, or China, kill a lot of innocent bystanders."

I agreed. I also agreed with Bobby's suggestion of one hour in twenty-four from the Portal Authority.

"Problem is," Bobby pointed out, "IC may be willing to risk some collateral damage, even a *lot* of collateral damage, if it means wiping out a Bug presence . If you think about Martinez's attitude last night, he was going to use that blockbuster regardless of who was in the area, unless

Brazilian authorities stepped up and forbade it. I think they were just as willing to kill civilians if necessary ."

"Yeah." I was ready to go home and hide under the bed. "I think we need to press for the time window from the Portal Authority, but stress we need to be careful to avoid human loss near a large population center. Thing is, what happens when we find that? We delay, they finish a big portal, and fly through a few tens of thousands of their fighters to begin a major attack. Then what?"

He shook his head, stumped. So was I. As the king muttered in the ancient musical *The King and I*, if memory serves, "It is a puzzlement."

Bobby, as down as I was, said nothing. After brief consideration, netting zero inspirations, I said, "Let's go get an early lunch, see if new ideas pop up, and then head to Fort Worth."

Stopping to check if Kaley had returned, no luck there, we jumped in my SUV and drove toward Billie Lou's. Rain still fell, perhaps a bit lighter, the sky dark gray and cheerless, but burgers awaited and we would not be deterred . Finding Alex at the counter, we ordered the usual, a cheeseburger and fries for me, a chili burger and jalapeno poppers for Bobby.

Alex was busy, not only drying glasses for the bar but serving a dozen or so customers strung along the bar. His first chance to talk occurred when he brought our orders. Setting them before us, he said more softly than usual, "It true we got Bugs on Earth now?"

I had no idea what IC considered secret and what they deemed classified, so I was prepared to issue a non-committal reply when Bobby blurted, "Yeah. We blasted a big colony yesterday, but I think there are a few still out there."

"That's classified info," I cautioned, knowing Alex had to be one of the most closed-mouthed people I knew. "Don't spread it around."

He surveyed us both. "Better not tell the wife then. She never kept a secret in her whole life."

Bobby and I both chuckled, although truth told, I hadn't seen her in the place for a year. A heavyset woman at the other end of the bar motioned for him, so he started in her direction. "Gets more service for smaller tips than any customer in history," he said, sotto voce, as he moved off. Bobby almost fell off his chair and I had a good laugh too.

We didn't talk much, knowing we couldn't make any plans until our meeting with McKissack et al. Bobby concentrated on his chili burger and double order of poppers. I managed to force down the burger, but didn't even finish the fries. Bobby didn't appear as worried as I was about the meeting, but he wasn't thinking about possible lost business. Somebody was going to figure out that Bugs were only a threat because they'd taken control on Titan and managed to invade. Now they had taken control of a pirate portal and done the same. How long until we were directed to take down the portal system forever?

Alex sidled up. "You guys lead an exciting life. One of these days when things quiet down, how about letting me take a portal to someplace off Earth? I'd provide lunch for your field engineers."

Bobby grinned. "You got it. How about a trip to Mars for you and the Mrs.? Once we get all these Bug problems straightened out."

Alex seemed a bit surprised and I thought for a moment he might have been joking. He managed a smile, unusual for him. "Sounds like fun. Not sure Marissa will go for it, but she might."

Shocked, I nearly gaped, realizing I had never heard Alex refer to his wife by her given name. As I recovered, I said, "Tell her it's on us. She'd never pass up a freebie, right?"

That got a solid har-har in return. "Hell, no. She'd probably take a hysterectomy or a root canal if it was free."

We joked around a bit more, then left, Bobby dropping a Fifty dollar bill, as he had since his kidnapping. Other than Kaley, me, Margie and Virgil, Alex is Bobby's next favorite person in the entire world.

The brass were gathered in McKissack's private conference room as we arrived by portal, not having to be concerned about the weather. Not a big group, just the boss, two aides the commander who had called, and a one-star I didn't know.

McKissack sounded apologetic. "Sorry to yank you guys over here. Last evening on Ganymede, you guys helped us pull off a coup. We're hoping you can help us do it a few more times."

I had detoured by the coffee pot. Seated, I said, "We just got the door open, Admiral. Your guys did the cleanup."

"And we need to do more," he replied.

The one star surveyed me. He didn't know me, and I didn't know him, so he didn't know how many irons we'd pulled out of the fire for McKissack and IC. After a pause, he inserted, "This whole can of worms is due to your own lack of precautions in opening your portal network, Commander."

Three things were made apparent by his statement. Number one, he'd thought about the problems our network had created and decided to lay the blame squarely on SSS. Two, he didn't want to concede we'd done anything spectacular last night. Finally, he knew I had served in IC.

I paused to look him over. He had a thin face, a ramrod-straight back, thinning hair, a slender build, and a big fucking attitude. I didn't let any irritation show.

"I don't believe we've met," I said.

McKissack spoke, sensing my underlying feelings and wanting to prevent a pissing contest to start our meeting. "Doctor Hays, this is Admiral William Weston Overton. He's our new chief of off-world operations."

I nodded. "Your old job, eh, Kinsey?" I wanted the one-star to know McKissack and I were friends. *Good* friends. "Is he any good, or does he just like to irritate guests?"

That caught McKissack by surprise. I'll admit I should have stifled the impulse to trade barbs with Overton but I was pissed. The one-star appeared affronted and McKissack didn't seem too happy.

Instead of answering, Overton observed to his boss, "Perhaps IC should recall the commander to duty. Then we could rein in his company's wild behavior ."

Not if you ever want another fucking favor from Triple-S, I was about to say. McKissack intervened. "Please, Bill, don't be absurd. Scotty Hays has done so damn many off-the-books favors for us that frankly, we could never repay him or his company."

I did speak then. "Thank you, Admiral." I glanced at his subordinate. "Here's the thing, Bill—may I call you Bill? I could make the same complaint about how your IC forces on Titan let themselves get overtaken and killed, but that would be *just* as unfair." I stressed the "just." "In fact, we're all still learning here, as we expand our portal network. We have to acknowledge mistakes will be made. They have been made. We can give up our portal network or we can keep working together to improve it and make it bullet-proof.

"I don't think it helps us to be at odds, of course. Working together is a lot more productive."

Overton didn't like my "may I call you Bill?" bit, which was why I'd used it. He swallowed hard, pushed one more time. "Working together? We serve the United States and the world to keep it safe. You work for money. Those aims do not seem compatible."

Oh, he was armed and ready to fire. If I'd been meeting with him, I would have walked out but this was McKissack's meeting and I was rather fond of him. "One thing you could do if you pulled me back in," I said, turning back to McKissack. "Promote me to one-star and put me in charge of off-world ops. I guarantee I could do better than this clown."

Overton levitated straight out of his chair. "I will not sit in this meeting and be insulted."

"Okay, stand and be insulted," I told him. "I came at your boss's request, and I'll stay at his request, but I won't respond to you. Why don't you go back to your office and finish your mental masturbation or whatever the hell else you were doing before you came in here?"

McKissack's face was a study and I couldn't figure out if he were angry or trying not to laugh. Bobby's expression represented a weird combination of horror and amusement, as though he couldn't decide which. I wondered if Overton were going to leave or assault me.

Quiet reigned. After thirty seconds, McKissack said than I would have imagined, "I think we need to do a reset.

"Admiral Overton, this is Doctor Charles Scott Hays, one of the founders of Solar Subway Systems and one of the inventors of portal travel. Doctor Hays, this is Admiral Overton, one of our most capable, and until today, one of the most articulate, field leaders in Intersolar Command. Both of you are valuable to IC and to this nation's defense. Do either of you have any questions?"

I dipped my head, no. Overton didn't move a muscle. McKissack prodded. "Admiral Overton?"

"No." A clipped, one-word response.

"Good. Let's get down to business."

The rest of the meeting was about what I expected. IC wanted us to attempt to takeover any number of portals and we pledged to do so, with the next attempt once again on Ganymede, exact time TBD. Overton spoke only when spoken to and ignored me. Bobby had nothing to say at all, still horrified.

As we finished, I reminded McKissack we were only a phone call away if IC needed anything. McKissack nodded and wished us well. We headed back via portal to our offices.

I apologized to Bobby. "Sorry to cause a dust-up. That new one-star got under my skin."

"Me too, but I never expected easy-going Scotty to blast him."

"That's *formerly* easy-going. Too much crazy going on in my life and not even Kaley to share it with."

He patted my shoulder. "Maybe she's back."

Supposedly she was, but I couldn't find her. Margie thought maybe she'd gone out for dinner, but she would have let me know. I decided to get on some of the million tasks, including lots of vendor calls I had been delaying, and hope Kaley would drop by when she returned.

At nine PM, with no Kaley, I decided to chuck it and go home. I waved to Bobby, still pounding his keyboard. The weather had cleared, but a hand out the car window revealed a chilly wind whining out of the northwest. Pulling into my driveway, I noted lights in the house, a clear signal that Kaley had made it home. Entering the den from the garage, prepared to kiss and possibly seduce my beloved on the den sofa, I stopped and stared. Kaley wasn't in evidence, although she must be around.

Alone on the sofa, and turning toward me as I entered, sat Glynnis.

CHAPTER 15 GLYNNIS VISITS

"Glynnis?"

Okay, that was stupid, I'll admit. Quite clearly, my ex-wife sat on the sofa in my den. I just blurted her name before I could stop myself. Finding a purple dinosaur in my family room, or a chartreuse alligator, or even the Cheshire Cat, would have been a shock. But my ex? I felt such a frantic surge of *wrongness* I had to restrain myself from running out to check if I had driven to the correct house.

She was as casual and conversational as if we were still married. "Oh, hi, Scotty. We didn't think you'd be home so early. Kaley said you were meeting with army top brass, and she had no idea when you'd make it ."

I could command nothing more to issue from my mouth. Glynnis. Here in my house. I simply goggled.

She looked much better than she had in the hospital. Her face had filled out and she didn't appear to be quite so thin. She was dressed as usual, in a trim business suit of deep maroon, with a lavender silk blouse. She'd visited the hairdresser as well. Her head of lush, honey hair done in an off-the-shoulder, casual style had always suited her. Longer than I remembered but appropriate to a business woman who met with advertising customers on a regular basis.

I had to say something. I stammered, "You're... looking better, that is, like you feel better." I paused, then blurted, "What are you doing here?"

She didn't flinch or blush or have the appearance of the slightest discomfort. "Oh, I wanted to drop by to see the house," she said, still casual, "My psychiatrist told me I need to see my world without you in it. I thought seeing the house with Kaley here would do me good. Doctor Mills says it's a good way to begin my recovery."

But you're inside my house, I wanted to scream.

Kaley saved me by breezing in with a tray of drinks and bottles of soda.

"Oh, hey Scotty, didn't hear you come in. Glynnis stopped by."

"I noticed," I said.

Kaley gave me the eye, paused, then set the tray down and handed Glynnis a glass of what appeared to be Coke.

"Thank you," Glynnis said. She shifted her gaze to me. "I'm still on meds so no alcohol."

Kaley had anticipated my arrival. She offered a glass to me. I like Coke well enough although my fave is Dr. Pepper, but I had been looking forward to Jack Black and water. Kaley took a seat on the sofa beside Glynnis. I sat in my recliner, swiveled toward the sofa, although I was tempted to keep it pointed at the TV on the opposite wall.

Kaley could sense the latent animosity. Glynnis could be so blasé she might or might not sense my mood but I suspected she did. Glynnis went on as though nothing at all were amiss. "I dropped by to see the two of you because Doctor Mills told me to visualize you post-divorce to help me get on with my life. I was hoping to find Kaley. We've had a very nice talk to my benefit."

She paused, took a sip of Coke, looked me over. "How are you, Scotty? Kaley says you're working hard and so is she. "

She turned to Kaley. "Try to force him to take more time off," she said with a smile. "His schedule was one of the reasons for our divorce."

Glynnis turned back to me. "I know I got snippy and hard to live with when you were gone so much. I wasn't understanding. I don't want you and Kaley to let your schedules drive you apart."

I didn't know whether to explode, throw down my drink, or run screaming from the house. The only reason I stayed seated at all was there was about one grain of truth in Glynnis's words. Kaley and I had been working too hard. We'd seen each other little to none in days, hardly more than a kiss except for the recent night. I sat there absorbing the words and wondered if it could happen to Kaley and me, as the Bug conflict seemed to be stretching into infinity.

Kaley came to my rescue. "No problem, Glynnis. Thank you for your concern. I do understand, but as we're in the same company, and understand the issues surrounding this new conflict, we can make it work."

Glynnis nodded. "I'm sure you're right. You're a lot more understanding than I was, Kaley. I wish I'd done a better job. Bravo to you for your kindness and patience."

Glynnis turned to me. " Kaley and I had a nice talk. I mentioned being just out of the hospital. She was so understanding in providing me a room here for the next couple days."

I felt as if my head were about to explode. Glynnis? Staying *here*? It felt as though I were Alice, and I'd just wandered into Wonderland.

I was back to gawking. As my head swiveled to Kaley, she said, "Glynnis is in a bad position, Scotty. She's out of the hospital and her condo management notified her there's a mold problem in their building. It will be closed for two weeks. She had no place to go. You and I are hardly here right now, so I said she could stay until she can get settled. All she has is a suitcase."

And a three thousand dollar Oscar de la Renta designer business suit, I thought but didn't say. Matter of fact, I couldn't say anything. My fiancée, the woman I loved more than I had ever loved *anyone*, had invited my conniving, sly, frequently-ruthless ex-spouse into our home.

Without asking me.

"Please don't be concerned, Scotty," Glynnis said. "I'll only be here a night or two, then in a hotel downtown. I love the Ritz Carleton, such a nice place to stay. Even if I get stuck there for more than two weeks, I'll be fine. It was so sweet for Kaley to as. I know I caused trouble during the divorce. It's wonderful for Kaley to be so gracious about it."

She turned to Kaley. "I won't be any bother. I'm trying to get back into the routine at work, so I won't be here much. I eat out usually, and as I get back to my usual schedule, I'll go to the gym to exercise, then on to work. I won't be any trouble," she turned back to me, "I won't bother you at all, Scotty. "I'll try to be invisible, so far as you're concerned."

There was nothing to say. I looked between my fiancée and my ex. I was definitely not in a dream. It felt like a nightmare of the worst kind. Living in the same house with both of them was a nightmare of proportions I had never imagined. I didn't believe, not for a moment, Glynnis hadn't planned the whole thing. I doubted her condo, an upscale, high-dollar habitation, had a mold problem. Even if they had, they should have been able to accommodate those living there without having them move out. I decided to call the condo the first thing in the morning.

Glynnis arose. "I'm sorry, but I'm tired. You know how hard it is to sleep in a hospital. They wake you up every hour for something or other. As quiet as it is in this neighborhood, I'll get a really good sleep."

Kaley got up with her. "Here, I'll help."

She took Glynnis by the arm and they headed to one of the extra bedrooms.

I sat.

I sat some more.

Trying to come to grips with my current situation seemed to be an overwhelming challenge. I had traded shots with the Bugs on Rhea and Ganymede—and come out on top. Along with Bobby and a bit of help from IC, I had dropped two nukes on our enemies—and lived to tell the tale. I had nearly died several time protecting our country from the insectile invaders that still plagued us. Nothing I'd done prepared me for facing Glynnis without the ability to walk away. She was in my house, by invitation, and I could do nothing about it except grimace and accept it.

It occurred to me I felt exceedingly tired, as though I had been up, oh, about three days. I stood, swayed right and left like a drunken sailor, and set off to the master bedroom. I threw off my clothes, showered a full three minutes, toweled off, and fell into bed. Shockingly, I fell asleep. I awakened once, alone. Kaley had either been afraid of my reaction, or perhaps too pissed at my attitude. I didn't think about it long, being too exhausted. Again, sleep claimed me.

I awoke, still alone, to see rays of sunlight creeping around the drapes. The master bedroom is large, with an oversize king bed, dresser, two armoires, a sitting area with sofa and coffee table, and a small desk and chair. Somehow, it felt very empty.

Realizing my ringing phone had awakened me, I cast about for it, finding it not on my bedside table but on the bedspread beside me.

"Yeah?"

"Okay, I can tell I woke you. Sorry, I know you're beat, but we got calls and McKissack wants to see us again."

Bobby. I tried to process, coming slowly out of the fog. I go under hard when I'm tired and come out of it painfully. I managed, "A new sighting?"

"A bunch of new sightings. That's one of the problems they're having. Yesterday, IC put out the call over broadcast news and net sources for the populace worldwide to be on the lookout. Now they're getting inundated, and I think the problem is differentiating between possible legitimate calls and run of the mill hysteria. You know, like the old UFO sightings."

I rubbed my eyes, managed to sit up.

"What time?"

"McKissack says come over at eleven and he'll have early lunch."

"I never eat lunch that early. I haven't even had breakfast. Will Overton be there?"

"Now really, you expect me to know? The meeting won't last long. Forget breakfast except maybe a Starbucks sandwich and coffee. It's already eight and you won't get in here before ten."

I stood and stretched, putting the phone back to my ear. "Won't be that long. I showered last night and today isn't an exercise day."

"Just as well. You pledged to have a go at another possible Bug portal today. We got a slot at one PM."

The day was already clogged. Where was Kaley? Had she...

Then it hit me. *Glynnis was living in my house.*

I said a slow, deliberate, "Oh, shit."

A pause. "What? You stubbed your toe when you got out of bed?"

"My Goddam ex-wife is living in my fucking house."

"Huh?"

"You heard me. My Goddam—"

He cut me off. "Okay, slow down, cut the profanity. In plain words, why is Glynnis now in your house?"

I wasn't sure if I could explain. "I'll tell you later. Kaley invited her, that's all I'll say. I may move to a hotel."

Silence. "Kaley...?"

"No fucking questions, Bobby, I'll see you in an hour or less."

I hung up, dressed, and went in search of Kaley.

Nowhere to be found, probably gone to work. I think she'd understood how upset I was the night before and decided to let me cool off. Glynnis was easy to find. She sat at my breakfast table—*my breakfast table!*—drinking coffee, and munching on a croissant. She'd slept well, and I had to admit , although not the glamorous Glynnis I had married, she'd reclaimed a good deal of her looks.

"Oh, hi, Scotty. Kaley had to get away early. She made coffee, said to make myself at home."

I stood in the opening to the den, silent, gazing at her. I told myself to be cool, not say anything I might regret. "I have to go to work," I said distinctly.

After a moment, I added, "Glynnis, I don't like you staying here. I know Kaley invited you, but you had to know that would irritate me. Please, please find a place to stay and move out."

She stared a moment, a bit nonplussed and perhaps nervous. I don't think she expected I would be that direct, as Kaley had issued the invitation. "I'm sorry, Scotty. I didn't mean to cause any trouble." Fat chance. "I was following my doctor's orders, and dropped by. I never expected to stay."

"Fine. I understand Kaley asked you to. Glynnis, you put me through a lot during our divorce. Now that it's over, *I don't want you in my life*. I'm with Kaley, not you, and that's the way I want it to be."

Glynnis looked down, looked back up. "Okay, Scotty, I get it. Kaley is a very nice person, although at her age, I never thought you and she..." But she must have seen my face, as she hurried on. "But love does what love wants, right? You two make a sweet couple.

"I'll do my best to be out of here today. I've contacted the Ritz, and one of their residence apartments won't be ready until tomorrow, so maybe one more night, and that's all. I promise."

Tempted to comment on her "promises," I managed to say only, "I have to go."

I stalked out, not looking back, feeling, Glynnis's eyes on me until I passed through the den and into the garage.

For the few-minute drive to the office, I thought of nothing as the autodrive conveyed me to the underground parking. On our floor, I stuck my head in Virgil's office but he was out, then went on down the hall, checked Kaley's office, which she rarely occupies, on the way to mine. She was at her desk.

I changed directions into her office. We stared at each other.

"Why," I asked, in as normal a voice as possible, "did you allow that woman into our home?" Not very normal, it turns out.

She started around her desk, her face clouded. "I could see you were upset. I should have left word, let you know in advance—"

"What you should have done," I said, voice rising, "was not let her in the fucking house!"

She stopped, stock still, staring at me. "She just wanted to follow her doctor's orders, try to get used—"

"And you believed that bull crap? The word of the most crafty, conniving Black Widow that has ever existed in the western hemisphere? Both times I went to the hospital, she said she wanted me back. Both times! And you believed she 'just dropped by' to acclimate herself to my new life? I didn't think you were naive."

Kaley's face had reddened, something I rarely saw. She was steamed, and I had passed "steamed" some time back.

She cleared her throat, trying to regain control. "She was different, Scotty. Quieter. Not superior-sounding like she used to. She behaved as if she wanted to be friends."

"Yeah, that's our Glynnis—everybody's pal. Let me tell you something: She never does anything without a well-thought-out plan. I don't think she tried to kill herself, I don't think she wants to be friend, and I sure as hell don't think her condo needs mold remediation. She's a conniving witch, and she always acts one hundred percent in Glynnis's self-interest, that and only that.

"She wants me back, God knows why, and that's why she's there—to get close to me and take me back."

The red now verged on purple. I don't think I'd ever seen Kaley so angry. "She wants you back, huh? Well, I'm about ready to let her have you, Buddy. You're acting like such a jackass, maybe you deserve each other! Why don't you get the hell out of my office so I can get to work? Or hadn't you noticed that I'm busy?"

She threw her pen at me, and, shocked, I backed out. Heads poked out of offices, bringing the realization that, like it or not, our "conversation" had been at the one-hundred-decibel level. The heads were withdrawn as I stormed down the hallway and into the joint office.

Bobby sat, as usual, at his terminal. We eyed each other.

"Kaley and I had a fight," I began, but he cut me off.

"Shit, man, you think you need to tell me? People in the building next door know you had a fight. People on effing *Mars* know you had a fight."

I stumbled to my recliner. "Could you catch what it was about?"

"No. Just loud screaming and a lot of cuss words."

I told him. He listened, eyes wider by the second. I finished and he moved to my sofa.

"Look, I concede what Kaley did could be... irritating. But holy crap man, she's trying to help. And your ex did try, after all, to kill herself."

I shook my head. I wanted to go back to sleep. A busy day confronted me, one that might be supremely irritating if I had to put up with Admiral Overton again. I glanced at my watch. Nine thirty. We had an hour and a bit more before we had to leave for IC headquarters in Fort Worth.

"I don't think she tried to kill herself, Bobby. She wanted to get my attention and that was the vehicle. Both times I visited, she wanted me back. It's a new tactic. Kaley says she's different, milder, more subdued. There's no difference. She's out to do something else drastic. I've even wondered if she wants to hurt Kaley."

"Nah—she can be a pain in the ass, and I'll grant she is a plotter, but that's it. She's way too proud of her own skin to ever do anything to put it in danger by breaking the law."

That had been my thinking before, but I wondered.

"Better get on any tasks you need to get out of the way," Bobby remarked. "God knows how long we'll be on Ganymede."

One hundred percent correct. I had vendor calls, a couple of parts problems to solve for our field operators, and a list of calls to return that stretched to two pages. I tried to put Kaley—and Glynnis, for God's sake—out of my mind and get down to work.

CHAPTER 16 SIGHTINGS

I would have to apologize to Kaley; she had a good heart. Glynnis had conned her, typical of my ex, but it wasn't Kaley's fault. Only I understood how subtle and insidious G could be.

A suicide attempt might have changed her, but I doubted it. I couldn't believe a master manipulator would give up on life. She would do her best to get whatever the hell she wanted, only throwing in the towel when another choice presented itself.

Kaley couldn't help but be a loving, giving person, always ready to help anyone in need. Glynnis, on the other hand, couldn't help but be a me-oriented, self-loving conniver, whose only purpose in life remained to satisfy her needs and wants, the rest of the world be damned. I didn't believe any of her posturing and I had begun to consider she might be a psychopath.

Glynnis might be a problem, but my current problem was Kaley. Glynnis put me through a lot, and I harbored a huge, consuming antipathy toward her, but that didn't excuse acting badly toward the woman I loved. Finishing a call to a vendor who had always been reliable but had now been late with deliveries due to the loss of key personnel, who had decided to start their own company, I paused in my task list to dash off a note.

Dearest:

Sorry for being such a jackass this morning. I deserve to be whipped repeatedly with a wet noodle. I just cannot see that woman without a hysterical reaction. You know what she put me through. I guess I've never really gotten over it.

No excuse. I behaved rudely and inappropriately to the woman I love. And I do love you, a great deal.

Very sorry and contrite.

Love,

Your fiancé and still, I hope, friend

I slipped away from my desk and peeked into her office. Vacant. I deposited the folded note on her desk and departed. Back at my desk, I called Margie to find Kaley was on her way to Baltimore, Kuala Lumpur, and, time permitting, moon Delta. She might not even get back today.

Bobby spoke up. "We need to leave. Better take a restroom break."

I always took a pee break before a meeting—sometimes they stretched out longer than planned, and I didn't want to leave and miss anything. I returned to the office and we made our way to the lab. The portal connected, and we walked through into the small IC portal and with an escort, to the command offices.

A lieutenant jg met us with badges, so nobody stopped us on the walk. Bobby and I knew the location of McKissack's primary conference room, so we went right to it. We were ten minutes early and the first to arrive. A commander I knew slightly showed up and took a seat. She informed us

McKissack and others were running late in the previous meeting, and asked if we would like coffee.

We never refuse coffee on principle, so we moved to the service stand, and I poured the commander a cup, which seemed to surprise her. There were some muffins and a blueberry bagel on a plate, from a previous pow-wow, and Bobby scarfed up the bagel and a muffin. The Glynnis business had me so stirred up that I had no appetite at all, so I sat and sipped coffee. It tasted strong and a bit stale, but it had caffeine, so I was satisfied.

The commander's name had slipped my mind, but she wore her nameplate, "Lt. Commander Sarah Savage." She looked us over, and said, "I hear you guys are going to take a shot at another Bug base."

Bobby replied, "That's the plan. My impression from our last meeting is later today. Don't know if we've got a potential target or we're supposed to go fishing and see what we catch."

She shook her head. "I don't either. There's a planning team that is going to consult with you."

Bobby beat me to it. "You working any with the new off-world ops guy, Admiral Overton?"

She shrugged. Blonde, slim, and rather pretty, although I understand we males aren't supposed to comment on such things, she wore one of those worldly expressions which battle veterans often have, a face that said she'd seen it all and didn't want to see anymore. "He's only been around a short while."

"What do you think of him?"

She grinned. "I heard you guys got into it the other day."

I corrected her. "Not 'you guys'. Just me. I didn't like his attitude and I told him so."

The grin widened. "We heard. Sounds like you won't be inviting him to your birthday party."

I grinned back. "Well, we're vendors, so we invite everybody 'cause we're trying to sell portals. But I doubt if he'll want me to come over for barbecue."

"Is he always a hardass?" Bobby persisted.

The grin persisted. "One man's hardass is another man's friend." She wasn't about to say anything negative about Overton. I doubted if she's say anything bad about any of her staff, higher- or lower-ranked. The politic thing to do.

McKissack strode in, harassed and irritated. "Sorry for the delay. The rest of the group will be here shortly."

Neither Bobby nor I had any idea how big the group might be. As this meeting was about new sightings, we might have a crowd. I wasn't far wrong, as a good group soon trooped in. Captain Martinez and Admiral Overton completed the group. I shook hands with Martinez, who was nearly as close a friend as McKissack, and we got down to business.

I won't bore you with the details. Overton and I didn't talk to each other, the junior officers gave us an overview of the statistics, literally hundreds of sightings. They requested a team be set up to evaluate the reports based on satellite info, to validate, or more properly invalidate, the information. Their take was many of the reports were like the UFO reports of a hundred years ago. That is, hysterical observations of weather phenomena, meteors, stellar objects, scheduled aircraft, and so forth.

Bobby and I agreed. Bobby also proposed a second team to correlate satellite scans, to investigate whether Bug spacecraft, or evidence of Bug activity, could be identified. Naturally, some of the bigwigs wanted to comment, but we still finished in ninety minutes and were quickly on our way to Ganymede. It turned out Martinez had stopped by our meeting out of curiosity. He'd attended the meeting to determine what the target of the day would be for our Ganymede operation. Appropriate, as he was the guy who was hosting the event.

We crossed to Ganymede together with Overton along. I assumed either Martinez had invited him or McKissack had suggested he get educated on what Triple-S and IC did together.

The Ganymede exercise was another non-event. We managed to latch onto a small Bug portal and blast it to smithereens, but there were only three spacecraft and a makeshift portal barely two meters in diameter. The site turned out to be in southern China. We left a five-hundred-pound bomb and closed the portal. The Chinese verified the kill.

I made it home by about eight . Kaley was still gone, and wouldn't make it home. Glynnis sat in my family room.

CHAPTER 17 A "QUALIFIED" SUCCESS—AND A PROBLEM

I eyed Glynnis, my face blank.

"Hi, Scotty. My hotel suite was being painted, but it'll be ready in the morning. My condo management tells me I'll be back in before the end of the month."

That put to rest any objections I would have voiced. Glynnis, dear, sweet Glynnis, had been waiting and prepared. I was stuck one more day.

"Kaley hasn't come home?"

" She wasn't here before I left for the gym or after I came back. There are phone messages. I saw your central unit blinking."

It was in the den, across from her, so it didn't necessarily imply that she had been snooping. "Thank you."

I crossed the room as Glynnis remained seated. Picking up the receiver, so that the messages wouldn't be heard, I checked to find Kaley had indeed left a message:

"Sorry I missed you at work, so leaving a message here. I'll try to get home later but may have to stay over. I passed through the lab at noon while you were meeting with IC, and got your note. Apology accepted. Please accept mine for not being understanding enough about your feelings. Love you."

At least we weren't at war anymore.

The rest of the messages were ads and a plea or two for charitable donations. As I have a manager at Guy's law firm who handles contributions to charities I favor, I deleted them. I had them on my list already, or I didn't approve of the organization.

Glynnis had gone to get a bottle of sparkling water from the fridge. "I hope Kaley is all right," she said, resuming her place on the sofa.

"Yes. She'll be home late, but she'll make it back tonight." I lied, as I didn't want Glynnis to know she and I might be alone for the night.

She nodded and stood. "Good. I'm tired. I'm going on to bed. I have to be up early to get my move done."

I was ready for bed as well, though not as exhausted as the previous night. I wouldn't have time for exercise in the morning, since IC wanted to recap today's mild success at noon, so I showered and threw myself into bed.

* * *

I must have slept soundly for hours. Suddenly awake, I saw the bedside clock showed five AM. I could catch a couple hours more z-time, as I had the alarm set for seven. I rolled over and motion next to me got my attention. An arm reached out to pull me closer. My outstretched left arm touched bare, warm skin.

Kaley and returned. Given our make-up, she was feeling affectionate. I pulled her closer, and kissed her as her hand began to remove my shorts. She pressed her bare upper body against mine. The kiss was soft, warm, enticing—and yet alien.

Glynnis.

I sprang from my bed as though beset by a thousand tarantulas. Fumbling for the bedside lamp, I managed to find the switch. Bathed in soft white light, Glynnis had sat up in bed. Naked, of course.

Words refused to come. I goggled at the form of my ex-wife in the exact position she'd occupied a year ago. Although about that time, our lovemaking had diminished. She stared back, eyes wide, perhaps the slightest bit afraid.

She needn't have been, at least not physically. Infuriated as I was, I would never strike a woman. And I was infuriated, or maybe past that. Enraged might be closer.

Finally I found my voice. "Out." I took one step toward the bed.

She fled, not even pulling up a sheet to cover herself. Out of the room, down the hall, I could hear her barefoot steps along the hallway, running toward her room. I went to the toilet, used it, drank a large glass of water, and sat on the edge of my bed, shivering.

It took me at least ten minutes to calm down. A host of conflicting thoughts whirled through my mind. Anger at Kaley—and myself—for ever thinking Glynnis could change. Revulsion for her intrusion. Beneath it all, the tiniest, tiniest bit of desire. She'd been naked. Her body was as lush and exotic as ever.

The last was the most irritating. I didn't want to be attracted to the devious, sly person I knew my ex-wife to be. All I knew was I wanted her out of my house, the sooner the better.

Recovered, I got dressed, brushed my teeth, and headed for the garage. I detoured past Glynnis's room. She was packing. She heard me and turned.

She saw the look in my eyes. "I'm sorry, Scotty. I know we could be great together again, I know we could. I was just trying to show you—"

I interrupted. "You showed me all right. You showed me the reason we ended up in a divorce. You're only interested in what you want, Glynnis. You never wanted to break away. You wanted to worm your way back to see if you could get rid of Kaley.

"It won't work. Do you get it? I can't *stand* you. I don't want to be near you, I don't want to see you. This is the last conversation we will ever have. You'd better be long gone, and never, ever come near this house again. I'll get a restraining order if I have to, but you are, by God, out of my life! Get it? Leave now and don't let me lay eyes on you again."

I stormed out. In retrospect, I should have seen her out and locked the door, but I felt like I was choking, gasping for breath. I rushed out the den door to the garage and on to work, not even stopping for coffee.

I calmed down by the time I pulled into the company underground garage. In the break room, I made a pot of Starbucks coffee, my favorite blend. Bobby often comes in early, so I hoped to find him, but our joint office was deserted .

I slumped into my chair, sipping coffee. How would I explain I had kissed my ex-wife in our bed? Well, our sometimes bed, as Kaley rarely stayed over. The point was: Glynnis had been where only Kaley should be.

As I fumed and roiled, in walked the object of my affection herself. She came across the office fast, bound for my arms, but stopped when she saw my face.

"What's wrong?"

Kaley looked wonderful, although her bubble-do was disarranged, her jumpsuit wrinkled as though she had slept in it, and her face showed a lack of sleep. I managed to elevate out of the chair. " Kiss first. Then talk."

She obliged. I felt a lot better when we both migrated to the office couch. She kept an arm around me, pulling so we faced each other. After another pleasant interval, she sat back, still facing me.

"You wouldn't be this upset about the Bugs. It's Glynnis, right?"

I explained and she grew more alarmed. As I finished, I discovered the cause of her alarm wasn't me. It was her.

"I can't believe it," she said in a low, disgusted voice. "I *believed* her. I wanted to *help* her. And all the time..."

She trailed off. "And all the time," I finished her thought, "she was trying, one more time, to try to convince me to come back."

Kaley shook her head. She didn't say anything.

"You have to understand her psyche, her motivation, her reason for living," I told Kaley. "She only cares about her needs, her wants, her pleasures. Making love, pardon, having sex, wasn't about my pleasure or even hers . It was about her mastery of the act. It was putting on a show. We went to entertainment *she* wanted to see. We ate at the restaurants *she* preferred. If you could watch her at work, she'd friend those who could help advance her career, discard those who couldn't, and leave a long, dirty trail of sell-outs and double-crosses behind. I'll bet she doesn't have any friends in her office unless you count the senior partners and they'd be just for show and what they can do for her."

Kaley leaned forward to peck my cheek. "Sorry for all I put you through. I assume she's gone for good. Just hope she doesn't come back and burn down the house."

I shook my head. "Not her style. She might get caught and put in jail. No, she may try to get back at us, but that won't be the way. She'd rather do financial damage to us than anything else, but the divorce failed in that. She has nothing to do with my finances now, or yours either."

Kaley smiled a wry smile and kissed me again. "We've both been working long hours. We could take the day off, go home, and I could try to reward you for your troubles the past couple of days."

That sounded to me, as the saying goes, like a capital idea. Before I could answer, however, Bobby bounced into the office. "Hey, I just—" He cut himself off as he spied Kaley. "Oh, you're back. Hey, I see you're getting reacquainted, but I gotta steal Scotty."

Inside, I groaned. IC had scheduled a noon meeting, which I planned to duck out of per Kaley's suggestion, but this was something different, I could tell.

"What?"

He glanced at Kaley, realizing, this had been a make-up session after our argument. She stepped in, before he could say anything else. "Bobby, if you need him, he's available. I need to get to my office anyway. There are a million calls to return, service gigs to set up, and who knows how many new problems that cropped up overnight."

She gave me a kiss on the cheek, sprang up, crossed to Bobby and duplicated the kiss, and left the office. Bobby shot me another guilty glance.

"Sorry. I didn't know she was back. An issue has come up with IC, plus we accomplished something amazing in the lab at UT Dallas last night. I wanted you to see."

I glanced at my watch. Already eight-thirty. "The meeting is at noon in Fort Worth, right?"

He shook his head. "Margie told me they rescheduled for one-thirty. McKissack's aide used the word 'urgent' about the meeting but they need time to get more data and allow for a few more bigwigs to arrive." Which meant Overton would be there. Ugh.

"Wendy and Ray will meet us at ten ," he added. "You can run us over to UTD in your SUV, or I can drive, we can see the demo I want you to check out. We can be back here by no later than one to take the portal to Fort Worth. I'm taking my bag." He meant I should take the travel case I always kept prepared, in case a trip to the out-worlds was mandated. "I got an odd gut-hunch we're going to be asked to go somewhere other than Ganymede."

I nodded and we headed out. We descended to basement parking L1, and soon were on the way north on IH 35E toward downtown Dallas and on to Richardson, Texas and The University of Texas at Dallas. Once we were on our way, auto drive activated, Bobby gave me the eye.

"You and Kaley all right now?"

Recalling Kaley's last kiss, I grinned and said, "One hundred percent." My grin faded a bit. "However, I had a bad experience last night."

I went through the whole thing again. Not that Bobby needed to hear it, but it felt good for me to work through the whole sequence .

I finished to a gaping face with pie plate eyes. "Holy shit. Just naked, lying there in your bed."

"Yeah. It's like I told Kaley. For just an instant, as I turned on the light and saw that beautiful body, the thought flashed through my mind: *She's beautiful, she's naked, and she's available.* It was nanoseconds, but it's still something to be ashamed of. I'll swear, sometimes I understand when I hear a woman say, 'You men are all alike.' I guess we are. We're programmed to react to any available female."

Bobby laughed. "Not me."

"Ha, ha. You know what I mean. But then, like big black headlines in some newspaper announcement of a famous death, 'My God, it's Glynnis.' *Glynnis*! I ran her out."

He nodded, sympathetic. After a moment, I said, "At least she went. But I was so goddam, *goddam* mad that I was really rude. She won't forget it. She'll probably find a way to get back at me, you, Kaley, or maybe Triple-S. Jesus, Bobby, I may never be free of her."

"I'm not sure of that. She finds a new sugar daddy she can manipulate, she'll forget you ."

I shook my head. Bobby could be right, but I doubted it.

In the lab Wendy and Ray were in residence, with a couple of grad students Bobby knew, although I had to be introduced. Wendy grinned and said, "The Portal Authority has granted a five-minute time slice. It's not an IC-mandated slot, just a brief slot they happen to have open. It's plenty to demo our new capability."

Ray was fuddling with the cross field controls. He said, "It's in about five minutes. We were worried you might not make it. Give me a hand, Dwane."

The tall, blond student joined him at the controls. "Bobby's trying to give us the credit," Wendy said, "but it was his idea. Much lower volage, even lower coil current, and a solid FlucGen pulse."

"Bobby hasn't explained it," I said. "What the hell am I about to see?"

She nodded, grinned at Bobby, and said, "Note the way our portal is set up."

I did. The portal was the standard two-hoop set of coils, connected by a gold mesh tunnel. The one difference was this was a test portal, and it was tiny, the portal diameters being only half a meter. This portal wasn't empty. A large glass cylinder filled it, suspended on heavy nylon cords between four towers, two on each side of the portal tunnel.

It was an odd setup. "What gives with the vacuum bottle/"

Before she could answer, Ray called out, "Time slice live. Starting up."

"Watch." Bobby pointed to the end of the glass bottle.

Ray and his assistant brought up the fields and readied FlucGen. Ray pressed activate, and the FlucGen system came up.

In the center of the bottle, a hole in reality opened. They had done it, opened up a one-ended wormhole, to another place. From its looks, it was somewhere in space, somewhere in the universe but was not on a planet or sun.

I glanced at Wendy. "A one-ended passage."

She dipped her head. "Yeah, just as we did, back in the beginning, when Ray and I and Charley and Grant discovered the effect. Then it was haphazard and we rarely knew what we'd get. This is one hundred percent repeatable. If we keep all the parameters the same, we return to the same place every time. No idea where it is, but photographs show the star patterns are the same.

"Change the cross fields, or the vacuum fluctuations, and we change the destination. We were afraid we'd hit space, so we set it up in the bottle. You've heard the story about those early tests when the bottle broke."

I had. Quite sad.

"The good news is we can be repeatable, and we can get not only a wormhole every time, but one to the same place. Problem is, we have no idea where it is or how to direct a single end portal to a known destination."

Still, it was a great accomplishment and I told them so. Since it was time to leave for the IC meeting, I hugged Wendy, shook hands with Ray, and told Dwayne and the other grad student, goodbye.

I discovered my mood was still foggy as we crossed the parking lot, but at least the day had turned bright and clear, the wind subsided and the air brisk but not icy. It was on the way back to the office that Bobby broke the news to me.

"Not certain about the subject of the meeting today," he said, looking troubled. " I heard a rumor last night via one of the officers on Ganymede. There's been a bug sighting on Mars."

CHAPTER 18 MARS SIGHTING

Bobby was right.

Five minutes of greetings and introductions complete—yes, Overton attended—and McKissack got to the point. "Last evening, while our Ganymede sharpshooters and S-Cubed were taking out another Bug site, I had a quick meeting in DC with the CNO and the joint chiefs. There have been two sightings via satellite of suspected Bug fighters on Mars. Both at night, of course, over rough terrain, but we're ninety-nine percent sure they were the real thing."

Overton spoke up. "I wasn't aware there were many surveillance satellites over Mars."

"There aren't—at least those exclusively for surveillance. But for com between the Mars bases, there are a few satellites sprinkled overhead, and they have scanners as a matter of course. Also, with this Bug problem continuing, a few more have been placed in orbit.

"The problem is the two sightings were almost a thousand kilometers apart. So, were they launching from a single base, or do we have two sites on our hands? At present, we have no idea."

Bobby held up his hand. As this was an IC meeting, I was somewhat impressed that first of all, McKissack had included us, and second, that

Bobby would even butt into the conversation. McKissack gave Bobby the nod.

"When we last had a problem on Mars, you had enough Seventy-sevens to do a full scan of the Martian surface in only three or four days. Do you plan to do that again?"

McKissack nodded. "It's in the works. Although we're building our space fleet to pre-war levels, it's still lower than before the last set-to. We've shifted a wing of the Seventy-Sevens to Earth to shore up our forces, and passed a few to Rhea, so they could get back to at least a fraction of what we originally planned. It will take some time."

That got a few raised eyebrows because some of those in attendance were surprised that McKissack would disclose such sensitive information in our presence.

There were comments and suggestions, and as is usual in such meetings, most everybody wearing a uniform wanted to comment. It went back and forth for twenty minutes, then a clerk opened the conference room door and brought in snacks and, thank God, coffee. Bobby made a bee-line for the food and drink, and since he's nearly as large as one of those SF-77's, everybody else gave way. I held back, letting the boss man and the other top ranks fill up. Overton held back as well, standing beside me, and surveying the grazing naval officers.

He spoke, surprising me. "I've knew you were in IC a while back. What I didn't know was that you manned a gun emplacement in fights on Rhea and Ganymede. Martinez told me you were one of the most natural artillery guys he ever saw. I thought you were a science wonk."

He was saying he appreciated my toughness, just like any good naval officer. I made a deprecating shrug.

"I had to get with it or get off the pot, Admiral. Want to know the truth? That's exactly what I am—a science wonk."

He disagreed. "Not *just* a scientist. You have a military heart, whether you want to hear it or not. You saw your duty and you undertook it, according to McCall and Martinez, with neither hesitation nor concern. I underestimated you. I won't do it again."

Our gazes locked. After a couple seconds, I said, "Same for me. I thought you were a typical spit-and-polish blowhard, but I was wrong. You're a good analyst, and you're not afraid to say you're wrong. Your only fault, mine too, is you say exactly what you're thinking, and you don't filter much. Glad to get re-acquainted." I grinned and extended my hand.

After a surprised pause, Overton took it, and I had one less enemy in the world, and one more friend.

"I need coffee," he said, and I followed to the bar, now rid of most of the attendees. Fortified with the largest container of caffeine I could discover, I returned with a couple of small canape sandwiches to hear the rest of the meeting proceedings.

The main concern seemed to be establishing a full court press on the Mars scans. A major Bug presence on Mars was almost as bad as the one on Earth, perhaps worse. On Earth, the good news had to be that resources of many nations could be brought to bear on the search for Bug sites. On Mars, the US had the major presence, and although France, Brazil, England, and Russia had small bases, the majority of any search efforts would fall to us.

The discussion beginning to lag at last, McKissack spoke . "I have a suggestion, if our S-Cubed guests will approve. Doctors Hays and Taylor have made significant contributions to our searches on Earth. I suggest you two be our guests on Mars to assist in organization of the searches. If you could lend a couple of days assistance, I would personally appreciate it."

Hmm. Had not expected that. First of all, my impression had always been that the US military doesn't like to see civilians mucking around in its business, even so-called talented civilians who have been of service previously. Secondly, I thought—and thought McKissack thought—that Bobby and I could probably be of better service doing our jobs back home.

Everyone paused and eyed us. Bobby, as shy as ever, glanced sidewise at me and his pleading demeanor said, *I don't have the time to be any part of this right now.* I agreed. His work had resulted in giving us the ability to snatch a Bug portal to our own uses, while keeping it active even if the Bugs killed power on their end. That work needed to continue. He, Kaley, and I worked best as a team, but Kaley was swamped with service calls, and we needed to leave Bobby alone.

I surveyed the faces, knowing I had to come up with a palatable alternative. Who was the most available and disposable? Me. A sudden inspiration struck me.

"Let me make an alternative suggestion. Bobby needs to continue his research with the research team at the state university in Dallas. It's the work that has given us the ability to be able to snatch a portal away from the Bugs and kill their site. As for Ms. Sellers and her field support group, they are close to overwhelmed with the number of proliferating portals. That leaves me. I'll make myself available.

"I suggest Admiral Overton and I go to Mars, today if we can swing it, to work with the scanning teams. After all, as he is off-world IC commander, he should be involved with the operation. I'll bet he's been looking for excuses to get out in the field. He and I would work well together on such an assignment, freeing up Ms. Sellers and Dr. Taylor to continue to support IC ops as the search for Bug sites on Earth continues."

I snuck a glance at Overton. He seemed surprised, but his expression showed he might be pleased as well. As for McKissack, he must have seen the conversation between Overton and me, so he considered, then nodded and said, "Bill, I like it. How do you feel?"

Overton smiled, and I caught the overtone of humor in his reply. " I was about to say I need to be involved. This makes sense, and I agree Doctor Taylor and the field support team need to keep on keepin' on. Doctor Taylor, if we leave you at home, can we count on your help to erase another bug site today?"

Caught off-guard, Bobby shrugged, and said, "If IC identifies a possible site, we'll give it a go."

So my suggestion, to my surprise, got a quick and total approval. We broke up after that. I asked Bobby for a second to huddle with Overton over plans. He hadn't moved from his chair at the conference table, so I sat adjacent and said, "How fast does the search start up?"

"Been checking on that," he said, as though he had expected it. "We have to shuttle in twenty additional Seventy-sevens to give us a reasonable search contingent. Still thin, but reasonable. We should be ready to go by noon tomorrow. Do what you need to do in the office to keep things under control while you're gone. Meet me at Mars Alpha tomorrow at noon local time. Get a good night's sleep tonight."

"See you tomorrow," I said. I grabbed Bobby and headed back to the office. Via portal, of course.

CHAPTER 19 GLYNNIS AGAIN

I went straight to Virgil's office.

Our CEO, sat at his desk, most unusual, as he normally meets with vendors, jawbones with investors, placates customers, or attends to important CEO functions. In a dark blue suit, cordovan shoes, cream shirt, and striped cream-and-blue tie, he looked the part.

He motioned me in and said, "You look tired as usual. How are things?"

I stayed in the door. "The usual fire drill. Possible Bug sighting on Mars. To keep Kaley and Bobby out of it, I've volunteered to spend a couple days at Mars Alpha to help supervise and make intelligent suggestions about the search. Although, I currently have none."

"Mmm. Sounds like a real party but not the fun kind. Okay, you want me to do my job and yours while you placate our biggest customer?"

"Exactly."

"Makes sense. It'll work me hard, but you harder, so I'll smile through my tears and continue." That was his form of a mild joke. Not true, however, as he would probably work as hard as I would on Mars.

"Yeah, I like to make sure you're earning the outlandish salary the company pays you." Also, not true. Like the rest of us "high-level company officers," he worked for a pittance, taking most of his remuneration in stock options. The way things were going, it didn't appear those options would ever be worth, as a technician in our lab used to say, zero-point-shit.

I simply waved and headed to the joint office. There, Bobby was hard at work on his computer, composing code to assist in our Bug search, oblivious to everything else. He looked up long enough to ask, "On your way?"

"No, it'll take time to get the fighters transferred, so we start in the morning. Kaley here?"

"She left for home before we returned. I don't think she'd slept, so I'll bet she went to take a nap."

I decided to check with Margie. Before I made it to my desk, she buzzed my phone.

When I picked up, Margie said, "Scotty, could you run down here a minute?"

Her office is next to Kaley's, so I walked straight down. She looked up, brow crinkled in worry, as I came in.

"What's up?"

She blurted it out. "Kaley just called. She wouldn't say much, but she said to tell you to come home at once. Emergency."

Kaley's the most level-headed person I know. If she had an issue, it must be *very* important.

"Thanks," I told her. She nodded, concern still evident. I added, "If there's something bad, if she's had a car accident or she calls again, call me in my car."

She nodded, and I sprang down the stairs to the underground garage. My only thought as I steered my vehicle out onto the streets was, *What has Glynnis done now*?

Approaching my house, which is set back from the street, I got my initial shock. The place was crawling with police cars, three on the drive, and another pulled up in the circle at the front entrance. A member of DeSoto's finest met me halfway up the drive, arm extended.

"Yes, sir? What's your business here?"

"I live here. I'm Charles Hays, owner of this house."

"I see. You need to park to the side of the drive, here. I can escort you into the house."

What in the devil was going on? "I'd prefer to park in my garage," I told him.

"Sorry, Mr. Hays, that's currently not possible. I'll be glad to escort you to the house."

You can't argue with the police, and you certainly can't let yourself get angry or upset, as that could get you arrested. Besides, I believe the Blue, of whatever municipality, put up with way too much BS from citizens in general. "Okay, officer. Give me a second."

I pulled off the drive, onto the lawn I pay about thirty thousand a year to maintain, along with the surrounding two acres. Locking the car and turning to the young policeman, I said. "Thank you. What's up here, anyway?"

I should have known better. Talking about the issue for which four police wagons were now perched on my grounds was beyond his pay grade. "I'm sure the lieutenant in charge will tell you, sir," he said and led off.

What could I do but follow? I did, up the drive, across the landing supported by four massive pillars, and to the front door. The officer didn't bother to knock, disconcerting, as it signaled that DeSoto's finest had taken charge of the premises.

My house was large and sprawling, a single story for most of its extent, with a second story in the center and behind the entry, mainly an office upstairs and a five-car garage below. To the center behind the entry was the den, with bedrooms and other rooms off to both sides, and a massive area adjacent to the garage for a gym and pool, which I had never bothered to install.

Three more officers were in the foyer. To direct right and left, respectively, were a massive living room and an equally large dining/banquet room that had never been used except for my ex-wife to give parties. At the dining table sat a lieutenant and a pair of policemen, discussing papers. As we entered, the two officers exited, and the lieutenant looked up .

I knew him slightly, from last year when Bobby had been kidnapped. I even remembered his name. I extended my hand. "Lieutenant Grissom. Don't believe I've seen you since the kidnapping last year."

He blinked, remembered as well, and took my hand. "Dr. Hays. I didn't realize this was your home at first. A Ms. Sellers let us in and admitted the home belongs to you."

I didn't like that word, "admitted."

"It's sort of joint occupancy, Lieutenant. Kaley, Ms. Sellers, is my fiancée. She has her own home but stays here sometimes. After we're married, she plans to sell her house."

"I see." Almost as if he were taking data.

I felt near to losing patience. "Lieutenant, I don't mean to sound disrespectful or upset, but could you tell me what the heck is going on? My fiancée has been off-world on important business for our company, she hasn't slept in a day or so, so she came here to catch a bit of rest. Then I get a frantic request to come home, there's an emergency."

He arose. "Fair enough. You know Glynnis Hays?"

"My ex-wife, although I wasn't aware she had kept my surname. What's she done now?"

His eyebrows rose. "Now?"

"Lieutenant, we've been divorced for more than six months. For the last several weeks, she's been very unstable. She tried to commit suicide twice, and when I visited her in the hospital, she tried both times to convince me to return to our former relationship. I am not interested in doing so and I told her in no uncertain words."

He gestured me to sit. I did, reluctantly, and he said, "How did your former wife come to be in your home?"

That got me. In my home? She had left, or so I thought. "She was here yesterday but she left at dawn. Ms. Sellers, invited her three days ago. Glynnis had just gotten out of the hospital and had no place to stay. She said her condo was being treated for a mold problem."

"Before you can see your Ms. Sellers, I need to ask you some questions."

I finally lost it. "Before you ask me one more Goddam question, I need to know: *What in the hell is going on in* my *house*?"

Far from being perturbed, he thought a second, nodded, and said, "Very well. Your former wife is in the guest bedroom where she had apparently been staying. And she is dead."

CHAPTER 20 SUICIDE OR MURDER?

Glynnis?

Dead?

For the tiniest instant, I felt a great and overpowering relief. Glynnis was *dead*. No longer would she plague me, bother me, torment me with her antics, her pleadings, her oppressive presence. She was gone.

Then the logic of the situation hit me, and reduced me to shocked silence. Glynnis dead in my home? When I had thrown her out of me bedroom, and, I had supposed, out of my house? When had she returned? More importantly, how had she gotten in? Unless Kaley had let her in on returning, she'd had to have a key. And given when Kaley had gotten home this morning, that appeared unlikely. She must have either stolen a key, or had an extra made.

"Kaley just got home this morning from being off-world. Did she discover Glynnis's body?"

"No." He didn't add anything.

"Look," I told him. "You're not being forthcoming. I'd like to cooperate, but I need to find out what was going on. My ex-wife had no right to be in my house. I threw her out yesterday. I told her I didn't want her back here under any circumstances. How she got in, assuming Kaley didn't let her in, is an interesting question. You need to tell me a good deal more before I say anything else. I don't know what my ex is doing here, but she shouldn't be. You haven't said how she died. Was it another suicide attempt? She's tried twice, did you know that?"

I saw his face harden.

"So you said. When did that happen?"

"I don't know the exact date, but I can find out. It happened twice, although Glynnis told me when I visited her in the hospital, the second time wasn't a suicide attempt, just some sort of mistake with the meds her doctor had prescribed."

He frowned. "Could you give me the history here?"

"Lieutenant, I'd love to, but I need to talk to my fiancée. I need to hear what she found and how she fell into the middle of this."

"Perhaps later. There are a number of... issues we need to clear up. Ms. Sellers is being questioned at the present and you know how this is done. We like to independently question the concerned parties to get the widest view of the situation."

Something else was going on, I felt certain. Clearly Grissom knew a lot more than he was saying but wasn't about to reveal anything else. In general, his statement about getting "the widest view of the situation" meant the questioners were trying to catch one or the other of the interviewees in a lie.

I began to suspect I might need legal counsel and wondered if I should call Guy. If I requested it, my questioner would have to comply, but that would put us into an adversarial position, so I decided to soft-pedal my approach.

"What do you want to know?"

" Give me the situation with your ex-wife, starting with the suicide attempt?"

I gave him all of it—Glynnis's attempted suicide, my visit, the second possible attempt and my second visit, including her pleas for reconciliation.

At that point, he asked me, "Had you initiated the divorce proceedings?"

"No, she did. I didn't find out until later she'd been sleeping with a member of her firm for months."

He nodded again, showing maybe the slightest surprise. "Yet she suggested trying again."

"She did, both times I visited."

"And you were not interested."

"Lieutenant, if you'd seen what she put me through in the divorce, you'd understand. I didn't even like to be in the same room with her."

He digested that. "Go on."

I continued. Kaley invited Glynnis to stay overnight when she showed up at our front door, our argument when I found out about it, Kaley going off-world as she usually did, and Glynnis ending up in my bed.

As I finished, he said. "In your bedroom, naked. With your wife-to-be off-world. And you threw her out. Weren't you tempted?"

For a perhaps a nanosecond, thought that was not what I said.

"Lieutenant, if you woke up and discovered there was a large, angry rattlesnake in your bed, what would you do?"

"Did you really dislike her that much?"

"Sadly, I did. I'm not proud of it, but it's so. She was one of the most manipulative, sly, me-first people I have ever met. I'm not sure I ever loved her. I was busy with the new company when we met. I was mesmerized by her beauty, and we got married. It was okay at first, but by the end of the first year, I knew it was a mistake. I hated the idea of divorce so I stuck it out for two more years, until she locked me out and started proceedings."

"Anything to add?"

"Only that I had no idea she'd gotten back into my house. Kaley wouldn't have let her in. I assume she stole a key or had one made."

"We did find a key. It appears to be new but we'll have to track down the maker."

"Could I see Kaley now?"

"She's still being questioned. It may take a while."

"I need to see her. Have the questioners take a break, you can stay in the room, but I need to see her."

He pondered. "Doctor Hays, I'm afraid we cannot allow it. If you were married, there might be a requirement for us to allow you to meet. As you are only engaged, you have no legal relationship."

I was beginning to heat up . "I think I need to call my lawyer."

He astonished me by affirming my comment. "That might be a worthwhile idea. You can call from here. Please do not leave this room."

He left and an officer stood in the doorway. Not only had he told me not to leave, but he had made sure I couldn't.

In seconds, I called Guy, who was available. "Did you call again to grovel and ask me out for steak?"

I brushed off his attempted humor. "I need you to drop everything and come out to my home, with a couple of junior partners. I just had a big, steamy pile of horse manure dropped in my lap. I need you to help shovel it off."

I'll give him credit, he didn't ask a lot of questions. "Your house?" He'd been here before, so at least he knew where it was.

"Yes. Come fast ."

"I'm about eighteen miles away."

"Take a fucking helicopter and send your two flunkies in a car. I need you here."

He didn't reply, simply hanging up. I sat and dithered for half an hour or so before I heard the whap-whap-whap of helicopter rotors. Shortly after, a uniform escorted him into the dining room. He sat on the opposite side of the table.

"You got half the effing DeSoto PD in your front yard. What's going on?"

I dumped it on him, the whole thing, including what I'd told Lieutenant Grissom. "I'm now regretting what I said," I finished. "Something's up. I think they may not believe suicide, think maybe Glynnis was killed."

He grunted, sitting back in his chair. Tall, broad as the ex-football player he was, gray-haired, and with a perpetual, world-weary expression, he actually had a fine sense of humor and better attitude than you'd think for someone who's spent decades in court. At the moment, he didn't project the slightest bit of levity.

"Assuming what you told him is the truth, which I am sure it is, no harm done. You may be overreacting. If Glynnis did attempt to, and succeed in, killing herself, they have to treat the situation as a death of suspicious nature and explore all the avenues. When they get everything nailed down, they may exit the premises, all smiles."

As he said that, Lieutenant Grissom came back into the room. He was all business.

"I see your lawyer is here. Mr., uh..."

"Smith," Guy supplied.

"Yes. Mr. Smith, Dr. Hays, I regret to tell you we are going to take Ms. Sellers into custody on suspicion of the murder of Glynnis Hays."

I elevated straight out of my chair. "What?"

Guy said, quietly, "Sit down, Scotty." To the lieutenant, "On what grounds, sir?"

Grissom hesitated. "Come, come," Guy told him, "You have to take her before a judge to arraign her, and evidence must be presented at a grand jury hearing for indictment. Might as well give us the big picture."

The lieutenant's eyes shifted between us. I had no idea of the proper legal procedures, but I suspected that an attorney in the district's attorney's office might have to release any info. Eventually he relented. I suspect it was at least partly because he'd gotten to know both Kaley and me a bit on the kidnapping case, and maybe held a bit of sympathy for us.

"Did you know that your former wife, kept a journal?"

No, I didn't. I said so.

"She made entries the days she stayed here," he continued. "Among the last daily entries is one that says you were having second thoughts about Kaley and wanted to reconcile. Her last entry states Kaley knows you want to remarry, and has told Glynnis if she doesn't forget you, Kaley will kill her."

CHAPTER 21 KALEY IN JAIL

The last police car left. In the den, I sat with Bobby and Guy, staring at them. Not saying anything. Staring.

Guy went over notes on his personal and he had taken quite a lengthy series of both voice and pen annotations. He seemed content to work. Bobby seemed equally content to stand by if I needed anything. I've remarked before that I loved him like a brother. I realized now I loved him more than most brothers could love. As I was an only child, Bobby took the place of surrogate brother, local father, and uncle. I felt close to tears.

I had barely gotten to see Kaley, as "the questioning would continue at police headquarters," as Grissom told me. He seemed sympathetic. "Come to the station later," he had told me. "We'll get you time with her."

Kaley left for the station with, Guy assured me, one of the most talented legal eagles he knew, a female, named oddly enough Sami Bridgewater. When I has asked why Guy himself wasn't accompanying Kaley, he patted my shoulder and said, "Women understand each other better, you know that. Sami is as scary an adversary as I have ever met."

Bobby spoke up. "As I got here, the policemen were carrying stuff out of your garage. Do you have to let them do that?"

I shook my head. "Don't know about police procedures, but Kaley let them in. I think if you invite police in, they have the run of the premises."

Guy smiled for the first time. "Best to let them take everything. Scotty's right. Kaley let them in. The thing is, Kaley has no legal standing, as either a co-owner or tenant in this house. If you were married, it would be different, but you're not. Whatever they took, saw, or discovered in your house may, in fact, not be admissible in court..

"I know you don't think Kaley did anything wrong, and I don't either, but if any action ever comes to trial, the DeSoto DA, or the Dallas County DA, wherever they decide to adjudicate this case, may have a hard time getting evidence admitted."

His remarks roused me out of my stupor. "That's just it. I know Kaley and I know Glynnis. Kaley would never do anything like that and Glynnis... That stuff in her so-called 'diary' is so much bullshit. What I don't understand is how she got in, and how she managed to kill herself and make it look like poisoning."

"Another thing," Bobby chimed in. "Glynnis was one of the most selfish, self-centered people I ever met. People like that do not commit suicide. Even if she wanted to get Kaley in trouble, she would have found some way to do it without hurting herself and making sure she got away scot-free. She wouldn't kill herself off to keep Kaley and you apart."

"She tried before," I pointed out.

"Yeah, but you said she told you the second time was not taking her meds correctly. The first time, what if she were just experimenting, finding out how to fake a suicide so later on, she could fake a murder attempt?"

I had no idea. I had to admit Bobby had a point. Glynnis was such a me-first person I had trouble imagining how she would kill herself to get back at me. I would have thought she'd have figured a way to kill Kaley and make it look like suicide. The trouble with that was Kaley had far too stable a personality to ever consider killing herself.

"The fact remains she killed herself and set it up to look like Kaley poisoned her," I said.

Guy stirred, finishing his notes. "We have no idea if poison killed her or not. we have no idea how she died. For all we know, she could have fallen in the shower."

I changed the subject. " Grissom said she had a key to my house."

"Really." Guy turned to gaze at me, then made a note. "I didn't hear that."

"Grissom told me himself."

Bobby stood and circled his chair. I got the impression he needed to move around. "So, she got a key, came back after you found her in your bed and threw her out, and then she decided to commit suicide and make it look like murder."

Guy consulted his notes and added, "That's speculation."

I hadn't seen the police in my garage. "What did they take from the garage? Did you see?"

"I had just arrived and the officers were coming around from the back of the house. I assumed the stuff came from your garage. I couldn't see anything, they had it all in boxes."

"The lieutenant is supposed to send me a list," Guy said.

From the garage. What could it have been? There was only my car, currently not in residence, Kaley's car when she came over, lawn and yard tools, and maybe a few quarts of oil in case my aging SUV needed one between changes.

"You don't keep any rat poison in your storage area, do you?"

I shook my head, no. "A pest control company comes out quarterly. They're good. I never see a spider, a roach, or rodents. No, nothing in the back like that. I don't like that stuff, anyway. Some of the old chemicals, like chlordane eighty years ago, are potent carcinogens. I don't touch 'em."

I turned to Guy. "What's the chance of getting Kaley out on bail?"

He shrugged. "Maybe possible. Harder in a murder case."

Murder. The word made me shiver.

He managed a smile. "It will be high but I'm pretty certain we can get bail *if* she's charged. That's a big 'if.' The Dallas County DA just doesn't go around charging people with murder casually—nor would an city DA like one in this burg. There would have to be compelling evidence. Given DeSoto's size, I wouldn't be surprised if the case was referred to the Dallas County DA.

"In any case, I'm sure Kaley has a clean record, and as she is somewhat of a local celebrity, as are you two as well, I would think that she could get out. It will take some time, maybe a day or two, but I'm pretty sure we can swing it."

"When can I see her?"

"Later today. They have to either let her go or charge her, generally in a day or less. You, Bobby, and she are considered the heroes of the last Bug war, so I suspect they'll act soon."

I looked around. I loved my house, the one thing I'd spent money on. Now, it felt gray, hazy, and worthless. Glynnis had invaded it and made it a place of disgust, leaving it permanently stained. I wondered how I could ever live here again.

"Hate to bring work up," Bobby started again. "You got your hands full, but we need to make work-related decisions. I'll cover everything I can. Thuan can help and I'll get Bets to be the field service foreman until Kaley gets back. That leaves Mars and you promised to help McKissack .

" He'll understand, but can you suggest anyone who might take your place?"

Not really. Bobby could, although at that sort of thing, I'm actually better. "You. Wendy's already active when you're tuning up to go prospecting for a Bug portal. Ray's good too. They can do a good job of running the pirate-portal ops."

He nodded . "Yeah. I don't love the idea of racing around in a Seventy-seven, but I could. Look, let me handle it, and if I feel overwhelmed, I'll call you for advice and consulting."

I agreed because it was about all I could come up with.

Guy's personal chimed. He answered. He talked. He frowned. He frowned some more.

Eventually he hung up. "That was Sami. She's working on bail, but they are playing hardball. Sami says they revealed they found 'a poisonous substance' in your garage. Not sure if there were fingerprints on the container, but fingerprints enter into the situation. She said given Kaley's spotless record and her standing in the community, they'll get bail, but it's be high as a cat's back."

"And how high is that?" I asked. I really didn't care.

"Maybe five to ten million."

"I've got that much in my fucking cash account at the bank. I'll get whatever it takes."

He grunted. "You don't have to worry. We manage your money and we're authorized to spend it with your go ahead." He pushed a button and held his personal to my face. "Do you, Charles Scott Hays, authorize release of funds from one of your accounts to be used as bail for Ms. Carrol Sellers?"

"Yes, I, Charles Scott Hays, so authorize you to fund bail for Ms. Carrol Sellers at whatever level is required."

"Good."

Guy's statement about the poison in my garage hit home. "Wait a minute. Poison in my garage? I do *not* have poison in my garage. None, nil, zip, nada."

He shrugged with his eyebrows. "They found some, whatever you believe."

I shook my head. "I tell you, Guy, I don't know how Glynnis did it, but somehow, that low, cunning, vicious bitch set this up to get Kaley blamed."

He regarded me. "Now, now, don't speak ill of the dead."

"I'm glad she's dead! I wish I'd poisoned her! She was the most manipulative, sly, cruel, ruthless person I've ever known. You'd never know it to talk to her, so soft-voiced, so innocent. God, how did I *ever* get mixed up with her?"

"Careful, don't go around talking about how much you wanted to see the big G dead. Could get you in trouble." After a moment, he added, " And it's beside the point. Now, we gotta get Kaley home and get her proven innocent. I'm going to join Sami at the county courthouse and get bail taken care of or force them to release her. I doubt if they will because that diary, true or not, is a damning piece of evidence." He stood.

I rose. "I'm coming with you."

"No, you're not."

"Now, listen—"

He stopped me. "No, *you* listen. Every time I talk to you lately, you're Mister Emotional. You're always upset about some damn thing, and I don't need you going off the deep end while I'm trying to get Kaley out of the slammer. Let me do my job. You stay here with Bobby, figure out how to help fight the Bugs.

"If some snafu comes up and I can't spring her this evening, I'll let you know. Then we'll get you a visit. Got it?"

I relaxed and dipped my head. "I want to see her today."

"You will. Now let me do my job."

He left, and I sat down with Bobby to try to clear my head and discuss the Bug war.

.

CHAPTER 22 TORN

I fell asleep.

Bobby left to deal with IC and make the required changes. After half an hour of sitting on the sofa, darkness arrived. I had one drink, watched the evening news, paying no attention whatsoever. Then I drifted off.

I felt, or sensed, or ESP'ed something, and woke with a start. There on the couch sat Kaley.

She watched me as I struggled from sleep.

"Are you a dream?" I asked.

"No. It's me."

She leaned over to kiss me, I grabbed her, and pulled us together. We held that clinch for some time, but it seemed only seconds. The mind plays funny games sometimes. I was struck with the visual juxtaposition of my revulsion at Glynnis, naked, on the opposite side of my bed, compared to Kaley, fully clothed but in my arms, and the sheer joy it brought me.

We managed to sit back. I regarded her, her bubble-do disarranged, her face free of makeup, her face showing the strain of the last few hours. She looked wonderful.

"Out on bail?"

She gave me an odd look. "I'm not sure. Guy put up a million bucks, but it's sort of an 'appearance bond.' I'm a 'person of interest' but they didn't want to charge me. I'm considered an upstanding citizen of DeSoto, never been charged with so much as a parking ticket. The locals turned me over to the county for arraignment, but I think the assistant DA on my case was uncertain how to proceed."

I said, "How do you mean? On the surface, you might be guilty of murder."

"Yeah. I think he was worried about the background of the case. Glynnis tried to commit suicide, twice. She'd just gotten out of the hospital. Her diary made it look bad, but she could have been hallucinating. The worst thing was a glass with my fingerprint on it in her bedroom .

"It was blurred a bit, and from my point of view I could have used it and got a fingerprint on it when I washed it and put it up, and I told them so. There was also a sort of two-thirds print on a bottle that they were concerned with. They call that a 'partial,' I think. Anyway, I'm still a person of interest, but given what you told the police about Glynnis in your—in our—bed, I think they had so many conflicting pieces of evidence they had to let me go for now."

"Guy is really good."

"Yeah, he is, but Sami is a tough customer. She was with me when I was interrogated downtown, and she pushed on the iffiness of the evidence. I got the idea the county lawyers were terrified of getting into a trial with her in my corner, with maybe Guy and a couple of others as backup."

"What now?"

"I'm going home. I don't want to stay here, not after today."

She flinched as she said it. "I'm sorry, Scotty, you know how I love you. But staying here, at least for a while, is just too upsetting."

"I was thinking about moving out myself. Glynnis in my bedroom. Glynnis dead in one of the guest rooms. Could I stay at your place for a while?"

"Pack some clothes and let's hit the road. I don't want to be here a moment longer than I have to."

Kaley only lives a couple miles away. Her house is smaller, maybe five thousand square feet, but plenty for us. I parked in her front drive, one of those circular things, and we squatted in the den, ordered barbecue for delivery and shared beers on her massive couch until it arrived.

"I have problem," she said once we'd settled in, giving me a kiss. "Wow, I'd like to sit here and do that for a couple of days. But first to my problem, which is, I can't leave the county.

"I'm sure we had twenty to thirty new calls today, and we probably still have a backlog of more than twenty, with only Bets and Kyle to help. I don't see how the company can manage to keep customers happy if I can't go into the field at all."

I kissed her back. "Don't worry. Bobby's setting things up. We discussed using some lab personnel, maybe Thuan, Evelyn, and Micah. We'll cover it. Bobby asked Wendy to oversee the nightly raids on Bug locations.

"That leaves Mars for Bobby. I can help you ."

She leaned away from me. "Help ? Are you kidding? There is nothing, absolutely nothing, you can do for me."

"I can sit by you on the couch and hold your hand."

"Scotty Hays, you're being just plain goofy. The best way we can help each other is to tend to S-Cubed problems as they come up. Period. You need to do what is required to keep IC—and S-Cubed—on the ball, and that does not and will never include sitting around here holding my hand."

She leaned forward to kiss me again, holding it this time. When she leaned back, she said, "Go. Go to Mars. Go wherever they need you. I'll feel better, knowing you're doing what my high-level, Vee Pee of Engineering fiancé needs to do. God's sake, do you think I'm poor little petunia in need of constant care?"

"No. Of course not."

"Then go to Mars. When were you supposed to leave?"

"Tomorrow. Look, Kaley, I don't want to leave you here with all this mess."

"I've got the best set of attorneys around working to help me. I'm not in jail, I'm home, and I'm comfortable. I'm fine.

"Yeah, it's irritating I can't do my job, which I love, right now. Especially since I think Captain Martinez on Ganymede wanted me to run by today, but he can wait. Or, if he can't, Bets can take care of him."

I knew she was putting on a brave show. At the same time, I knew if she thought I was doing one of those "poor little girl, let me take care of you routines", she'd take a baseball bat to me. I'd been on the verge of doing just that.

" I'll call McKissack." As I spoke, my personal chimed. Guess who?

I answered. "Hays."

"Good. I got you. You've been hard to reach today."

"Had this thing turned off for a while, Kinsey. It's been a rough day."

"Ah. No one ill or out of commission, I hope."

"I'll tell you when I see you. What can I do tonight?"

He got to the point ASAP, like he always does. "We'd like to move the Mars effort up. Can you meet Admiral Overton here in the morning at six?"

"Why so urgent?"

"More Bug sightings, all in the same area, all at night, when they think we can't detect them. We need to move, fast."

Oh, joy, another emergency without a good night's sleep. "Kaley just gave me a pep talk. I'll see you at six."

"I'll be in DC. Get there early so you can be fitted for a flight suit. By the way, you'll be flying in one of the new, Super-Seventy-sevens.

"Thanks for your help. Good hunting."

Hanging up, I said, "Speak of the devil. McKissack. They've moved the op to very early."

"Then we need to get to bed early. I'll—"

The doorbell rang. "Food," she said. "I'll get it."

She hopped up, grabbed her purse, and headed to her front door. While she was away, I called Guy on his private number. He'd had a hard day acting in my (and Kaley's) interests, but I needed to speak to him.

"Scotty?" he answered. "Jesus, not another problem, I hope."

"Not exactly. This will take only a minute, but we need to talk."

"What you mean is, *you* need to talk. So talk."

"Fair enough. I'll be away tomorrow, location classified, to work with IC on a very important part of our current conflict. I could be gone several days, and Kaley wants me to go—frankly, I think she'll be upset if I don't"

"Knowing her, I understand."

"Good. First of all, thanks for what you and Ms. Bridgewater did today. Kaley verified what you said—I think the whole Dallas County DA's office is terrified of your associate."

"Possibly. She's very effective."

"Anyway, thanks again. I now have some instructions for you. How much am I worth right now?"

"Who knows? Maybe three to five bill."

"How much of that is easily available?"

"Maybe a hundred mil plus."

"More than I thought. Listen, I could be out of pocket for some days. *Really* out of pocket. Incommunicado, even. You are hereby authorized to procure whatever funds you need to prove the innocence of one Carol Sellers. You've bragged about that crack detective bureau you retain. Use as many operatives as you need, as many as it takes. Five, ten, a hundred, I don't give a shit. Use the whole fucking outfit if needed. Explore every avenue, find out what evidence the DA has and take it apart, looking for holes.

"If you need another ten of your gofer attorneys and legal assistants, use 'em. Hire another firm to help, if necessary. If you need two hundred people, get 'em. It's a cliché, but don't spare the dollars. Use every resource you need. Got it?"

He paused. "Well, we can always use a few more hands and heads, and the detective service can help. Scotty, I gotta tell you, if we go all in, you're looking at tens of thousands of dollars per day. That's big bucks."

"Seriously. If we spend a hundred thousand a day, that's peanuts. Do it for six months and it's only a few million. Maximum effort, maximum headcount. Don't leave a single stone unturned. Okay, that's another cliche, but do it."

Kaley returned with two sacks of really aromatic goodies.

In reply, Guy said, "You know, I think this is the only time a client has ever given me carte blanche."

"Take advantage of it. Go rack up those billable hours."

He laughed. "You'll be sor-reee."

As I stuck the phone in my pocket, Kaley said, "Guy?"

"Yeah. I authorized him to ramp up the legal efforts. I want our problem fixed now."

"It's my problem, Scotty, not yours."

"I can't believe you'd say that. You're in trouble because psychopath of an ex-wife framed you for her death. I won't have it. Guy and his outfit won't rest until you are free and clear. At least I can go to Mars feeling a bit better."

"Come on." She carried the bags of food to her kitchen table. We ate a pound of meat, her turkey and me brisket, a bushel of slaw, barbecued beans, and potato salad, plus peach cobbler, before we headed for bed.

We undressed down to a T-shirt and shorts for me, my version of pajamas, and baggy sweats for her because she always got cold in bed. She said, "I need a favor."

"Anything."

"I know guys like to bond with with sex. I understand, we're programmed for it, men especially. I have to tell you, I'm pretty shaky. It's been a helluva day, and I'm still shook up.

"Could you just hold me tonight, hold me close and not let go? I just want to know you're beside me and everything is going to be okay. I promise to make it up to you. "

As a matter of fact, I felt pretty shaken as well.

"Nothing to make up. I know how you feel. It's been a terrible day. So bad that I'm not sure I ever want to stay in my house again."

I climbed onto the bed and held out my arms. "Come here, Ms. Sellers, and give me a kiss."

She fell asleep in my arms. I couldn't sleep, at least, not for a while. I lay beside her, tracing the profile of her face in my mind, her strong nose, equally strong chin, high cheekbones, and rumpled bubble-do haircut. It was a peaceful interval. For a time,

Worries intruded. Tomorrow, early, I had to go to Mars. I felt restless with a bad feeling about the coming day.

CHAPTER 23 SEARCH FOR THE ALIENS

Kaley insisted on rising with me to see me off. Still in sweats, she kissed me at the garage door, clinging to me . The taste of her mouthwash made our last embrace very minty.

" Listen to me," she said. " Bring back my engineering genius-slash-boss-slash-fiancé in one piece or you're gonna catch hell from me. Got it?"

"Got it. If I get myself killed, you're gonna punish me severely when I get home." I had started to say "kill me," but given the circumstances, decided to change that statement.

I left, parked in the SSS underground parking, picked up my travel bag in my office, and arrived in our lab at zero-five-five-eight hours. Our small portal sat open, connected to IC headquarters. I waved at the night op, a slender Latino named Luis, and walked through to find Overton waiting. He was already in his flight suit.

"Very prompt," he said.

"It's all that good military training."

"So, you admit it did you some good." Overton didn't smile much, but he did manage a slight upturn of the lips.

"I assume we're going straight to Mars," I said. "You waiting on anybody?"

"Nah. I have two aides coming through later, to help with logistics. A couple of my staff wanted to participate, so I figured, the more the merrier. McKissack has decreed, however, that all higher-level officers ride in the new Seventy-sevens, which have more firepower than an M1A2 Abrams battle tank. As they're limited in quantity now, there won't be any more available until tomorrow, so they'll have to wait their turn."

"I hear I get a new a flight suit. I hope it arrived."

"Yeah, it was with mine. In the cubicle over near the wall."

So no "fitting" required. I stripped to underwear, slipped on the soft sweats that went under the flight/vac suit, donned the suit, stowed my clothes in a locker with my bag and pocketed the key I joined Overton by the portal, helmet under my arm.

As I approached, a portal operator terminated the portal connection to the Triple-S lab and started the connection to Mars. The tunnel fogged, swirled, and cleared to reveal the opposite side of the Mars Alpha hanger. I waved to the operator and we strolled through.

Mars hangars, like the rest of the structures, are like big, rusty barns with few windows. Air pressure on Mars is something like 2% of Earth's, give or take, but winds can be well over a hundred miles per hour, kicking up sand storms of prodigious size. Make a building out of high-strength plastic, such as those on the various moons or even Mercury, and they'd be sand-blasted opaque in short order. Mars buildings are therefore metal and painted a rusty red to match the prevailing ground colors. Big, ugly, quite utilitarian.

The base commander met us at the portal on/off ramp. As I knew him, I introduced his new boss. "Admiral Overton, this is Captain Calvin Alford, base commander. Don't know if you've met him."

Overton nodded and they shook hands. "Once, actually, a couple of years ago. Haven't had time to hit all the out-worlds since I got the appointment. Didn't remember until you said the name. Good to see you again, Captain."

Alford grinned. "Your memory is good, Admiral. It's been a while."

He led us toward the exit, and to his office in the adjacent building. Crossing the hangar, I noticed a group of Seventy-sevens in the far right corner of the hangar, near the small hangar doors. Like other off-world bases, the hangars had two sets of doors, separated by an airlock just big enough for a '77 to scrunch in and then move out without having to evacuate the entire hangar of air. In an emergency, the hangar could pump out air quickly for a mass launch, if needed.

I thought I spied our '77, as one ship stood taller than the others. Two mechanics were crawling on it, so crews were still making it ready. The rest of the hangar was monstrous, at least two football fields long and one broad, with two portals, the one we had traveled over, and a jumbo in the opposite corner, large enough to transfer an SF-77 if necessary, which it frequently was. Including spacecraft, portals, equipment racks, repair areas, and personnel cubicles for the inevitable paperwork, never mind it took place mainly on terminals, and the hangar could be termed comfortably full, if not crowded.

We passed through a short tunnel, up a couple flights of stairs, and into Alford's office. Once there, he said, "We've got half a dozen Seventy-sevens set up to start the scan today, but yours is the only one that's one of the new super-models. It developed a slight problem with com circuitry after it arrived."

That got our attention. McKissack had not wanted us to fly in one of the older models, because the new models were "safer." A thought struck me from an article I'd read—never buy a new model of any automobile, because it won't be as reliable as one that the assembly line has been turning out for several years. Could that be true of '77's also?

Overton echoed my thoughts. "A serious problem?"

"Thank God, no. Although the new models have a revised airframe, a bigger engine, and more armament, they use most of the same electronics. Give us half an hour."

Alford picked up his cup. "In the meantime, I pride myself on my coffee, and we've got time for a cup." Overton seized on the opportunity, as did I.

Alford's coffee, his pride and joy, was up to expectations. I blissed out, as my sleep quota was far under-served, and I wasn't about to get any nap time for the foreseeable future. We sat around a small conference desk in his office, plopping our helmets on the table beside our chairs, me listening as Overton asked about Mars operation, boning up on one of the major bases for which he held responsibility. Alford didn't say a lot I didn't know, but he did surprise me by claiming Mars now housed more than a hundred SF-77's, though none of the new Supers, except for the one we would be chauffeured around in.

A knock on the door jamb announced a master chief, age appropriate to the stripes on his work tunic. He saluted. "Ready to go, sir. The com unit was on the fritz, but we had a replacement module."

Alford nodded. "Thanks, Davis—and my thanks to your crew for getting on it. We need that bird in the air today."

Not much air out there, but I got the gist of the comment. Overton and I stood .

"Your pilot is Lieutenant Dawson," Alford told us. "He'll have overseen the repair, so meet him there. Davis, I've got a conference with McKissack . Could you see Admiral Overton and Doctor Hays to the hangar?"

"Aye, sir."

The chief headed out. We hurried after Davis, who wasn't wasting any time. Crossing the hangar toward the group, or mob, or herd, or whatever a bunch of '77's are called, I saw our ride, even bigger than its fellows, had been pulled to the fore, our pilot beside it, talking to one of the aircraft mechanics. They, saluted as we came up, a bit surprising, but Overton was an admiral and also their commanding officer. We thanked the chief, got a quick nod, and he began to confer with his tech.

Overton held out a hand. "Lieutenant Dawson, Captain Alford said we'd be with you today. We appreciate your ride."

"Yes sir, glad to be of service. I understand we're going Bug-hunting. If we find any, are we allowed to be pest control?"

Overton beamed. "Appreciate the sentiment, Lieutenant." He turned to me. "This is Doctor Hays, one of the inventors of portal travel."

The pilot's eyebrows lifted a fraction and he took my hand. "Glad to meet you, sir. Are you the expert who knows where Bugs like to burrow?"

Up close, he stood three or so inches shorter than I am, though he had plenty of bulk in a solid body. His face, showed mixed-race, a dark tan skin with no beard or mustache. His accent carried a hint of the south, maybe Georgian. A very likable sort.

"Not sure about that, Lieutenant. I may have a few ideas."

Overton asked , "What's your first name, Lieutenant? What do you go by?"

The lieutenant hesitated and said, "First name Herbert, sir. My parents called me 'Herbie,' but I never liked it. My call sign is 'War Eagle.' The guys in the cockpit call me 'Eagle,' 'cause I went to Auburn."

Overton grinned. "The Tigers who cry 'War Eagle.' Never really understood that, but I like the call sign. Eagle it is. This guy goes by Scotty," gesturing to me, "and I'm Bill. I refuse to put up with all that Admiral-Lieutenant-Doctor BS in the cockpit. Got it?"

Eagle nodded after a second. "Sounds good. Okay with you, sir?" Looking at me.

"Great. We don't want to refer to the admiral's rank too often—he might get a big head."

That got a shocked expression from the lieutenant, but Overton added, "Same goes for a Ph. D. geek. Don't want him to think he knows everything."

Tit for tat. "Well, I don't know everything, only most everything."

That got a laugh. We popped on our helmets, faceplates open. Eagle moved to the right side of the Super 77, and we followed him through the hatch, up a ladder that held a couple more steps than the older-model '77, and into the short tube-cockpit that had the same seating layout, pilot in front, followed by nav, and weapons control. I assumed Bill would take second seat, but he gestured to me, taking the weapons position. I knew to plug into ship com, as my experience in Brazil had me familiar with the basic cockpit procedures.

Eagle came across com. "Scotty, connect to the oxy supply. Just curious, either of you checked out on a Seventy-seven?" The ship mechanic had closed the hatch, and as Eagle asked the question, I felt the jerk as a truck began to haul us toward the airlock.

"I'm fully checked out on the standard Seventy-seven's," Bill answered. "Not on this model, although the controls look the same."

"They are, sir—sorry, Bill. You shouldn't have any trouble in an emergency."

"Just flew in my first seventy-seven recently," I told him. "Not checked out, but I could probably figure stuff out in a pinch. Trained on F-X-Two's and Threes, and have a civilian pilot's license. Believe it or not, I knew enough to connect my oxy line."

"Glad to hear it. As Bill will tell you, these things practically fly themselves. Four of the first search group have launched and two will follow us. They hope to have thirty or so birds up by the end of the day."

Once in the airlock, it evacuated and we were towed a short distance out, then released, as the truck went back for its next ship. Eagle hit the gas, and we began to lift. Like the previous model, this one could go vertical, although it could take off on a runway if in an atmosphere that would support flight. Having runway capability was a good deal more important on Earth, where vertical took a lot of fuel due to the weight of the ship, but not so much on Mars, where it weighed considerably less. We were airborne, or spaceborne, considering the miniscule atmosphere, the barns of Mars Alpha dwindling below.

A pang of regret assaulted me. Kaley sat, stranded, at home, restrained from travel and facing potential murder charges. Here I was, some hundred million kilometers away, facing who knew what kind of danger. What if the unthinkable happened? What if I didn't come back?

The thought of death has never concerned me. I figure what happens, happens. Worrying about death is worse than death itself. I've got enough problems without inviting extra. Now, if anything happened to me, Kaley would have to face the results of Glynnis's treachery on her own. It was a devastating thought .

I swallowed hard and said a silent prayer I'd make it back, something I'd never ever done before.

We had headed north, so far as I could tell. "How far to Grand Canyon?" I asked.

Valles Marineris, the "Grand Canyon" of Mars, is one of the grandest of all canyons in the solar system. Wider than the US, it spreads across thousands of kilometers, not just a single canyon, but a group of rifts and gullies, many larger than Earth's Grand Canyon. Not exactly straight, it wiggles and squiggles generally west to east, but also north and south to a degree.

I didn't know our assigned area, but Eagle did, proceeding generally northeast and ultimately descending over a network of dry canals, a sprawling mass of gullies and ridges which I estimated would cover thirty or forty thousand square kilometers. We stabilized at two thousand meters, high enough to get a good overall vista, low enough to catch details.

"Scotty, you're our resident expert," Bill announced. "Any suggestions on how we operate?"

I addressed our pilot. "Eagle, you got metal detectors on this baby?"

"Yeah, Scotty. Take a gander at the screen to the far upper left of your console."

It wasn't labeled but I recognized the format. "Gotcha. Okay, Bill, we're over the canyon for a reason. The Bugs need to build a portal about fifty meters in diameter, minimum, maybe twice that. If they do it on the plains, it's too darn visible."

"I see. Makes sense. They want to locate in rough terrain to mask their work."

"Righto. Now, we know they will keep their fighters grounded during the day, and they probably have camouflage to screen their site. Our best chance to spot them is to get a flicker on the detector and and get as good a look as we can from current altitude. We spot anything, we don't let on, don't do a one-eighty to check, nothing. We move on, notify IC command, and they either try to get our team back home to hijack their portal or maybe send in a quick strike to knock them out."

"Boy, I'd love a shot at them," our pilot commented.

"Yeah," I replied, "but if we botch it, they know we're onto them. They'd move the site and try to get a large portal built before we catch them again. Lemme tell you, they get a big portal built, they could have thousands of fighters on Mars in a flash. And we is, as the saying goes, the screwee."

"Okay. Gotcha. What about our elevation?"

" It's good. Just follow your assigned route and keep your eyes open."

We proceeded to scan the canyon for several hours, meandering on a pre-planned route, never backtracking, always moving forward. Eagle exchanged radio com with our fellow searchers, none of whom were any closer than forty klicks away. We were too far over the horizon to contact

Alpha. We had just changed course for about the forty-leventh time, when Eagle interrupted himself.

"Okay now, proceeding—" He stopped in mid-sentence. "Well, crap." In synchrony with his exclamation, our nose began to drop.

"What?" Bill said.

"These Goddam super models," Eagle said, his voice dripping with acid. "The rumor was top brass was pressing to get them in the field, and they cut short some of the testing. I've heard they're having engine problems already."

In the process of doing a one-eighty, he let the nose drop, lost a little attitude. "Other engine seems okay, but we got to go home, right now. I'll call the others, get them to give us an escort. Dammit, I don't know why the brass are so anxious to get us in these bolt buckets. The older Seventy-sevens are far more reliable. Sorry, Bill."

Bill growled. "Nothing to apologize for. I'll give McKissack hell about this. It's *my* bacon about to get fried as well."

Eagle and I gave a nervous laugh, then lapsed into silence, as neither of us had anything to contribute.

We had to get back to base with all alacrity or risk getting stranded. I figured we were more than four hundred klicks out. Eagle brought up the nose and we climbed, heading south. The good news: our ship could make it back to base on one engine, no problem.

I sat back. Nothing to do .

"Sonovabitch." From Eagle.

"Problem?" From me.

"Forward view to port, about ten o'clock low. Three Bug fighters coming in."

Bill swore, as I glanced to my left and tried to find the bogies. There they were, streaking out of a canyon, coming fast, headed right for us.

"I don't get it," Bill said. "Thought they liked to stay in during the day."

"You got me," Eagle said, and I had to agree.

Then I got it. "The engine problem," I said. "When it happened, you circled and dropped the nose of our ship. There must have been a site right below us and they thought we spotted them. They're coming to defend their base."

The other two were silent. I could scarcely believe it, but it was the only explanation. A Bug site lay beneath us, and its defenders launched to protect it.

Coming on fast.

CHAPTER 24 DOGFIGHT

Not an expert in air-to-air combat, I thought Eagle would make for higher altitude, which could give him maneuvering room. No, he angled our fighter into a dive, heading toward the rising enemy. I wanted to ask why, but it seemed an inopportune time.

"Hang on," he called out. He broadcast, "This is Mars Alpha fighter Seven-Seven-Alpha One Two One. We have major engine failure and are under attack by three bogies. Sending current position." The Bugs closed in, and he had no more time for chit-chat.

He let fire with his cannons.

I knew the older '77's had beam cannons. Our new fighter had projectile cannons, by the sound, twenty millimeter, as the bub-bub-bub of their fire shook the ship. He did a dive-and-pass-across maneuver, sweeping all three positions with what was essentially a field of flack. As he pulled away, the three fired beam weapons, but we weren't there anymore, streaking south, speeding with every bit of thrust our single, fully-functional engine could give us.

Not enough. They screamed after us, gaining fast, and I remembered Bug ships not only had extreme range, but exceptional acceleration. Checking the rear radar, I saw only two ships pursued us, the third falling off. It disappeared into the canyon. I realized Eagle had gotten a hit.

The remaining Bug ships opened up, and even though we zigged and zagged, one beam clipped our left stabilizer. I didn't feel anything, as there wasn't enough atmosphere. Eagle was banking and flying an evasive pattern with our forward and rear side thrusters.

"We can't outrun them," he called out. "I'm going to try a spin maneuver, try to knock one of them out, maybe discourage the other."

I had no idea what a spin was, but I quickly found out. Although we were in the atmosphere, even at a couple klicks up, there wasn't a lot. Eagle cut the engine to idle, hit forward port thruster full, and we began a flat spin, bringing our nose toward the bad guys. He socked starboard thrusters full and let both ships have a broadside, continuing the spin back toward our direction of motion.

"Got you, you son of a bitch," he yelled. Sure enough, rear radar showed one blip falling off hard. The other continued the chase, firing all beam cannons. We hiccupped in flight, our bad engine dying as the good one sputtered and began to fail.

"The other engine took a hit," Eagle yelled. "I can't keep us up, got to find a place to land."

Despite our difficulties, he spun us , gave the remaining chase ship another twenty millimeter salvo, then spun again. On the rear screen, I saw our pursuer climb and turn. We were alone.

We were still falling fast, with no rear propulsion. We sank beneath the rim of the canyon. I knew we had thrusters, forward thrusters to slow us and vertical thrusters for lift, but did we have enough in the tank to get us safely down? No idea. I could only hope.

The sun sank toward the horizon, and we passed into shadow. We would be hard to spot by rescuers, assuming we were in one piece after landing.

"There's a wide spot below, with walls high enough to make us harder to find. I'll try to put down there."

"How's thrust?" Bill called out.

"Rear number one is gone. Number two is ten to fifteen percent. Forward speed is below a hundred kilometers per hour. Ground coming up fast. Slowing... Now."

Forward and bottom thrusters chimed in with throaty whines, as I braced myself. I've heard in crash, you should try to relax. Ha. Try it some time.

Canyon walls stretched above us, the Martian soil seemed to be approaching at an alarming rate. Bill spoke up. "There are air bags and force deflectors all around you Scotty. Lean back and hold onto the grab bars to your left and right."

He didn't even sound nervous. Strangely, I didn't feel nervous either. My only regret remained I might leave Kaley without my help.

We sank.

And sank.

It seemed to take a long time, although the chrono showed it had been seconds, not millennia. The forward and nose thrusters came on full. Our nose came up, we slowed, and time seemed to stand still.

Then all propulsion failed, and we were in free fall. We hit, hard, as all the restraint mechanisms went off, and I felt batted up, down, and side to side.

Wham! Bounce one.

Wham! Bounce two.

Wham, wham, wham!

WHAM! We stopped with shocking severity. I felt as though my stomach might bounce right up my throat and land in my lap.

And abruptly we were still, me too stunned to move. I heard air escaping and realized cabin pressure had been compromised. I felt my suit pressurize, as the various protection devices flattened. I stared at a blank control panel. Eagle lay sprawled in the front of the cabin. One or more of his protection devices had failed, as well as the seat structure. The back of the seat was securely connected to his upper torso but had torn away from the lower seat. Looking at his crumpled body, head at an awkward angle, I feared the worst.

Outside the canopy, canyon walls stretched away and up, more gradual than they appeared at a distance, seeming to stretch to the sky. I thought I heard breathing behind me, and hoped I was right.

I was alive. At least one of my companions was gravely injured and we were stranded, near an enemy base, hundreds of kilometers from Mars Alpha. Eagle's last radio transmission had identified our position, but we were at the bottom of a canyon, and with the stealth coatings on every '77, we were virtually invisible.

And the enemy was nearby.

CHAPTER 25 SURVIVAL

Frequently in an emergency, my mind seems to speed up. Don't ask me why; such a situation simply gives me focus that I lack—or fail to use—in everyday situations. It's not that I can't focus the rest of the time, but an extreme situation somehow juices up the problem-solving part of my brain to hyper-speed. I become, so to speak, a sort of mini-Bobby.

Oxygen. My suit would keep pressurized, so long as I had something to breathe. My normal oxygen source had been the ship supply, now apparently off, as the engines were dead. Where...? My mind resurrected a sign. There, lower right, below the switches and panels near the floor. "Emergency Oxygen Supply" had been stenciled on a small panel. I pressed in, it opened, and I extracted a small backpack. It had explicit instructions on its side, showing how to connect the tubing to my air input and attach it to my back. A small note below the instructions explained that the oxygen was stored in a chemical process and released by the unit with mild heat. It cautioned that the supply was good for only twenty-four hours, which seemed quite respectable to me given the small size of the pack.

The oxy supply attached to my air line, I could immediately tell the difference, so my suit supply had already gotten stale. Supposedly one person could attach the pack to one's own vac suit, but I put that off. Perhaps Overton and I could help each other.

Overton. My next problem: to determine the condition of our crew.

"Bill, you conscious?" I called over ship com.

He stirred, moved, groaned, but his voice was strong. "Yeah, I'm awake. Got a problem. My leg. Not sure how bad, but it smarts like the very devil. Might be broken, or muscles or tendons torn."

Not good. I stirred, unbelted, moved gingerly out of my seat. Amazingly, I seemed to be whole, although aches and pains told me my body would be a patchwork of bruises tomorrow.

I twisted toward Overton, moving toward him. His suit appeared solid, and I didn't see damage to the legs, even on the limb that he kept absolutely still.

First things first. I reached down to the appropriate panel, removed the oxy pack and told him, "Connect this to your input line. The ship air supply is dead."

I helped him connect, then had him lean forward, which caused a massive groan, and attached the pack to his suit. I handed him my pack and had him do the same for me. I could stand close enough to his seat he could do the fastening without undue discomfort.

I surveyed his form. "Looks like moving could be a real problem."

"Yeah, maybe, but I'm gonna have to. Bug forces in this area know we're around, so maybe best to get the hell away from the ship."

Good point. I hadn't gotten to that yet, focused on our health and safety, but I'd have arrived there pretty soon. I didn't know how many Bug fighters there were in the area, but we had to assume if they sent up three, they had more.

"Gotta check Eagle," I said. "I'm worried about him."

Overton hadn't been able to see with me in the way. "Oh, Jesus, that looks bad."

I agreed, going forward, still moving with care. Sure enough, the pilot seatback had sheared off the support base and seat itself. I'd never heard of a fighter having such a problem, so I began to wonder if this were another of those "early production" problems, like the engine issue Eagle had referred to.

The closer I got, the worse it looked. Up close, I couldn't even understand how his head could be arranged at that angle, given he wore a helmet. Inside the helmet there is a "personnel health and condition" panel, but of course I couldn't see it. The suits are a sort of elastic material and cloth, far too thick to feel for a pulse.

Behind me, Overton spoke. "On his left sleeve, a connector. Plug in with the line you can pull out a few centimeters from your right sleeve."

So, there was a way to check the condition of flight personnel in real time.

"Gotcha." I did as directed, and a display sprang up above my left eye:

> Respiration—Not measurable.
> Pulse—Not measurable.
> Body temperature— <30° C

A string of data flashed onto the display in sequence, followed by a final verdict:

> Deceased.

There were a lot of feelings I could have experienced, but I was in focus mode, so I stuffed feelings into a dark place and turned to Overton. "Sorry, Bill, he's gone."

A sigh. "The position of his body, the way the head is jammed back. Could hardly be anything else. I'll put him in for the highest decoration I can get."

"Hell, he should get the Medal of Honor, from my point of view. He saved us both."

"No argument there. What now? Do you agree staying in the ship could be dangerous?"

"I have mixed feelings. Granted, if a Bug fighter came along and spied us, this would be dangerous. Think about it. The ship is coated with stealth materials, there are no shiny outer surfaces. Might be a good place to hang out."

"Yeah, but near here, we know for sure, is a Bug site. I'd feel more comfortable staying near the ship, but hidden."

If he felt more comfortable, so be it. "Sure you can make it out?"

He snorted. "Shit, I don't have a choice."

"Okay, let's move. We can't take Eagle, but we can come back for him, once we get a rescue crew in here."

His helmet bobbed. "Right. And we Goddam sure *will* come back and get him as soon as we can."

No man left behind. I could appreciate that. "Okay, I'm going first. Unbelt and get ready to move while I set things up."

"Check your local com panel—your right sleeve."

"I see it."

"Set to Channel Two. That's local radio, suit-to-suit. Right now, we're still hooked to the ship com, which has battery backup. Outside, we'll need to connect via the suit radios."

I did so. "Do you read?"

"Roger."

I nodded, though he wouldn't see it, then moved to the hatch, going down two ladder steps to reach the latch. I'd been worried about it jamming, but it opened readily. Shoving it open, I climbed down, looked around.

Above me, the canyon rims towered, almost a vertical cliff behind the fighter, but far more gradually on my side of the cliff. The slope didn't appear that harsh, but the top of the canyon might be two or three kilometers away or maybe more; it was hard to tell. In full sun, the rocky, graveled canyon bottom and the striated walls might be a colorful sight, but now, they were only a muted gray. Above me, stars had begun to appear.

I stepped back into the fuselage, climbing up several ladder steps. To my surprise, Overton stood near the ladder.

"Thought I'd have to get you up," I told him.

"I should have waited. I'm sweating inside this suit, just from that little effort."

"How do you want to handle this?" By which I meant, how did he need my help to descend?

"Get me positioned on the ladder. I think I can use the good leg and my arms to maneuver down. My arm strength is good."

"Okay. Coming up."

Once I stood beside him, he said. "We've got a twenty-four-hour supply of oxy, but there's no food aboard. There are three emergency weapons, plus an emergency radio. Take those."

The radio was fairly hefty, though not too heavy in the gravity of Mars. The weapons consisted of two seven-millimeter long-barrel machine pistols plus a beam weapon. Each had its own holster.

"Okay. You know your vac suit has a water pipe in the helmet."

I nodded. I knew that from using vac suits on the outer moons. "Should have heaters, too," I added. "Never had to check before, but is there a status panel?"

"Yeah—left arm, small screen. Toggle the red button."

I did, and it showed everything operational. And a good thing, as given our current position, the temp would edge toward a hundred below zero Fahrenheit, before dawn. "I'm good," I said. "How about you?"

"Good to go. Help me onto the ladder and stand back. I don't want to take you with me."

"I can hold on to you as you go down. It's not like we're on Earth."

A big advantage. At only about a third of Earth's gravity plus a little, holding onto a man Overton's size, tall but not hefty, didn't present a huge problem. I helped him onto the ladder and he began to descend. As the ladder didn't go all the way to the ground, he had to use his arms

Alone for the last two steps, he negotiated it with no problem. I hopped up and down said ladder a couple of times to get the arms and radio, and we started off toward the shallower slope, him with one arm on me, limping and groaning.

"Leg may not be broken," he said. "Probably fractured. Hurts like hell to put weight on it."

The closer we got to the canyon wall, a gradually sloping barrier that seemed to go straight up to the rim, the more rugged detail made itself visible. The slope appeared smooth and gradual in places, but there were ruts, indentations, and outright gullies spread along the slope, obstructing progress.

I looked back. The ground seemed rough enough that we hadn't left a noticeable trail, a great relief. We proceeded higher, and I stopped Overton, assuming he needed the rest. He was beginning to breathe hard, as much from the pain as from the exertion.

"Let's see what the radio tells us," I said. I managed to get him seated, putting the com unit between us.

The radio box opened to reveal a microphone connection on a cord to the unit, an antenna, which we lengthened to its maximum extent, and a set of legs to prop the radio upright.

"You know how to use this thing?" he asked.

"Not a clue. I can probably figure it out."

"No need. Remember, I came out of naval air."

He reached down, flipped a switch, watched as various lights and a small screen activated, then attached his vac suit mic cable to the radio mic connection. "This is the crew of Mars Alpha fighter Seven-Seven-Alpha One Two One. We have ditched near the following position over sector One Four Three Alpha." He proceeded to give our coordinates, then signed off and we sat back to wait.

Nothing. We listened for a few moments, but not a thing.

"Not surprised," Overton commented. "Look at the status screen. No incoming signals of any kind detected, and this baby can just about sense anything across the spectrum.

I looked up that long, dark slope. The sky was filled with stars. Our eyes now accustomed to the night, the ground appeared well lit, almost like Earth during a full moon, although you couldn't call it bright. With no dust or pollution—and no air to speak of—the firmament above provided quite a light show.

I made the decision. "We'll never be found down here. I have to make it to the rim. I should be able to send out a good distress call from there."

"It's a good distance. What, maybe three klicks or so? And a decent slope."

"Doesn't matter. Besides, I'm in decent shape and Mars gravity is a big help."

"Okay, help me hide and good luck on your way."

I turned to stare upslope again. The rim, brightly outlined by the starry sky, seemed a million miles away. I remembered the twenty-four hours of oxygen we had. I needed to get on my way. "Okay," I said. "Let's get you situated."

CHAPTER 26 CALL FOR HELP

Not a hundred meters away, I had spied a deep rut in the slope. Actually a gully, it stretched a good kilometer to our left, several meters deep in places and a perfect place in which to hide. I helped Overton to the gully, got him well hidden, and he took one of the machine pistols ("I don't want that damn beam tinker-toy").

The other machine pistol plus the beam sidearm strapped to me, the radio on my back, I started upslope. On Earth, my load, including the oxygen backpack, would have been uncomfortable and possibly unsupportable. On Mars, I could handle it, although I knew it would get a lot heavier before I reached the summit.

I made good time, moving with a solid, loping stride The slope was no more than five to occasionally ten degrees. I also hit occasional flat spots, giving me a breather. Still, the going began to get tougher as I went on, and on, and on.

Even distances on Earth can be deceiving. Here, in the dim light, and with few points of reference, it had me bolluxed up quickly. I soon decided, regardless of my first impression, the far-off rim lay a good three to four kilometers distant, not the two to three I'd assumed.

I took a break, sat and puffed, about halfway up. With a sip of water, I was ready to stand when a flicker of movement caught my eye. Glancing up, I saw a Bug fighter slip by, moving at a slow search pace. I ducked and hoped the pilot wasn't looking down.

The fighter disappeared to the east. Breathing a sign of relief, I hopped up and moved as quickly as I could manage up the slope. The chrono in my helmet showed another twenty minutes, a good three-quarters of an hour after I had left Overton in his hidey-hole. Finally, the summit appeared to be getting close. It was at the hour mark I arrived at what had been the visible rim.

Not the rim. Here, the slope flattened dramatically, but stretched on another kilometer to a farther rim that might or might not be "the" rim. Still, I had made it to a relatively open area. Turning, I discovered I stood higher than the cliff edge on the opposite canyon wall. I had enough clear sky to have a good chance of either hitting one of our '77's passing by, or catching a satellite in place.

Overton had coached me on what to say, either via SF-77 ship-to-ship channel, or on a sat link. I set up, turned the radio on, plugged my suit mic into the input, and started my pleas for help on the normal fighter channel.

"This is the crew of Mars Alpha fighter Seven-Seven-Alpha One Two One. We have ditched near the following position over sector One Four Three Alpha." I repeated the coordinates twice. Waiting about thirty seconds, I performed the call once more, and then, in succession, ten more times. I got no response.

That made sense. More than likely, the Mars Alpha fighters had returned to base. Assuming some of our fellow searchers heard our SOS earlier, they might have lingered to search, but my sense was we had moved some distance from the coordinates Eagle had broadcast at the beginning of our encounter. They could easily have missed us. Now, in the dark, any exploration would seem futile without some hint as to where we went down.

I decided to try the satellite link. I had to change the transmitter frequency and and modulation type, as ship-to-ship was spread spectrum, but satellite links used an FM technique that provided good communication, provided you were in line-of-sight of the satellite. I had been careful to listen to Overton's instructions, and there was a small manual, but I was successful doing it from memory.

"This is the crew of Mars Alpha fighter Seven-Seven-Alpha One Two One. We have ditched near the following position over sector One Four Three Alpha. Have not been able to rouse a response on ship-to-ship. Please respond if you read me."

I repeated the message twice only, getting a response with cheering rapidity.

The speaker in my ear came to life. "Alpha Fighter Crew Seven-Seven-Alpha One Two One, we read you loud and clear. Glad to hear from you guys. We called off search for the night, although we have an approximate position."

Another voice took over. I recognized Alford. "Who is this? Over."

"This is Hays, Captain." I spoke formally, as I didn't know who was on the line with the base commander.

He surprised me. "Scotty, thank God you guys are okay. They are pinpointing your location now via satellite GPS, and we'll have birds in the air ASAP."

"Sir, hear me out. We are very near a Bug base, though we do not know its exact location. We were attacked by three fighters. War Eagle knocked at least two of them out."

Alford laughed. "We knew you found a nest or stirred up the hornets somehow, Scotty. Any idea why they came out at you during the day?"

"Sir, we lost an engine, so Eagle did a one-eighty, to head back to base. I think we did it directly over a Bug site. I suspect they thought we spotted them and that's why they launched."

I heard him mutter under his breath. "Bad luck."

"Yes, sir. As I said, three of them, but with our engine failure, we were boxing with one arm. The ship was further damaged in battle, but Eagle managed to bring us in. Unfortunately, we came in hard."

Silence. "How hard?"

"Sir, I am sorry to report War Eagle has been killed. Admiral Overton has, I believe, sustained a broken leg but he'll be fine. I suffered no injuries when we crash-landed."

Alford sounded incredulous. "No injuries *at all*?"

"Nothing serious, sir. Bumps and bruises, but I'll be okay. We need to get the admiral medical care. And sir, we need to get Eagle home. I'm not sure Admiral Overton will leave without him."

Another silence. "Understood, Scotty. The first Seventy-sevens are within minutes of takeoff. We had more in the area but were unable to trace you. They had to return for fuel. Are you close to Overton so I can talk to him?"

"No, sir, sorry. I left him about three and a half kilometers down in the canyon. Had to get up high enough to get a radio signal out."

"Can you get back to him?"

"On my way there, sir. He's not far from the landing site."

"Good. When you get there, turn the radio on full, ship-to-ship channel seven, and leave it on. It could help us locate you faster."

"Plan to, sir. And sir, bring plenty of firepower. That Bug base has to be near here, and unless they've had time to run, they'll throw everything they've got at you."

"Mars Beta is sending reinforcements too, Scotty. We'll find those bastards and send them all to Bug hell."

"Anything else?"

"We should be to you within an hour at most. Going to have to do a bit of looking around, but we'll find you."

"Thanks. When we get back to the base, drinks are on me for the whole damn outfit."

"I hope you got a big bank account."

Not quite as big after Kaley's legal expenses, but big enough. "Don't worry, Captain, I can cover it."

He laughed. "I'm sure you can. Alford out."

I sat back, satisfied. Now we had a good chance of getting home in one piece. Kaley. I hadn't had much time to consider her the last few hours. I'd better make it back, or else. I couldn't imagine the shitstorm that would hit IC, McKissack, and Alford, if I didn't.

Turning off the com unit, I shouldered it and started downhill.

Moving down seemed much tougher. Climbing, if you stumble or lose your footing, you simply fall forward onto the slope. Descending, there's nothing to catch you, and given the lower gravity, you can catch a bit of momentum and really pick up speed. Earth's gravity can pull you down the same way, but it's heavy enough to stop you. Mar's gravity is light enough to pull you downhill, but not give you much braking power.

Realizing if I fell, I might tumble a long way, I went down much more slowly and chose a route that wiggled back and forth, not directly downhill but on a slant left, right, left, right. Slower but safer.

I had gone no more than half a kilometer when, once again, a flicker caught my eye. My glance up revealed a Bug fighter, almost directly above, proceeding west. Only, it slowed and began to make a sharp bank to port, coming back.

I'd been spotted.

This stretch of slope sat at a shallow angle, with little or no rough ground, boulders, or other places of concealment. I didn't want to go downhill at this point. Downhill led straight to Overton and the ship. I headed left, toward rougher ground, spying shallow ravines three hundred meters off and at my elevation.

Glancing back as I sprinted, I saw the Bug fighter complete the turn, stabilize, and dive, headed for me. I increased my speed, but saw I'd never make it. I turned and faced the diving craft. Its beam weapons opened up, scoring the ground, twin continuing divots of soil and rock racing toward my position. I hesitated, then sprang to the right as the sizzling rays neared me. They missed by a meter or so.

I was running for the shallow ditches, trying to reach them before I was a target once more. Even as the ship climbed and banked to starboard, I dived into the trough, sliding for meters, worried I'd abrade the suit. I came to a stop in the shadow of the trench, well-hidden and able to catch my breath.

Huddled in the hollow, I saw the ship pass over, although clearly the occupants had lost sight of me. After it passed, I raised up to peer after it, saw it bank again.

It was coming back.

CHAPTER 27 HIDE AND SEEK

Now began the deadliest game of hide and seek I had ever played. The enemy, untiring and deliberate, continued passing overhead, taking its time in the deadly search. I had about decided that as long as I stayed well hidden, I had a good chance to wait them out.

No. Very quickly, two additional fighters appeared, and they began to crisscross the area, back and forth, scanning a set pattern that centered on the position of the shallow troughs and rough area where I had chosen to hide. I could barely raise my head to check one ship before another passed over at a different angle. They seemed uncommonly determined to find one singular Earth soldier, with no apparent reason to give up. Did they believe that I had been "dropped" in the area to spy out their new site? That seemed ridiculous to me, but who knew how paranoid the Bugs cold be?

I changed position several times, moving deeper into the ravine, and found to my pleasant surprise the bottoms became deeper, the walls more jagged, the terrain easier in which to conceal myself. Eventually, I found a narrow, deep trench with a broad overhang that concealed me completely. I slipped into it, crouched down as small as I could, and hoped they'd eventually give up and go home.

After about half an hour, I peeked out, to find nothing overhead. Ducking down, I waited a few minutes, then began to worm my way to a position where I could get a good view of the sky.

After ten minutes of scanning, I decided my pursuers had given up. I began to move out of the trough, back toward my pathway and on to Overton's position. I went slowly, glancing back a lot, trying to stay alert for any danger.

Only a final glance backward saved my life. The bug ship had nearly caught me. I jumped sidewise just as the beams passed exactly where I had been standing only a second before. There appeared to be only one ship. Perhaps the others had returned to base while this one lurked, trying to catch me when I emerged.

I was so angry at the deception that as the ship passed overhead, I yanked up the machine pistol, set to auto, and put about ten rounds toward the fuselage, only tens of meters above me. I almost stumbled and fell in surprise as I saw the ship jerk, stutter, and fall off to my left. It turned, straightened, and began a descent, coming toward me. I ran for the troughs.

Hidden among ruts and piles of rocks, I watched as the ship thumped hard twice on the Martian soil, coming to a halt no more than two hundred meters from where I cowered. The hatch at the top popped up, two figures emerged and leapt to the ground, each carrying some sort of medium length rod, surely some sort of beam weapon.

I didn't wait, but faded farther back into the maze of ruts, ravines, and tumbled ground. The last time I peeked, the two Bugs had entered the first gully, peering left and right but not spying me yet. I continued to flit back and forth between good positions of concealment, retreating. I was determined to lead them farther from our ship, hoping Overton remained well hidden.

I was ducking down when, at some distance to the rear of the two Bugs, two more ships appeared. The single ship appeared to have recalled the its two companions. Or perhaps now that darkness had set in, the nearby base had called for help. I hesitated a heartbeat too long. A beam weapon blast cut the rock to my left, and I dived for safety. Picking myself up and bending as low as possible, I fled to the east, hoping I wouldn't be visible from overhead.

I felt, rather than saw, the presence above. I crouched as the two shadows passed over. They would no doubt return, so I ran again, my retreat taking me into an open space on the upslope side, where the troughs emptied into rougher ravines, with deeper sides, and greater areas of concealment.

There, in a hollow to my left, lay a monstrous cave, retreating into the canyon side. In it, more than half-completed, an enormous Bug portal stood, more than twenty meters high. It would be more than twice that if they were allowed to complete it. Various Bug crew were at work. I couldn't tell if any of them, some no more than a hundred meters away, spied me or if they were even on the lookout. I scuttled to the safety of the deeper ravines, stopped, and took shelter, as the two fighters glided overhead again, still not catching sight of me, or so I hoped.

I decided to wait. My pursuers would soon appear on the other side of the open space. If ever there was ever an opportunity for an ambush, this was it. In less than a minute by my chrono, they emerged, the lead Bug a good three meters ahead of the second.

My projectile weapon, one of the newer US arms, was a seven-millimeter US/European machine pistol, with a thirty-round magazine. I took aim and sent the remaining twenty rounds toward my enemies. They dropped instantly, one moving frantically, as I saw I had hit both helmets. I couldn't be sure how badly I had injured them as I'm no expert in Bug physiology, but they didn't move long. My silent sidearm, combined with our distance from the boundary of the Bug portal site, had perhaps not drawn the attention of the various portal workers.

It was fully dark, and although the starlight made the scene relatively clear, I hoped the Bugs, somewhat blinded by the lights around their work site, wouldn't notice. Those lights weren't very bright, but they were enough to ruin the night eyes of those working on the portal.

I remembered Bobby saying that the Bug's compound eyes were bad at detail but good at catching motion. That meant even though they wouldn't catch their fallen comrades lying still and silent, they would more than likely see me as I tried to cross the open space. I had to return to our ship and Overton, who I hoped remained hidden.

Meanwhile, the two Bug fighters passed overhead twice more, each time at a slightly different angle, but didn't seem to either see me or spy the dead crew of the fighter. I counted the time between passes. Almost exactly two minutes. Two more minutes passed. Then another two. Then two more. The ships appeared to have vanished.

Had they returned to base? Suspicious they might be hovering just out of sight, I remained in place another full ten minutes. After that full count, I waited another five minutes, all five groups of sixty seconds seeming to pass in roughly a century each.

I lifted up, peered a full three-sixty degrees, saw nothing.

I had to take the chance.

Moving slowly, I crept out of the deeper ravines to the east of the Bug portal site. I had to cross a solid hundred meters of flat, relatively clear ground. I didn't walk. I crawled.

It was impossible to see the workers to my right in the well-hidden cove. They must know the enemy lurked nearby, but they might be too disciplined to do anything more than their assigned job. I hoped that was true.

Creeping beside the dead crew members, I examined one of their weapons. I had no idea if I could figure out its operation, deciding I didn't have the luxury of time to learn.

I had no warning. Two laser/particle beams streaked past me, missing by an eyelash. The two enemy ships streaked overhead. Looking up, I saw several Bugs at the portal turn toward me, gesture, and point.

I did the only thing I could do. I jumped up and ran into the troughs, back towards our ship, fleeing for all I was worth before the enemy above and those on the ground coordinated their efforts to pursue me.

CHAPTER 28 DESPERATE RETREAT

I had to return to the ship and Overton, even though I led our enemies directly toward them. I was committed to having my transmitter activated, to guide our '77's to us. The rescue team would arrive soon. I had to be nearby when the good guys showed up to light up the beacon.

The troughs were a parallel grouping of gullies that ran east-west, shallower and not as jagged as those to the east past the Bug site. My cover would be marginal at best, better against the airborne enemy, not good if the Bug workers at the portal grabbed weapons and joined the chase.

I had two more magazines for the machine pistol. Tossing the empty one aside, I loaded another as I loped down the troughs. To the west, the ships banked on thrusters and headed in, diving toward me as I ran. As they neared, I ducked just as their beam weapons opened fire, digging small trenches on either side of me, but missing as I lurked beneath a large boulder.

As the fighters passed overhead, neither traveling fast, I thought. *It worked once, Maybe it'll work again.* I emptied the entire thirty rounds at the bellies of the two craft. One of the ships jerked, but both continued east. To my right, another beam sliced past, so the workers had armed themselves and were in pursuit .

I ducked, bounding west, trying to stay beneath the trough crests. I attracted no more fire, so my pursuers were far enough back they couldn't spy me. I thought crazily, *Kaley is never gonna forgive me if I get my ass killed.*

Reaching a larger trough that ran at an angle, I ducked into it, stopped, and lifted my head. The two ships split up, one moving to north and away, while the other readied another run at me. I hoped that meant I had damaged the retreating ship. I could see no other figures to the rear, though I had to assume some of the Bug workers must be out there.

I decided to stay in place a moment, to at least give the fighter a chance to pass overhead. I loaded the final magazine, then extracted the beam weapon from its holster. As hand weapons, I had no strong affection for the small blasters. They could do damage, but it took a multi-second shot to penetrate even a vac suit. I didn't have many more rounds for the regular sidearm, so I had to try it.

I peeked out of my gully and there were two Bugs, not twenty meters away, both holding the same type of longer beam rifles my first pursuers had used. Blaster in hand, I fired, a solid two seconds each. The second Bug swung up his weapon as I switched my aim. It shook, retreated, and fell.

The first had dropped, so I assumed the beam weapon had worked. I still didn't have a lot of faith in it, so I set the pistol to semi-automatic fire and scrambled to my left and into another very shallow trench, this time moving back toward the two enemy I'd hit. Foolish, maybe, but I felt I had to know if they were capable of pursuit.

Peering over the edge of my shallow hiding place, I saw nothing. Based on their position a moment ago, they should be to my left and about ten meters west and five north, give or take. I crept into the next low spot, passed another trench wall, and peered in the direction of the pursuit. Nothing. Had only two of the Bugs come after me? I found it hard to believe. Nothing emerged from the shallow culverts stretching away from me.

I had come two hundred meters from the open space that looked into the enemy site. With no idea of the personnel complement, I assumed there were dozens of the Bugs, if not a hundred. Surely a larger group must be after me.

The single Bug fighter slipped by to my right by a good half a klick, as though the pilot had begun a sort of grid search. It flew too far away to spot me in the darkness. Looking left, I saw two scenes .

On the other side of the ridge, my pursuers lay. Dead? At least, not moving. I spied three more, long beam weapons in front of them, moving down the canyon. Bringing up the machine pistol, I squeezed off three rounds. Two of the bugs jerked and flew back, falling. The third spun frantically around, trying to move sidewise.

A moving target is harder to hit, but I'm a good shot. I qualified as sharpshooter in arms school many years ago in basic training. One round, two rounds. The last Bug dropped, legs shaking, then its body relaxed and stilled.

All the enemies I could see were down, dead or injured. I sprinted toward the ship and Overton's concealed position. Every few yards I glanced at the sky, hoping to see an SF-77 or two coming in for a look-see. Where the hell were the good guys? It had been an hour since I called and no sign of them. It occurred to me that as I had yet to set up the com unit, the good guys had no way of zeroing in on our position.

My last glance skyward saved me. Four Bug fighters came out of the east, two to my left, one to my right, and one headed directly overhead. I threw myself to the side, burrowing into the gully behind a low pile of jumbled ground. Rock and soil exploded around me, as bright flashes of light told me how close the beams had come. I ran, the sky clear, as all four fighters pulled up and headed back at me.

So much trouble for one little human? I thought as I raced toward the fighters. From their point of view, I could be the pilot of the ship they downed, and who had downed their craft. If I were them, I would be a lot more concerned about packing up and getting the hell to a new location. Surely, they would realize our pilot had messaged our base and other IC fighters nearby.

Whatever the reason, they weren't giving up. The Bug fighters neared, and I couldn't very well keep running, or they couldn't miss me. The troughs in this series of gullies weren't deep enough, the deepest two or three meters. I found the biggest ledge, coiled in a ball and hoped the Bug beam weapons weren't strong enough to cut through it.

All four had seen me before I went low. They fired, their beams crisscrossing in a pincer move designed to raze the area. If the right one don't get you, the left one will. Dirt erupted around me and one beam missed my left foot by two centimeters. As the four ships passed overhead, I hopped up and continued west.

I was near the end of the troughs. Only a wide stretch of open ground separated the ever-shallowing grooves and Overton's position. I had to lie in place, hope the ships would give up , and assume they missed me.

They four ships flashed over three times, still close, as I held on for dear life.

Another pass.

I kept quiet and tried to take regular breaths, as if frantic gulps for air might give me away.

No sign of anything overhead. I ventured over the lower of the two ridges. Where could they have…?

They were coming in, each from a different direction. I saw them, they saw me, and they opened up in unison. In front, behind, and on both sides, all around me, dirt and rock erupted like a geyser. I was thrown up and back, landing hard against the adjacent ridge. It felt like several tons of debris landed on me, and I found myself buried under the red Martian soil.

CHAPTER 29 THE BEST DEFENSE...

Stunned, I laid under the piles of dirt and rocks. Had I not been in the vac suit, I would have asphyxiated. My head began to clear. *Good thing I'm well concealed*, I thought in a dizzy haze. *No one can possibly see me.*

My right arm could only move a limited amount. Shifting it back and forth, I began to dig my way out from under the dirt and debris covering my helmet. Frantic efforts finally resulted in clearing my helmet and the right side of my chest. As I cleared the faceplate on my helmet, one of the Bug fighters flickered overhead and I froze.

Two others slipped above, higher than before. I was more than likely well camouflaged from above at that point, so I ceased movement and waited. The fourth was either patrolling farther off or had returned to base. I began to dig once more, freeing my left arm so it could be of use to move dirt and rock. I managed to sit up, spying one of the three fighters starting a return pass. I scrambled to free my legs as the ship began its dive. As it neared, I lay back, my lower body covered, frozen in place .

The fighter slowed, too near to fire at my position, but close enough for a visual scan. It passed over me at a crawl, and I had to believe the pilot spied me or recognized the pile of soil and rocks as the previous target.

Frantically, I began to move my legs. The left one burst free first and I concentrated on the right. A warning icon began to blink on my internal status screen: *Oxygen leak detected.* I couldn't hear hissing, nor did I feel the internal suit pressure drop, but that had to be bad news. I managed to stand, looked east but didn't see any pursuit on the ground. If there were any more of the enemy pursuing me on foot, they had to be at the series of troughs unless the pilots in the Bug fighters had communicated with them and warned them away.

No enemy fighters showed to the east, but I saw three to the west, banking for a return pass. I had been too far below the adjacent ridges to see the other two. I moved enough to my left to be under the slight overhang and froze as the ships neared. They slipped over quietly.

I stood, glanced behind, and headed toward Overton's position in the giant, loping strides that low gravity allows. He should still be hidden in the tumble of boulders that made up the only decent hiding place in the area. I had to be hidden among those rocks before the Horde fighters could return. My oxy read okay, but I still had a leak. I was making great time when a beam blast just missed taking off my right ear.

I dove into the soil, sliding and possibly making the leak worse, although the warning didn't change on my status panel. I saw a dozen Bugs scatter out of the gullies, most with beam weapons. Raising my pistol, I let fly with a half-dozen rounds. Three Bugs did the death dance, one pirouetting twice before it fell. As the other two dropped, the rest were bringing up their weapons when they began to jerk, slip, and shake.

I looked behind me and saw Overton's machine pistol spitting out rounds. As he continued to fire, I sprang up and head toward him, frantically casting glances skyward to locate the enemy fighters.

There they were, in a unison dive, aimed at me, ready to fire. I lengthened my strides, exerted every muscle to make it to the rockpile before they opened up, making my kangaroo hops even longer, straining every muscle. They were almost on us. I hoped Bill ducked. At least he might be safe.

I wasn't going to make it, I could tell. Sweat beginning to drip into my eyes, I made an instant decision to stop, turn, and bring up my automatic pistol, prepared to empty the few rounds left toward the enemy.

Kaley, I said in a silent apology, *I'm sorry. I tried, I really did.*

I didn't have to fire. AS I took aim, the three ships skidded right, two collided, and the third broke in two. The conglomeration of debris spun past, a hail of descending meteors. It crashed to the south in a massive eruption of parts and dirt. Simultaneously, huge splashes of dirt flew up as several cannons opened at once, the trail of bullets marching toward the remaining group of Bugs. What had once been a group of pursuers suddenly became a large collection of miscellaneous body parts.

The good guys had arrived.

Picking myself up, I hurried to the rockpile, to find Overton, still on his knees, looking over the devastation. I felt rather than heard a massive explosion up-slope. Almost surely, that meant the end of the Bug portal site. I was right, as I saw a cloud of dust fountain into the air.

Overton turned as I squatted down.

"Good shooting," I told him. You saved my ass."

"Fair is fair. You saved mine."

Just then, two of the '77's approached, went into vertical, and descended, stirring up a blizzard of dust as they settled on thrusters. They finally alit, and two figures leapt from each ship, hurrying toward us. I realized the two fighters, instead of carrying a normal crew, had flown medical teams to tend to us. One spoke over the com channel. "I'm Commander Ahmadi," he said, waving so we could distinguish him. "I'm field surgeon and MD for Alpha Base."

I pointed to Overton. "I'm okay. Admiral Overton has a broken leg, we think."

He knelt beside the admiral, gave his staff instructions and had Overton stretch out, as much as possible, for a quick field exam. The other three acted like part of a well-oiled machine, setting up instruments and scanning the area for more enemy.

The good doctor asked questions, probed the leg, sat back. “I think you’re right, looks like a fracture. Not a full break.”

As 77’s carry a crew of three, I realized the third member of each crew was the pilot, no doubt remaining aboard. In no time, they had Overton’s leg immobilized and held rigid by stays and a clamping mechanism.

The commander turned to me. “You seem fully mobile. Any problems?”

“Bumps and bruises. I have a small leak in my suit, so I need to get connected to a permanent oxy supply on the way home.”

“Easily done.”

He paused, surveyed the area. “Your Seventy-seven isn’t visible. Is it nearby?”

I managed a relieved chuckle. “Actually, it is. To your left, down slope maybe three hundred yards, right in the bottom of the canyon.”

He turned to survey the downslope. I could imagine his squint through his faceplate, trying to find it.

Overton spoke up. “Damned hard to see it in the dark. Fix your radio compass on ninety degrees, find the large boulder to the right, follow it down.”

Good directions. I wouldn’t have located it without the info. Earth-type compasses won’t work on Mars, which has almost no magnetic field, but a compass utilizing GPS signals from the satellites and orienting on the stars did the trick. I located our downed 77, as the commander nodded, said, “Got it. I understand War Eagle did not survive.”

He said it with a solemn look on his face. I got the idea Eagle had been popular and well known by everyone. I let Overton answer.

"Sorry, Commander Ahmadi, he was killed in the crash."

The commander dipped his head. "He was a good pilot and a warrior. He will be sorely missed."

I didn't let myself feel sorrow now. I had too many other things to worry about. Later, I would mourn our brave pilot.

I caught motion above and glanced up to see another '77 coming down. "Here comes our taxi, Commander," I told the commander. "If you need help with the admiral, I'd be glad to assist."

CHAPTER 30 NO ONE LEFT BEHIND

Overton was one hundred percent adamant.

He wouldn't leave without War Eagle. He sat, back against the boulder that had protected him, and told the commander how it would be.

"Sir, we'll come back for him. I guarantee it. But first, I have orders from Captain Alford to get you back in one piece. Do you understand? Those are my orders."

Overton snorted, at least that's what it sounded like over com.

"I understand, Commander. Let me ask you something. What's my rank?"

"Admiral, sir."

"And what's Alford's rank?"

"Captain, sire."

"And which is higher?"

Ahmadi, got it, whether he wanted to or not.

"I understand, sir. Problem is, every other Seventy-seven has a full crew, including the two that brought us. Each has a pilot who is still aboard, keeping watch for the enemy. The Seventy-seven coming in now to pick you up only has room for two additional passengers."

"Bullshit. Scotty, there's a good, solid stow space behind the crew seating, right?"

I didn't know why the admiral had sucked me into the conversation, but what the hell, I decided I liked the admiral better than ever, especially with the stand he tool about War Eagle's remains.

"Absolutely. He can fly back with us. That's what you want. Right?"

"Goddam straight. Got that, Commander?"

The commander knew when to surrender. Also, I think he felt that same admiration for Overton that I did.

"Loud and clear, Admiral. I'll send a team—"

"No, you won't. You'll go yourself. Scotty will be glad to help. Right, Scotty?"

I'd squatted down. Now I stood. "Come on, Commander. You and I are enough to do the job."

Commander Ahmadi arose as well. "Simmons, get the admiral ready to go. The taxi is coming."

As she spoke, it settled to the ground in another cloud of dust, beside its hangar-mates. I started downslope without another word, the commander following.

A hundred meters downslope, he commented, "The admiral has strong opinions."

"He's also on this frequency," I added.

"Not really," he replied. "These are near-field radios. They're only good for about thirty to fifty meters. Understand, I'm not complaining. I like it he's loyal to those under his command. Besides, War Eagle was one of the good guys. He'll be missed for certain."

"I wish we at least had a body bag," I lamented.

He held up his pack. "Got a multi-duty sheet in here, which will serve well."

We approached our fighter. The fuselage had several cracks, and the left landing gear had partially buckled, although I hadn't noticed the slanting fuselage before. I'd had too many other things to worry about just then. Looking it over, I was amazed that Overton and I were in as good shape as we were.

At the hatch, I levered it open and stepped aside.

"I'm sure you want to check his body," I said.

"I have to. IC regulations."

He sprang up the ladder, entered the cabin, and moved forward. I climbed only high enough to see where he knelt near War Eagle.

He didn't take long. "I pronounce Lieutenant Dawson deceased. So entered in my log." To me, a parenthetical comment, "I'll need time of death from your suit log when we return to base, Commander Hays."

So Alford had let it out—at least to Ahmadi—that I was former IC.

"Certainly. Let me come help you with his body."

"He's not heavy. I can bring him to the hatch."

And he did, with seemingly little distress. Once near me, he said, "I'll leave him here for a moment. Help me spread the covering."

He came down, retrieved the sheet from his pack, a sturdy plastic, folded into a very small square, and we spread it to the left of the fuselage. Despite the compact package, the sheet extended a full two by four meters.

He climbed back into the cabin, over my protest.

"The admiral told me to get him. I will get him."

He did consent to pass Eagle to me, and I held the limp body, with mixed feelings. Ahmadi jumped down and shared the weight. We wrapped the body carefully, I might even say, tenderly. A bit of dust clung to the outer surface of the sheet. Hefting it between us, we carried it back. Not a heavy load. Sharing it, we each supported only thirty pounds or so. We laid it a few feet from Overton.

"Admiral," Commander Ahmadi said formally, "The remains of War Eagle are prepared for shipment." He saluted.

The admiral returned it. "Thank you, Commander. We take our fallen back. No one left behind. Ever."

I found myself standing at attention, as were the other IC personnel. Overton himself stood ramrod-straight, even though I bet myself that he paid a serious fee in pain to keep himself upright.

The admiral leaned toward the shrouded remains of our pilot. "Lieutenant Dawson, call sign War Eagle, we salute you. Your bravery and daring destroyed our enemies and saved your comrades. God speed to you new assignment."

Ahmadi and the EMT's saluted and I found myself joining in. Grissom regarded me oddly leaving me to assume that Alford had not shared my service with him. As he did, Overton said, "Although Scotty is a civilian now, he served in IC six years, leaving service at your rank." The MD nodded and turned to his men.

"A moment, Commander," Overton said.

"Yes?" Ahmadi hesitated.

"I would like to assist in the loading of War Eagle's remains."

"As would I," I interjected.

"Sir, with your injury..."

Overton shook his head. "I'll be fine, Commander."

So together, the six of us grasped the shroud, lifting our brave and fallen comrade, as Overton had termed him. I wasn't sure the admiral could carry his portion while supporting himself on a fractured leg. On Earth, I don't think he could have pulled it off, and he would have probably turned the fracture into a clean break. As it was, he limped along, at God only knew what cost, and we arrived at our taxi.

At that point, I insisted Ahmadi and I lift the remains into the back cargo area of the fighter, securing it with straps against any movement in flight. The pilot boarded. I hadn't met him, but "Brooks" was stenciled on his vac suit, alongside a lieutenant jg insignia. I helped Overton up the ramp. He was shaky as he took the rear seat. I couldn't imagine the pain he had experienced. We'd gotten off to a rocky start, but I'd grown to like him a helluva lot—and a great deal more after our shared mission.

Descending the ladder to secure the hatch, I waved at the staff and told Ahmadi, "Thank you, Commander. We'll never forget Eagle, but likewise, we won't forget the team who came to get us."

He shocked me by saluting. "Likewise, Commander. Thank you for your bravery, service, and for saving our admiral."

I secured the hatch and climbed back to my seat ahead of Overton.

I felt very odd.

I found I was having trouble with a lot of moisture in my eyes. It must be, I finally decided, all that pollen in the air.

CHAPTER 31 AN EXTRAORDINARY DISCOVERY

I stayed at Mars Alpha only long enough to see to Admiral Overton and the disposition of War Eagle's remains. Then I made a special request for emergency portal service to our headquarters. Even though Alford secured priority service, it still took half an hour. I had time for a shower and fresh clothes from my travel bag.

Carrying the bag and feeling refreshed, though tired from all the exertion plus lack of sleep over what had become nearly twenty-four hours, I watched the portal cloud, swirl, and open to our lab. I walked through to find Bobby waiting and to my astonishment, he hugged me .

"Hey, pal, I'm glad to see you, too."

He had some moisture around his eyes also—those allergies must be going around. "Man, you are pretty damn calm for somebody who got reported MIA in an engagement with the Bugs. We've all been worried sick. They just sent word a couple hours ago you were okay."

My heart vaulted into my throat. "You got word... You were told... Jesus, Kaley found out, didn't she? Holy crap, I gotta call her, make sure…"

He patted my shoulder. "Hey, it's okay, I called her a while back to tell her."

That didn't serve to calm me down a lot. She would have been frantic, hearing nothing, for hours, while I... "What time is it?"

"It's about ten AM. Don't worry, you can be on your way to visit Kaley and grab a nap. We've got everything under control here. Bets and Kyle have taken care of a huge number of calls and field service is getting back to normal, so tell Kaley not to worry."

Even though I had figured out the equivalent time on Mars, it still came as a jolt that I'd been gone only about a day. It had been an action-filled, stressful, twenty-four hours.

"Before you go," he said," I gotta show you something."

"Man, can it wait? I need to see Kaley."

"It'll just take a moment. Last night we did a brand new experiment at the university." He referred to the project team at UT Dallas. "We set up one of our personals and took a video as we did it. You *have* to see this!"

I signed and mentally threw in the towel. A video couldn't take long. It had been a while since I had seen Bobby so excited. "Okay, show me."

"It's in the office."

I followed him down the hall and to the office, waving to the portal attendants, two of our newer employees. In our joint office, he gestured me to the sofa on my side and went to his desk. As he joined me, he fiddled with the touch screen, calling up the video from storage.

Plopping onto the sofa beside me, he held out the screen for me to share. His personal was one of the new units, a double-fold that opened to a full twenty-five-centimeter screen, more like a baby TV unit than a com. The video came up, a picture of the project team vacuum bottle. They had modified it some time ago to make the end portal heavy-duty plane glass, six centimeters thick, that gave a clear view right down the center of the column.

"Now watch as we bring up power," he instructed.

I did, expecting to see what occurred, a medium-sized circle in the center, showing a clear view of a star field, one particularly large red giant centered in the view. It was a similar scene to the one I'd seen before.

"Looks the same," I commented.

"Wait."

The video continued. As I watched, the picture in the hole shifted left with a jerk. It was partially the same view, as the red giant had shifted to the far left of the picture.

"What the hell happened?" I asked.

"I created a pair of crude adjustments to the FlucGen amplitude and frequency. What you just saw was a change of the FlucGen frequency. Keep watching."

Again, the view shifted, this time to a new star field. It hadn't been a jump, like what might occur by killing power and re-establishing the wormhole. No, the entire view simply panned to the right, as though we were manipulating the aim of a powerful telescope. After rushing sidewise for what might have been ninety degrees, the view stabilized .

"Here, we changed the static electric field a bit."

The impact had me almost breathless. Our big complaint about a single-portal wormhole had always been the inability to predict the opposite end point. Here, we still couldn't do it for sure, but the team had just demonstrated a repeatable way to influence the end point in a predictable way. Perhaps there could now be a route to a useful single-ended wormhole.

"How in the world… who figured that out?"

"Me, Wendy, and Ray together. Me and Wendy, mostly, though Ray made one aces suggestion. There's a lot of work to do. I'm working like hell on a highly accurate FlucGen control mechanism, both amplitude and frequency. It'll have to be computer-controlled with agonizing accuracy. Wendy and Ray are developing methods to control electric and magnetic fields with the same precision. If this works, we can create a wormhole with a single portal to at least some degree of accuracy."

"How much accuracy?"

"Not sure. But now there's a chance to have a subway tunnel with only one transmitter."

Our long-time dream. "You're a genius, no doubt about it."

He grinned. "And I'm handsome, too. Seriously, don't discount the contribution of our two university partners. I can make big leaps of logic, but Wendy can nail down details and ferret out important values I miss. And Ray, he may not have the highest native intelligence, though he's a lot smarter than the average bear. He thinks in more detail and figures out hardware implications better than either of us."

I stood. "Okay, Dr. Genius, you've done it again, you and the team, that is. But now, I have to go see the woman I love."

"Gotcha. Give her a kiss for me and tell her she'll be out of this mess before she knows it."

I waved and hit the road. In my car, I set it to auto on the way home, meaning Kaley's house. I wasn't sure I'd ever enter my house again, except to pack up. Above me, the sky was sunny and a clear blue, very different from the velvet-black, starry bowl I had experienced over the last twenty-four hours.

On the road, my personal binged, and McKissack's face came on. "Glad you're back among the living," he told me.

"Not nearly as glad as I am. It was an interesting last day or so."

"Just wanted you to know. We got both those Bug sites, the one you found and the other about thirty klicks away."

"I assumed there must be another one nearby to supply the additional fighters that kept showing up to search for me. Glad to hear you got 'em."

"Better news. Full scans indicate we have rid Mars of Bugs. Congratulations."

"Due to Lieutenant Dawson, War Eagle, more than either me or Overton. You ought to put him in for the Medal of Honor."

"Already done. Given the circumstances, it's a slam dunk."

"Good."

"Also, you've been officially recalled into IC service for twenty-four hours to be awarded the Silver Star. As has Admiral Overton."

"I don't deserve it. Overton, I agree with."

"Pardon me, Scotty, but bullshit. And remember, for today, you're talking to your commanding officer, Admiral."

"Admiral? Sorry, that's Commander."

"Not anymore."

"Huh?"

"Scotty, you've been working for nearly a year with IC, helping us save the world. Your assistance has not only been crucial, but significant and invaluable to our effort. I've had to bend, twist, spindle, and mutilate a lot of rules to keep you in the loop. Much of the information I wished to share had such a high military classification I had to ignore about a dozen laws and hundreds of regulations to do so.

"So, I've decided to solve the problem with an ingenious solution that was actually suggested by the CNO. You were officially recalled to duty today to receive your decoration of valor, while at the same time being promoted to Vice Admiral, Lower Half, or a one-star. Tomorrow you will officially retire as a one-star. There is a huge difference between a retired Lieutenant Commander, and a retired Vice Admiral."

"What, we get more pay?"

"Hah. As if you needed more money. What're you worth, anyway, ten billion?"

I had to chuckle. McKissack knew more about me than I thought. "Nah. Maybe three. What's a few billion among friends?"

"True. Anyway, no, not a lot more pay. You didn't stay in that long. As a flag officer, we can treat you differently than a retired lieutenant commander."

About to turn into the alley behind Kaley's house, I took control and pulled to the side of the street. "How differently?"

"You don't pay attention to such things, but congress recently passed a law that flag officers may be recalled to active duty at any time to serve during an emergency. For now, we let you retire. Should the need arise to share certain highly-classified military data, we can recall you. Congratulations, Admiral. I hope you enjoyed your day as an IC officer, and I hope we don't have to call you back any time soon. But we can if I need to."

"I can't figure out if that's a threat or a promise."

"Probably both. Sorry I didn't get to consult with you on this, but I didn't have the luxury when the CNO came up with the idea. Go see Kaley. I imagine she's been pretty worried ."

We disconnected, I drove the rest of the way, and parked in the garage. Unlike mine, the garage opening into the kitchen. I went in to find it empty, but heard bare feet in the hall.

Kaley burst into the kitchen, clad only in a T-shirt and shorts, and launched herself at me.

We didn't say a word, just held each other for about an hour or two, locked in a kiss that could have gone even longer, so far as I was concerned.

Pulling away a fraction, she whispered in my ear, "Thank God, you're safe."

She took my hand and pulled me into the bedroom. By the bed, she whispered, “I want you to hold me, make love to me, and tell me everything will be all right. I don’t want you more than ten inches from me until we get up in the morning. Now come to bed.”

So I did.

CHAPTER 32 SEARCHIN'

"I made a decision," Kaley told me as we ate breakfast the next morning.

We were stuffing ourselves. We'd slept in until almost eight AM. Kaley called Alex at Billie Lou's and had breakfast delivered. I had no idea Billie Lou's delivered breakfast—hell, I'd never heard they had a delivery service. Alex was fond of Bobby and me, I'll admit, but he didn't break rules. I had to assume Kaley had used her legendary powers of persuasion . Breakfast included two waffles, scrambled eggs, about a pound of bacon, hash browns, fresh blueberries the size of small plums, fried apples, and a bowl of oatmeal for you-know-who.

Kaley brewed coffee, so I felt in heaven. All my favorite things on the table, including fresh cream and a bowl of sugar. Maybe Kaley for dessert? I could hope.

I let my focus swim back to her original statement. "What have you decided?"

"As soon as this murder thing is behind me, and you've convinced it will be behind me, we're getting married."

That deserved a kiss, so I arose, rounded the table, and gave it to her. "I can't wait for dessert after breakfast."

"You horn dog, you got dessert about six times during the night. Not that I didn't enjoy it, but you have things to do in the office. Bets is coming by to brief me on service status at ten."

"I'm not going in unless Admiral McKissack insists. As you probably noticed, I'm sore a bunch of places, and as creaky as a ninety-year-old. By the way, you have to show me proper respect from now on. He recalled me to IC service yesterday and promoted me to admiral."

She gawked. "You're shitting me."

"Cross my heart and hope to get heartburn. I'll expect you to salute me each day when I get home."

"If you're lucky, you might get a kiss."

"If you're really serious about hitching up, I'll suspend saluting requirements after you say 'I do'."

"You better be careful, bucko. You might get a different sort of salute if you're not careful."

"Very funny. I'm not working today. I'm going to meet with Guy and get an update on what he's doing on your behalf."

"Did he call you yesterday?"

"Not as far as I know, but I'm still dropping by for an update. Which reminds me, he's probably in his office by now."

I stepped to Kaley's old-fashioned internet landline wall phone and called the number I knew by heart. As usual, I had to fight my way through secretaries, clerks, and aides, but my name worked wonders. In only a scant four minutes, he came on the line.

"I thought you were on Mars."

"It was a quick trip. We scragged a bunch of bad guys, then I came home."

"Congratulations on your scragging. And glad to hear you are back in one piece. Any problems?"

"I'll tell you about it some time. I want to drop by for an update."

"An update? Give me a break. We've only been balls-out for about thirty-six hours."

"And you haven't finished up? What kind of a legal service are you running? I figured by today, all the gofers you have working the problem would have solved it."

"Listen, the improbable we do immediately. The impossible takes an extra hour or two."

"So when can you brief me?"

He sighed. "Come over about three."

"I'm bringing Kaley."

"Go for it. I got Jack Daniels in my cabinet. We can celebrate whatever you want."

I started to say, "Just being alive," but on second thought, I decided I really didn't want to get into all that yet. "See you at three."

As I returned the receiver to the wall, Kaley said, "Okay, what do we do until two? And don't make any lewd suggestions."

"I wasn't. I'm going to check with the police to see if the crime scene tape has been removed from my house. If so, I'd like to go over to my house and look it over. You don't have to go with me, but I'd like you to, if you don't mind."

Frankly, I hated to even go inside my (former but never again) home, but I wanted to check out the room where Glynnis had stayed—and come back to, even though we thought she was gone for good. I hoped Kaley would come, because she could provide some context to the weird and terrible occurrence that day.

Kaley nodded. "I'll come. I love my house, I really do, but if I have to stay here another hour, I think I'll scream."

I helped her clean the kitchen and store leftovers in her zillion-cubic-foot Sub-Zero fridge, even bigger than the one in my house. She went for a quick shower and change, as she still wore the T-shirt and shorts. I still marveled at her youthful appearance. Nearly seventeen years my senior, she appeared to be maybe thirty. She'd mentioned, once, a minor genetic boost. GB's had gotten a lot more popular, but I knew for a fact that although they did help set back the clock a few years, they certainly didn't take it back to your youth. A simple truth: some families have better genes than others.

She came in, fresh and damp, surrounded by the fragrance of flowers.

"Ready."

"Maybe we should stay here," I murmured, kissing the back of her neck.

"Boy, I can tell that once we're married up, I won't be getting much shuteye."

"What can I say? I'm under your spell."

She punched my shoulder and we headed to the car.

A call to the DeSoto PD verified that my house was no longer an active crime scene. It was only minutes away. We parked in front, as I wasn't about to enter the garage unless I had to. True to the report I had gotten, the crime scene tape had vanished. We climbed the steps to the landing, past the massive columns. Although the door has a key-lock, I said my name and gave a four-digit code, and the door opened.

The house seemed oddly quiet and still, with a stale feel to it. Kaley followed me in, shivered, and said, "Bad memories."

"You never saw her, right, until the police arrived?"

"Right. I had no idea she was even here. I'd been to bed, woke, had it in the back of my mind I needed to clean the guest room and wash the sheets, but I hadn't gotten around to it. I answered the door, and there the police were, to tell me about an emergency call about a poisoning.

"I didn't know what the hell they were talking about, until they asked about Glynnis. Had she been a guest? I said yes, but she'd gone. They asked me to show them the guest room, we walked in, and she was on the bed, in a pile of vomit."

"What could you see?"

"Not much. In seconds, the policeman rushed me out, called his partner, and they radioed for assistance. Pretty soon the whole house was full of cops."

"That's weird. You didn't call she certainly didn't. Who did?"

"Don't ask me. The next thing I knew, they were ready to charge me with murder. I still haven't figured out how Guy and Sami managed to spring me after they took me downtown."

"Guy and I both provided info. Her first attempted suicide helped your cause, as it was well documented by the hospital."

"Still, I'm not in the clear by any means."

"Don't worry, we'll get there. Now let's go to the guestroom," I suggested.

As we entered the hallway, I said, "The thing I just don't get is, Glynnis was a real me-me-me person. In her view, she always came first. Why would she kill herself to get back at you or me, when it ends her life and we happily go on about our business?"

"Not if I get convicted of murder."

"Even then, it wouldn't do her any good, from her point of view." We entered the bedroom. The bed sat as it had been left by police, sheets and covers stripped, Glynnis's one piece of luggage taken, the small items on the dresser removed as well. The rest of the furniture had been moved. Police crime scene analysts had given it a thorough going-over.

I finished my thought. "Think about it. Glynnis was all about her priorities, her desires, her pleasure. If she died, she'd never know if you were convicted of murder. And she'd want to know. She'd *have* to know. I can't imagine she would kill herself."

"Great. You're doing all you can to figure out how to convict me."

"Don't be silly. Somehow, she died here, and her journal, diary, whatever that book was, tried to implicate you. She wanted you to be found guilty of *something*. But consider," my mind formed conclusions as I spoke, "What about convicting you of atte*mpted murder*?"

"But she didn't do that. She killed herself."

"What if she didn't *mean* to kill herself?"

"Huh?"

"What if she decided to concoct the diary story, then ingest enough poison to make herself ill? Not enough to die, but enough to make her symptoms real."

"She didn't do that. She died."

"What if only getting sick is what she planned? She procured poison. Have the police said anything about what kind of poison?"

"No. Neither Sami nor Guy mentioned it."

"We can ask when we see him. Say Glynnis reads up on some poison or maybe a medicine, decides it will work, and when she gets here and sneaks in, takes a carefully-measured dose, just enough, or so she thinks, to make her ill. She somehow manages to bollux up the dose and ends up killing herself. That makes sense to me. Her plan is to damage us but live to see how her plan screws up our life. It would be the perfect revenge."

"But Scotty, that is so... twisted. How could she ever...?"

"Because, as I'm coming to understand better in retrospect, Glynnis was a genuine, gold-plated psychopath. She didn't care about anyone but herself—her happiness, her success, her pleasures. It makes perfect sense. Why did she divorce me? I discovered the many liabilities of marriage to her, and her sexual performances no longer dazzled me. She wasn't the center of my attention, my universe. So, she'd show me. She'd divorce me and damage me monetarily.

"The thing is, it hurt her worse. I think she realized she didn't have the patsy, me, around anymore, didn't have me to squire her to important events. She decided he'd get me back. Then, if I began to pay less attention, she'd invent new ways to string me along. Only I wasn't buying. That first suicide attempt was a ruse to get my attention and increase my interest.

"And then the horrible realization, for her. I didn't want to come back! All that was left was to extract all possible revenge. Somehow, she miscalculated the poison dose and ended her life as she was attempting to end ours, at least as a couple."

Kaley surveyed the room, shaking her head. "It sounds so Machiavellian and awful. I suppose she could have been that evil-minded and corrupt. It's just hard for me to imagine."

I understood Kaley's feelings; she had a straightforward mind and a generous spirit, always willing to give someone the benefit of the doubt. On the other hand, I could imagine Glynnis's devious and underhanded tactics with no trouble at all.

Enough chitchat. We needed to go over the room once more. But first...

"Maybe I'm onto something, maybe not. Let's go back to the moment the police arrived and you took them to the room. Tell me every single thing you remember until they made you leave."

Kaley frowned, concentrating fully, resurrecting every shred of memory since that awful morning three days ago.

"Um, okay. I was still in bed, still exhausted from my last trip. I heard the doorbell, got up, threw on sweats, and went to the door. A DeSoto policeman stood there. He said the police department had gotten a call about a possible poisoning—"

I interrupted. "Did he say who called?"

"No. He only mentioned the call. I told him I was the only one home, my fiancé was at work, and I had no idea about any call. His partner came to the door. I guess she'd been sizing up the place. She asked if I knew the owner of the car in front of our house. That was the first time I had noticed it. It looked like Glynnis's car, but she'd left, so I said I had no idea.

"He asked if he could come in and check, and I didn't see anything wrong with that. Remember, I thought I was alone in the house. I said sure, come on in. His partner didn't come in, but headed toward the car. I trailed along as he poked in the kitchen, den, and so forth.

"When he started into the guest room section, I noticed the door to Glynnis's room was open. He looked in all the rooms, even the half-bath, checked each, and got to the open door. I entered behind him.

"He said something. I think maybe, 'What the hell.' He rushed over to the bed. His body shielded me from seeing very much, but I could see a form lying partially on the bedsheet and partly underneath it. He examined Glynnis, though I didn't know it was her at the time, then turned to me and said, 'Please go back to your family room. This may be a crime scene.' I tried to ask a question, but he shooed me out.

"I only stayed in the room seconds when the policeman had me leave."

Sure enough, her presence had been so brief that she couldn't have seen much. I considered. "Go back over those few moments you stood in the doorway. Tell me exactly what the cop did, what you saw, what you smelled, what you felt."

She hesitated. "Well, I just—"

I stopped her. "Go back for a minute, in your mind. Describe ever single iota, no matter how small."

"Uh, okay." Another pause. "I heard the cop's exclamation as I turned into the room. He rushed across to the bed. I saw a body, but I couldn't even tell if it were man or woman. I recognized Glynnis's bag on the chair and I remember thinking, 'What's Glynnis's bag still doing here? She'll be upset she forgot it.' Then I smelled a terrible, sour smell, vomit. The sheet and bed cover were tangled, and the bed cover had been partially thrown on the carpet.

"I went to the den and sat, as requested. I decided the body must be Glynnis. Her car had been in front and her suitcase was on the chair. I was there when you arrived. The only other thing the police said was to stay in the room and not move, until they started to question me."

Her recounting hadn't helped, although I found myself hewing strongly to my previous theory. Glynnis's death had not been suicide, but an accident in her plan to convict Kaley of attempted murder. Still, it was only a theory, and a shaky one at that.

"Okay, let's check the room , though I assume the DeSoto crime lab has been thorough."

We plowed every bit of ground in the cubical space. Looked under bed, furniture, investigated all the drawers, most empty, checked the small guest closet, also free of contents. I even looked under the small rocker, going so far as to check the underside of the seat.

Nothing.

"You got me," I said, sitting on the edge of the bare mattress. A slight disagreeable tang lingered in the air, though I could discern no stain on the mattress cover nor on the gray carpeting. "I can't find anything of interest. The police lab did a thorough job. Either that, or there was nothing to find."

Kaley attempted a smile, failed. "What did you expect? A note saying, 'I'm going to pretend to poison myself so I can get Carol Sellers convicted of attempted murder?'"

"That would have helped. Anyway, we're done here."

I locked things up and we headed to my car. I turned for a final look at my home for the last five years and thought, if I never entered it again, it would be too soon. I made a mental note to tell Guy to put it on the market.

Then I got in the car, and drove us to Kaley's house, to await the meeting with Bets and the later rendezvous with Guy.

CHAPTER 33 MORE SEARCHIN'

After the brief meeting with Bets, who appeared to have field service concerns well under control, we grabbed a bite at Billie Lou's. I wasn't in the mood to exchange barbs with Alex and was glad to find it was his day off. The waitress, Mary, who had served us before, had a sweet demeanor and no inclination to chitchat. I gave thanks and had the usual. Kaley, Ms. Healthy Eater Extraordinaire, had a BLT and a chocolate milkshake. It occurred to me today was April Fool's Day. Somehow, it seemed appropriate.

As Guy's offices were across town, we headed out early and were in his waiting room by two. One of the admins, Claire, brought us fresh coffee and tiny chocolate croissants. I managed to eat two despite my latest meal.

We didn't wait long. At two-forty, Guy entered the waiting room, grabbed coffee as I refreshed mine, and we strolled back to his office.

As we got seated, I asked, "So, what's new?"

He took a second, sipped. "Not a lot. Kaley, your bond holds and you are still a person of interest. In bringing up the suicide attempt Glynnis made, we shed a good deal of doubt on you as a killer. Especially as you are a model citizen, have donated substantially to many worthy causes, and are one of our folk heroes due to the Bug wars.

"By the way, did you really donate ten million dollars to build a new playground and athletic field in DeSoto and the same amount for one in Dallas?"

Even I hadn't heard that. I glanced at Kaley, She flushed, embarrassed. "I wasn't keeping it a secret, really," she said. "Hey, you know what I'm worth. I never spend a penny. I haven't even bought a new dress or any fancy makeup in a year. Like Scotty, the only substantial money I've ever spent is on my house. Might as well let a bit of it do some good."

He gave a sage dip of the head. "True. Didn't do your PR any harm. Anyway, you keep the appearance bond and must show up in court if summoned. Also, you have to stay in the county. I think the police are less interested than they were. The local papers have been pretty kind to you."

She didn't react, simply stared at her hands. "Good to know the public is on our side," I commented. "What else ?"

"We learned a little about the poison," he said.

That got Kaley's attention. "Really? What was it?"

"It's a brand-new drug, been out only a year or two. Used to treat Alzheimer's, and like most new drugs, it's been relatively effective in some cases, usually depending on the genetic makeup of the patient. It's potent, chemically. Too much of it can kill you. It's the sort of drug you'd never let the patient self-medicate. For many Alzheimer's patients, especially those further along in the development of the disease, many might have forgetfulness, lack of task-orientation, confusion, and so forth. The medication would be given via a caregiver, who could mete out a correct dose, and make certain it is administered properly.

"A dose is four small pills. Up to eight, max. Twelve or more could induce stomach distress, twenty or so could provoke a severe illness, leading to hospitalization, and more than two dozen could kill you. The exact fatal dose depends on the patient's size, body weight, and condition of health. Of course, it's all by prescription and monitored by the doctor."

That description seemed to play into my guess as to Glynnis's death. "Taking maybe twenty tablets could make a large man sick, but the same dose to a small person could result in death."

"Exactly."

The other thing that bothered me was the source of the medicine. "Where would somebody get a prescription drug like that? Surely it would be difficult to acquire."

"Yeah. Expensive, too. Glynnis had a prescription that was forged, or *somebody* had a fake prescription. It was ordered from a reputable on-line source."

Kaley said, "You said expensive. How expensive?"

"A dose is four tablets, patients take a dose every third day. One month's cost? Forty-two thousand dollars."

I whistled while Kaley goggled.

"She had a bottle of a month's dose of that stuff?" I asked.

"Actually, three months. Plenty to kill her."

I interrupted to bring Guy up to date on my theory. "You're saying," I finished, "That she had far more than enough to kill a bunch of people."

"Yeah. The evidence is she ingested quite a bit."

"What evidence?"

"Stomach contents. The pathologist thinks it was a fatal dose."

"But what's 'fatal'? Say Glynnis determines a dose of, say, twenty-four pills is the dividing line between death and serious illness. Glynnis wasn't a large woman; Kaley, for instance, outweighed her by thirty pounds."

"I do not!" The outraged response from my true love.

I made a placating gesture. "Come on, I'm not saying you're fat. You're four inches taller than she was. Glynnis claimed to be five-six, but she barely made five-four. I doubt she ever weighed more than one-twenty.

When she left the hospital after the first suicide attempt, if that's what it was, I doubt if she tipped the scales at one-oh-five. Let's say she thought eighteen to twenty pills would make her sick, so she decided to take sixteen to be safe. In her current condition, that might be a fatal dose."

We all chewed on that a bit. After a minute, I asked, "How did she get the prescription?"

"We, and the police, are working on that. It was supposedly from a respected geriatric doctor but he denies prescribing it. Generally, either PAs or nurse assistants call in prescriptions, so Glynnis or someone could have faked that part. The transmitted form was correct. As this drug is somewhat experimental, Medicare and many health insurance companies have not approved it. It's not like the drug is some sort of addictive painkiller or opioid, so some of the checks and balances for such drugs don't apply. Paid via a funds transfer with no identifying tag."

Well done and typical of Glynnis. The spider had been cleverly weaving her web. She had not, I felt with a wry and sad satisfaction, remembered to include her weight loss in her calculations.

"Where was the poison, that is, the medicine bottle found? Was it in Glynnis's guest room?"

"Oh, no. It was in your garage."

Kaley and I stared at each other, astounded. "I hadn't heard that," Kaley muttered.

I felt at sea over the location of the poison. No wonder the local gendarmes had carried all the boxes out of my garage.

"Also in the works. As I said, the fund transfer was not traceable to anyone—you, Kaley, Glynnis. Such transfers can be set as totally anonymous now days. It will take time to trace a source, if it's even possible.

"One thing. The bottle was suspiciously clean of prints. Police isolated a partial, however. It's a match to Kaley's left index finger."

Again Kaley and I goggled at each other. I stuttered, "But... isn't that in itself suspicious?

One part of a friggin' print, the rest of the container clean, and the single print is Kaley's?"

Guy shrugged. "Sure. It's why Kaley isn't in jail right now. It doesn't help a Goddam bit either."

We exchanged glances. "We're not giving up," Guy said. "I'm spending thousands of your dollars every day to uncover how this went down." He shifted his eyes. "Kaley, I don't have a doubt in the world you had nothing to do with the death of Scotty's ex. We'll keep digging. We'll get it straightened out. Glynnis could have 'stolen' a fingerprint of yours off something and planted it on the bottle. Hell, it can be done with plain adhesive tape. Don't worry. With the amount of effort we have going, we'll solve this ."

Kaley looked exhausted and I felt the need for rest as well. We had nothing more to say, so we bid Guy adieu, and I took Kaley home.

CHAPTER 34 BAD NEWS

We stayed in at Kaley's home the rest of the day. I called the office, but Bobby and the team were hard at work on their new discovery, and didn't need me. Virgil encouraged me to take time off, as field service was manageable by Bets and her team. Calls were edging up, but they handled priority calls first, and the rest could go to the backlog for now.

I sure as hell wasn't about to return to my house. We watched old movies and took long naps. Both of us were closer to totally frazzled than to well rested.

I tried to reach McKissack, to ask about the Bug threat on Earth. He had been confident that the Mars threat was dead, and there had been no reports of sightings on the out-worlds. The main concern remained pirate sites on Earth, especially in China and Russia. Since McKissack remained unavailable for the present, I'd have to tamp down my curiosity and appreciate another viewing of *Casablanca.* As it is my favorite, that made a satisfying evening. I can quote dozens of lines from that movie. My favorite: "Of all the gin joints in all the world, she has to walk into mine."

At breakfast, with only toast, coffee, and oatmeal, not my favorite morning menu, Guy called on my personal. I answered. "Yeah? Anything new?"

"Can you run over here?"

"Now?"

"Yes, as soon as possible."

"Sure, Kaley and I—"

He stopped me. "Just you, as soon as you can."

He hung up.

Kaley eyed me. "What was that about?"

"Guy. He wants to see me. Alone."

After a moment's thought, she said, "That doesn't sound good."

"Maybe not. But I think I'd better go."

I was already dressed. She came around the table and kissed me. "Then go. You can stop by Starbucks or McDonald's for your favorite breakfast."

I laughed. "It's not my *favorite* breakfast." I kissed her back and headed out.

At the law office, I only had to wait a moment, just long enough for Claire to get me a hot cuppa plus cream and sugar. I had taken my first sip when she gestured, and I went down the long hall to the last office.

Guy sat behind his desk, frowning. I expect he perfected that look over years of courtroom maneuvers. When you're a solid six-three, weigh at least thirty pounds more than Bobby, and spent several years playing pro football, that's a pretty intimidating combination.

His expression lightened when I strolled in.

"That was fast."

"You said as soon as I could make it."

" I did. My crew picked up... an interesting piece of information. Perhaps I should say an interesting potential piece of evidence. I wanted to consult you about it."

"If it's evidence, you need to notify the police, right?"

"Well, yes and no. The police will eventually need to know. It concerns the medicine that was purchased. It was done by a private, encrypted cash transfer, which is supposedly untraceable, as I told you. Even though credit cards can be kept anonymous when they are used to authorize a cash transfer, there are ways of tracing said transfer back to the card. I'm sure the authorities will eventually do that. However, our detective bureau was able to one-up them. They traced the card."

That perked my ears up. "For God's sake, the police missed it? Where did they find it?"

"Glynnis's car. It was taken in when the police gathered evidence and of course they searched it thoroughly. Found nothing. Since then, it has been at the Dallas pound.

"Our operatives submitted a request to go over the car, and since it had been searched, they got permission yesterday. They found the card."

"How did the police miss it?"

"Cleverly hidden. A piece of the floor carpeting, under the floor mats, had been pulled up and the card secreted, the carpeting put back in place. Hidden well and cleverly."

"Where is it?" I asked, my pulse increasing.

"Here."

He reached into his drawer, pulled out a small box, opened it, and passed it to me. The card lay on the bottom of the box, face up. A familiar logo showed in the upper left corner:

American Express Business Card
Solar Subway Systems, Inc.
Dallas, TX

Beneath that, the responsible party's name was stamped: Carol Sellers.

I stared at it, first without comprehension, then, without belief. "Kaley's business AMEX card? How the hell did Glynnis get that?"

"No idea. It is Kaley's card. As it was in the possession of your ex, I think that's a big plus for you and Kaley."

I nodded in agreement.

"One thing," he cautioned. "It appears to have been wiped clean. Understand, we didn't touch it. It potentially helps Kaley, but why is it clean? It would be a lot better for Kaley if it had Glynnis's fingerprints all over it. It would help your theory about Glynnis, if it had Kaley's prints on it, like she was framed. As it was wiped, it could appear Kaley planted it after removing her prints."

I thought that over. "Guy, that's just too damn convoluted. I think it helps Kaley for certain, no matter what."

"I wanted you to know about it. We could put it back, let the police find it, if they can."

I thought it over. "No. That's not right. I know Kaley didn't try to kill Glynnis. Therefore, any evidence, no matter what we may think, has to be valuable in proving Kaley is innocent. Turn it in to the police."

"I wanted to get your opinion."

"No, you wanted to know if I wanted you to break the law. I don't, either to help Kaley or to keep you and your private eyes out of jail. Turn it in, explain the circumstances."

"Okay, we'll do it."

"One more thing. Make sure the detective who turns it in is the one who found it, and that he assures them he did not wipe the card, and he volunteers to take a lie detector test if necessary to verify that."

"All right. He'll have to say he reported to us first rather than turning it in ."

"That's okay. You're the client, and they always report to you prior to doing anything on their own. They might take heat, but the police will get it."

He took the box, closed it, and put it in his upper left drawer. Pushing the intercom button, he said, "Claire, get Ralph Abernathy of Investigative Services on the line."

He turned back to me. "I'd hoped you'd say that, but I wanted you to understand the potential problems."

"I think it's all upside," I said. "The police can bring a lot more resources to bear on our problem than we can."

"Fine. Want us to keep spending bucks like somebody at Mardi-Gras?"

"Full speed ahead and don't spare the gas," I told him. "Keep us in the loop."

"Okay. Tell Kaley I said to marry you. You're clearly the most love-drugged man in this area."

"Right you are." I gave him a grin and left.

Inside, I was thinking, *How could Kaley's business credit card have been used to buy the chemical that poisoned Glynnis?*

CHAPTER 35 A WEIRD CLUE

I called the office again to find I could stay away with Virgil's blessing. Hanging up, I reflected although the April day was clear, warm, and sunny, my disposition came nowhere near that bright. It seemed every time we uncovered new information, it did Kaley little or no good, or was neutral, at the best.

Returning to Kaley's, I explained the situation, and she agreed with my suggestion to Guy and the fact evidence lately wasn't helping. I joined her in watching old movies, politely suggested a trip to the bedroom, was put off politely, and settled for putting my arm around her while we watched another old, old favorite, John Wayne's The Quiet Man. Yes, I do love a number of recent old movies, but the ancient ones always draw me back. I'm a huge fan of the Marx Brothers, and so is Kaley. We might need those as backup if things didn't improve.

We slept side by side, and I awakened to smells bacon frying—Hallelujah!—and coffee perking. I arose, showered in fifteen seconds, and made it to the kitchen in sweats, matching Kaley's. As I had gargled with minty mouthwash, I bestowed a long kiss until she shoved away and said, "Hey bucko, want to burn the bacon?"

"No, Ma'am," I said contritely, noting that two of the bagels I had bought on the way home yesterday from the law office were grilling. With plenty of butter, making my heart leap for joy.

"Set the table," she directed. "I've been too busy to get to it."

I put out plates, glasses that I filled with ice and water, and two thermos-style cups, filling mine and doctoring it with a proper amount of sugar and cream.

"Want coffee?" I asked.

"No, too busy." She was, cracking eggs in a bowl with a small amount of water, then whisking them. She cooked scrambled eggs in butter, though I frequently did them in left-over bacon grease when I cooked .

I watched the bagels, turned them once, and added more butter while Kaley wasn't looking. They were browning well, and as the bacon was about ready to drain, she turned that over to me as she added cheese and chives to the eggs and poured them into the melted butter in a fresh pan.

We finished in unison. I began to apportion the bacon while she served the cheesy, bubbly eggs. I was salivating as I added the bagel halves.

Sometimes Kaley, who is far more religious than me, said grace. Today, she leaned across the table, kissed me again, and sat to eat. The food was wonderful. She cooked six eggs and about a half pound of bacon. I gobbled in silence, adding a bit of Tiger Sauce to the eggs. She put out a serving bowl of blackberry jam, so I polished off my bagel with aplomb.

"That was wonderful. Marry me today, cook that every morning, and our marriage will be perfect."

"Yeah, until you die of coronary artery disease. You won't get that treat often, Doctor Hays, but I felt in the mood. Somehow I felt better than in a long time."

She sounded better, even though I had been rather down. We discussed the credit card further after our glorious meal. Kaley refused to worry about it, seeming even a bit excited about the news. Great news, she insisted.

"Why is that?" I asked.

"I never used that stupid card. I have my own. Actually, it's a debit card. I keep around a hundred thou in my checking account, so my debit card is the go-to expense card. I never carry cash, other than a couple hundred in the bottom of my travel bag, for emergencies. They can check the account and see I haven't used it since I got it. When was it issued, maybe three or four years ago? I wasn't even sure where it was until I thought about it. Then I remembered, it was in the bottom of my pack, that the one I carry when I run around the solar system.

"All Glynnis had to do was poke around and she'd find it while at your house, 'cause I stashed my pack in the den. I'm going to call the police and suggest they fingerprint your desk and my pack. I'll bet G left her prints all over it."

Good thinking. I decided to call Guy, but he beat me to the punch. When I answered, still at the breakfast table, he said, "I'm going to set up a conference call via our computers. I assume you're still at Kaley's I have her coordinates. Is her ISP the same?"

"No changes."

"Okay, you and Kaley get to her desk. I'll send the invite in about five minutes."

We did and he did, me pulling up a chair beside hers as the invite came through. She clicked it and in a moment, we were looking at Guy. He had on sweats, his hair mussed, so he hadn't left home, probably just finishing morning exercise.

"And a bright good morning once again," he said.

"Must be big news to get with us this early," Kaley observed.

"It is, it is. Our detectives turned the credit card over last night and the PD got right on it. I got the info before I went to bed last night, so I thought you might want to hear it. Kaley, you're not totally in the clear , but this certainly helps."

"Let us have it," she said.

"Okay. The police processed the card thoroughly. We already knew the card had been used to authorize the cash transfer, all one-hundred-plus-thousand-dollars of it. Odd thing, however, the credit card had been carefully wiped."

"As in cleaned off," Kaley qualified.

"Correct. Almost nothing on the card."

"That's not a big help," I commented.

"Ah." he grinned. "I said *almost* nothing."

"For God's sake, tell us," Kaley burst out.

"Sorry, I get it this is your future we're talking about. You know how I love to be theatrical."

"Out with it," she persisted.

"Okay, okay. The police found one small, slightly smudged partial on one edge of the card. It's technically not enough to validate a match—you know how there have to be so many so-called minutiae matches—I think they're sometimes referred to as Galton Points, although I'm not familiar with the source of the name. Anyway, there aren't enough points for a verifiable match, but enough to make it likely that it's Glynnis's left index finger."

I sat back, exchanging glances with Kaley. "That would seem to be very, very good news."

"Yeah, about as good as it could be without absolutely letting Kaley off the hook. I think that, together with your expenditure record on the card, plus the partial, I can get bail reduced to personal recognizance, and even remove the travel restrictions so you can get back to work. Just wanted you to know. The way things look, if you authorize us to keep on keepin' on, I think we can wrap this up quickly. I talked to one of the ADA's and she's getting close to calling it a revenge suicide."

Kaley smiled far more broadly than she had for days. "Boy, is that good news."

"Agreed," I chimed in. "Keep spending at the current rate or increase it if necessary. We want to get this puzzle solved."

"Got you. I'll call if we get more news."

He terminated the video, and Kaley and I stared at each other, kissed, and Kaley whispered, "Might be about ready for that bedroom trip."

After another kiss, she said, " You've been spending a lot of money on this business. I have my own money. I can take over."

"Bullshit." I'll admit I was adamant enough to raise her eyebrows. "You got into this mess solely because I was married to Glynnis. It's my fault and the expenses are on me."

She reached up and caressed my face. "That's sweet, Scotty, but it's not your fault. The fault is solely on Glynnis. God, if she were still alive, I'd be tempted to kill her myself." She laughed. "You know, it is sort of hilarious she was trying to screw up our lives, and killed herself in the process."

She leaned in, kissed me again. "Now, if you're ready, we can—"

The buzz of my personal stopped her. I pulled it out, checked it. "McKissack."

"Well, crap." She knew what that meant.

I answered. "It must be a big problem."

"It is. We got a jumbo Bug portal open in China and fighters are poring through. Already a couple hundred. We need all hands on deck on Ganymede. This time that has to include you."

CHAPTER 36 EMERGENCY

I explained to Kaley and she told me to get the hell to Ganymede.

"I'm all but cleared now," she said. "Go rescue Earth and be a hero again."

I kissed her goodbye and headed to our lab and the small portal. Bobby announced Ray was out of town, but Wendy would join us on Ganymede. She and Thuan had gone ahead to IC headquarters. It occurred to me, I was about to risk my ass for the second time in 48 hours. Waiting a dial-in, Bobby handed me my vac suit.

"We might need these."

I nodded and we put our suits on, helmets included, faceplates open, as we waited.

The small portal took us to the IC headquarters in Fort Worth. There, a crowd had gathered, awaiting transit to Ganymede. Additional laser cannons, loaded on trucks were, hurried through the jumbo. Wendy waved.

I'd been too hyped up to notice, but Bobby's face, through the open faceplate, was twisted into one of his worry frowns, eyes narrowed as though working on a problem. Wendy beat me to the question, and raised her voice over the commotion of equipment movement, babble of voices, miscellaneous noise of hangar operations, and the restricted hearing with a vac helmet in place. "What's the trouble?"

I moved closer to hear his answer. To the rear, I spied McKissack giving orders to aides. I suspected he'd just issued a stern directive to get the hell on with it. If his earlier description had been accurate, the buildup of Bug fighters could be a hyperbolic function. I hoped China was throwing every bit of firepower they could muster at the Bugs until we could arrive.

I turned my attention to Bobby as he said, "I have a... a concern. Maybe it's nothing, but..."

The last of the armament arrived, and a host of people, including naval techs, SSS staff, including Bets, plus a full platoon of Marines, began to move up the ramp toward the portal .

I missed a few words due to the uproar but caught up to him as he said, "...and the portal mismatch is larger than we've ever dealt with. We've been able to snatch control from their smaller portals, which they erect first as a parts conduit for building their big portals. Now, we have to work our magic on one of those jumbos—something we've never even tried."

Trust Bobby to hone in on the big concern, something I hadn't even considered. Matter of fact, I'd never even thought about it. In our own portal system, we could connect a normal two meter portal to a six by ten jumbo with no trouble. Bobby and the project team had perfected the technology and techniques to do a "snatch and grab," that is, wrench control from a Bug site and take over portals that were shaped and sized like our smalls, or one that averaged the size of a regular and a jumbo.

Now, we were going to attempt snatching control from a portal that might approach fifty meters in diameter. The Ganymede jumbo was our largest size wormhole maker, but it was only twenty percent the size of the Bug ring. What that meant in the mismatch of the apertures, or the differences in power utilization, I had no idea, and Bobby was saying effectively that he didn't either. We might be picking a fight with a bully, armed only with a few twigs.

We transited through the portal, personnel taking their places. I was shocked to see Admiral McKissack bring up the rear of those making the transit. The Ganymede jumbo was near the center rear on the Ganymede Beta site hangar. Across from me, the jumbo control systems were in position along the far hangar wall. The portal faced right from the front of the hangar, so those of us exiting took places as we had for the other exercises. The Marine platoon sat along the far wall to the right of the jumbo. A host of weapons, far more than for any exercise, were placed in front of the portal front ring, aimed dead center, with control personnel in heavily-armored pods at each weapon. Dead center was a rocket-controlled superbomb. The operator only had to press a button on a remote controller to send it up the ramp.

The portal techs, both ours and IC, huddled near the portal excitation panels adjacent to the Marines. Those of us in command or tech support positions stood behind the concrete barriers we had become accustomed to. Massive, heavy, waist-high, they made excellent shields if battle ensued during our takeover. I looked around. Bobby had disappeared. I had no idea why.

The hangar speakers blared a horn blast, and everyone quieted. Captain Martinez's voice followed. "We are about to attack an active site with plenty of in-place defenses, according to Chinese observers. We must be prepared to evacuate the hangar and open hangar doors to the surface vacuum, should a major counter-attack result. Please check your suits for integrity and heater performance. Tune suit radios to channel two, our on-site emergency band. If evacuation is necessary, the roof vent will open, and will reduce internal pressure to Ganymede surface pressure in less than a minute. Doctor Taylor of Triple-S, please."

So that's where Bobby had gone. I spied his highly elevated head to my left, thirty meters away. Given his concerns, I guessed what his message would be.

"We need to prepare for the worst in terms of the coming encounter. We are attempting to take over an enormous portal with one less than a third its size, something we have never attempted. There are clear dangers in making this attempt, but we must do so. Therefore, as our portal is powered up, please take refuge behind the barriers. I would urge everyone to avail themselves of a weapon. IC personnel will be passing out personal weapons immediately."

Over channel two, Martinez's voice rang out. "Martinez, to all personnel. Check around you to see everyone has clear reception, should hangar pressure evacuation be necessary."

People checked left and right as Bobby arrived. Wendy stood close by, as did Bets and Kyle. IC personnel were handing out hand weapons, but mainly to Ganymede personnel. They ran out before any were distributed to civilians.

"Begin the attack," Captain Martinez called out. Across the hangar, I saw Faye, our long-time Ganymede support tech, gesture to the IC personnel, who gave their attention to the controls.

As they brought up cross field power, I saw warning lights blink on the first portal ring. When a green light atop the ring flashed, electrostatic and magnetic fields were set. The red sister light started to blink, signifying FlucGen power was increasing. Soon the connect would begin, and you did not want to be near the portal entrance, let alone inside, as connection occurred. I'd seen that situation months ago, as a spy being returned to his native land transited the tunnel just as the portal disconnected in a swirl of brown fog. We'd never found a trace of him.

Martinez's voice blared. " Take your places behind the barriers."

We knelt, Wendy and Bobby side by side, twenty meters from me. I found myself wishing I had Kaley at my side, as she had been so many times before.

A bright yellow light on the ring signified portal contact had been made and our portal and the enemy portal were engaged in a fierce battle for control. I crossed my fingers realizing we were about to grab a tiger by the tail. I hoped we could hold on.

The first jumbo portal ring sat at a heavy angle from me, but I could still see the brown fog beginning to swirl, the interior darkening, as our portal controller began to gain the upper hand. The enemy portal didn't give up easily, and for thirty seconds, far longer than any portal connection I had ever experienced, the fog swirled, the inner luminosity pulsed irregularly, dark, then lighter, then dark again, in a jerky, sporadic cycle.

Then it pulsed, almost black, and began to clear...

Fire erupted into the hangar, beam weapons sweeping the interior, one piercing the far wall, as air began to scream out the puncture. I felt the pressure lower. My suit compensated, as I slammed the faceplate closed. I could see the upper exhaust open and both inner and outer hangar doors began to rise.

Our beam cannons returned fire, but I could see that two were out of commission. Three fired up, although by that time, pressure had fallen so low I heard nothing, just felt the floor vibrate as it raked the interior of the tunnel with fire.

A Bug fighter careened into the hangar space, flying at an angle. The cannon must have hit it, as it careened in a lightning pirouette, spinning out the open hangar door, and exploding into a thousand fragments as it crashed headlong into the surface. An enormous number of bug soldiers spilled through the entry, firing beam weapons in every directions.

The Marines opened up. I threw myself prone, realizing my head had foolishly been above the barrier. I felt bullets slam into the barrier. Heavy firing of our beam cannons made a bright series of flashes on the hangar roof. I hazarded a peek, to find the enemy fighters down, as our beam cannons continued to fire.

Before I could catch my breath, another fighter streaked through the tunnel, weapons flashing, high enough to miss most of the cannons, but it caught the back one. Torn from its mooring and carrying the entire emplacement with it, the remains of the beam cannon and the entangled fighter crashed through the hangar wall. The roof sagged, and for an awful instant, I was convinced it would collapse on us. The side structure held, merely bowed in the center. Thank God for the low gravity of Ganymede.

None of the Marines had made it into the tunnel, as both enemy beam cannon and small weapons fire continued to pour from the opening. The only thing that saved us was the position of our weapons below the tunnel axis. Martinez voiced a command, now over channel 2. "Launch the bomb. I say again, launch the bomb."

No response. Was the bomb damaged? I chanced another peek as Martinez commanded the launch. I knew where the launch officer had stood. The location was empty. He had been to my left, across two of the barriers, maybe ten meters away. Where was he?

I had to duck or be cut to pieces as more Bugs came through the portal and the Marines returned fire. This time, the attacking sortie was a bit smaller, but they came in fast, spraying beams in every direction. I knew our soldiers couldn't all dodge the assault.

Where was the launch officer? The only way to reduce the onslaught was to get the bomb headed through the portal. If we couldn't stop the raids, our defensive capabilities would erased. Instead of us taking over the enemy site, they would overtake us.

I chanced another look. Three of our beam weapons fired almost continuous blasts into the tunnel. That worried me even more. The lasers that powered the beams heated up quickly. If they didn't get to "rest," they shut down on their own.

I stared at the launch officer location. No sign of him. The IC people had a problem. Most of them were across the hangar, on the other side of the weapons emplacement. McKissack and a few of his fellow officers were on our side, but too far to the left, not able to get close. It struck me that I was nearest to the weapons officer's position.

Oh well, I thought, *you are a full one-star now. Time to call yourself back to duty.*

Bending low, I prepared to race to where I had last seen the guy with the launch control.

At the same instant, thirty more Bug soldiers poured through the portal. The Marines opened fire at them. And at me.

CHAPTER 37 SURPRISE ATTACK

I ate dust as Marine shells whined overhead and ricocheted off the concrete barriers around me. Friendly fire. As the enemy soldiers streamed down the ramp, the choices were defend the hangar or give up. I hoped those near me, including Bobby and Wendy, were safe, but I couldn't be sure we could avoid all the metal being thrown around.

One bullet ricocheted off something higher up and pinged a second time off the barrier directly in front of me, missing me by a hair. I saw reflections of the bright flashes of our beam on the sagging ceiling of the hangar. I heard the faint voice of Martinez in my headphones. "Launch officer, fire the rocket. Report."

No answer. I squirmed around to get a bearing on the last place I had seen him. He was a full lieutenant. He had been holding the remote control device, something like an ordinary TV remote, except with a small screen at the top.

I couldn't see. Too many barricade chunks stood in the way. Bobby crouched a couple of concrete blocks away, his body covering Wendy's as they tried to avoid friendly fire. The firing lessened, but rounds continued to whine overhead and bounce around in the hangar.

Bobby might be closer to the launch officer, but I preferred he keep Wendy safe. My last sight of the commander had him about ten meters away, almost forty-five degrees to port.

I started to crawl, inching my way right, around the nearer end of my protection. I knew another block lay something like man-height away. The coast appeared clear. There being an apparent lull, The enemy foray had ended, temporarily. I crawled left, to the end of the barrier.

Our hiding places were similar to traffic barriers. A good meter and a half tall, they had the same basic cross-section, a modified, narrow trapezoid, three meters long. On Earth, they would weigh well over a thousand pounds, but in Ganymede's gravity, close to two-fifty. The way they were laid out, spaces between barriers on one row were covered by barriers on the next row.

I got to the forward row. Firing started again with a great deal of flack overhead. On my stomach, I moved up another row, and snaked left. I could see two IC personnel lying ahead. I snaked toward them. What would have been a cacophony of noise remained eerily silent, as we now operated in vacuum. One of my legs felt cold and I hoped a heater had not died. With no heat on that limb, it would be subject to frostbite.

As I crawled near the IC officers, I stopped in shock. Blood covered both, already frozen on their vac suits. Both caught several rounds. They had been dead before they knew what hit them.

I noticed I was breathing a good deal harder, although my exertion was minimal so far. In addition, just as on Mars, a trickle of sweat edged down my neck and another across my middle.

Shaking off the feeling of Deja vu, I edged through the space to the next row. The weapons office should be here.

It was deserted. I edged left, to look for the next space, and got another shock. There are no spaces in between. They butted together in a solid row. I realized this row must be the last before the beam weapons and artillery. The launch officer must be inside the barrier, unprotected from friendly fire, God help him, or with with only a single block for protection.

The flying bullets and laser fire seemed to subside. I couldn't hear any gunfire in vacuum, but the constant splashing of concrete dust and blinking light of the beam weapons had made a good warning that the conflict proceeded. Now, all seemed still.

I had to look over the barrier, and that meant exposure to possible fire from the Marine contingent. I hoped they were safe, but as they had been in a serious engagement, there were probably losses. I rose to my knees, watching the ceiling, eyes alert for random bullets bouncing off upper surfaces.

Nothing. I held my breath and raised my head above the edge of the block.

The Marines remained in place, ready and watchful. As I lifted my head, one raised his weapon, but another gestured and it dropped. The beam weapons were the worse for wear, three out of commission and a couple more with damaged personnel pods. Two cannon emplacements appeared operative.

Satisfied I remained relatively safe, I stared left. Sure enough, a single barrier sat about its own length away from me. Behind it, the commander sprawled, his blood-covered body in splayed disarray. It didn't take a Ph.D. in engineering to figure out he was down for the count.

No wonder he had been hit. He had stood at such an angle that the Marine contingent, firing at advancing Bug soldiers, could hardly have managed to miss him if he had been exposed. Holding my breath, I leaped over the barrier and hustled toward the smaller block and its protection.

Just as another enemy foray occurred.

I didn't hear a thing. As I dived toward the edge of the block, I felt a slight shock to my left shoulder and arm. I didn't realize what had happened until I reached the dead officer. A sharp spark of pain had me staring down in surprise at my suit. Blood bubbled out of a small hole. I had taken a hit to my upper left shoulder.

It wasn't necessarily fatal wound, I could see. Except, I was bleeding like crazy, and my vac suit had sprung a dangerous leak. I clamped my right hand over the hole, pressing hard. Could I use my left arm? I could, pain sharp but bearable. The remote lay beside the downed officer. I stretched to reach it, uncovered the hole and felt air escape from my suit. The oxy unit increased flow, but not enough to compensate.

I pulled myself to my knees, cradling the remote in my left hand. Could I trigger the launch mechanism from behind the block? Nothing like experimentation. I uncovered the red guard on the toggle and hit it.

No good. It might be a laser trigger and require direct line-of-sight to the missile to activate. I was going to have to raise up, aim, and hope it worked. It had hit the concrete floor when the commander fell, so that was not a trivial concern.

Lightheaded and dizzy, I force myself to press harder on the perforation of my vac suit. My oxy supply was going to lose the pressure battle, if I didn't get some assistance. I knew there were emergency patches for vac suits, but whether any were available in the hanger was a question with no answer for me.

A sudden shove pushed me further behind the barrier, and onto the dead officer. I looked up as Bobby crowded behind the barrier, trying to shield his extra-large body from fire. "I knew it," he said, "you came after the launch control." He spoke louder. "This is Hays and Taylor of S-Cubed. We have the controller and request launch permission."

A moment's possibly astounded silence was followed by, "Bobby, that you?" It was none other than McKissack.

"Aye, sir. Admiral Hays"—later, I would remember Bobby's reference with humor and satisfaction—" is wounded. We need assistance immediately. Please order all defenders to cease fire as I trigger the launch."

I was grateful Bobby was speaking, as I seemed to be out of breath. McKissack's voice boomed across com. "All defenders, hold fire. I repeat, cease fire regardless of further incursions. Take shelter. I say again, take shelter."

A pregnant pause. Then, "Doctor Taylor, launch the missile."

Bobby stood, and there's a lot of him to stand. Aiming the remote, he toggled the switch.

Another pause. Bobby flattened himself as the hangar remnants flared with brilliance. The ground vibrated to the extent I bobbed up and down. lames licked over the barrier, just not quite able to reach us. Then it was dark and I felt relief. Until I realized I couldn't breathe. Bobby turned to find me gasping. He pressed hard on my shoulder. I tried to say something but failed.

"We need help here," Bobby yelled, and I wondered vaguely if he were hurt too.

People crowded around me. I realized both Martinez and McKissack were in the crowd. I could do nothing but stare. A medic knelt over me and a tech joined him, to put a small patch over the hole in my suit. I wondered if there was a hole in the back of my suit too, but the front patch seemed to alleviate the pressure issue.

No exit wound, I decided. Which meant I had a slug in my body. A souvenir. Poor Kaley. Now she gets to find out I'm hurt again. Or maybe dead. Even as I thought it, the world sailed away in a spiral of gray and black.

CHAPTER 38 RECOVERY

I awoke to find Kaley sitting by the foot of my bed. My bed in what was clearly a hospital. I stared at her a moment. She had been reading, but now dozed, the book in her lap having apparently closed on its own. I shifted to ease my arm and her eyes flew open at the slight sound.

She grab my right hand. "Hey there. How do you feel?"

I felt fine, only a bit of tenderness in my shoulder, and seeming no net damage from my lack of oxygen. My mouth, however, was parched as the desert.

"Thirsty," I rasped.

"Goodness." She grabbed a sippy cup compete with straw and lid, filled it from a small water and ice pitcher. She hesitated. "Do you need help?"

"No," I croaked, " Just hand it to me."

She raised the bed to a slant so I could sip without spilling or choking. The water tasted like champagne.

I took my time, sipping until a good half of the cup was empty.

I looked around. The hospital room appeared quite decent. A single; I had no roommate. A large TV, now off, a row of windows that looked out onto a sunny lawn about two stories down, every surface covered with flower arrangements. I handed the cup back.

"Where am I?"

"The IC hospital facility at headquarters in Fort Worth. You've been here a couple of days."

Astonished, I muttered, "Two days?"

She assumed what I referred to as her "nagging wife face." "You big doofus, do you know how badly you were hurt?"

"It wasn't that bad."

"Are you kidding me? You had a nicked artery in your shoulder, you lost half your air. The surgeon who fixed you up told me he was surprised you got here in time"

"Hey, all's well that ends well."

She gave me her super exasperated stare. "Boy, I can't wait until we're married. The next time you go off and get yourself killed, I'll inherit a jillion bucks and be wealthy for life."

I grinned at her, not my best grin as I still felt more than just a little weak, no matter what I'd just told her. "Think what a great catch you'll be for some fortune hunter."

"For some—" She choked up, tears streaming down her face. "You son of a bitch. Do you think I'd really last a week if something happened..." She launched herself, just like the missile, at my bed, covering my right side, bawling, kissing, and wetting my face with her tears.

I managed to work my right arm around her, the left one bandaged and also tied to an IV. I whispered I loved her and I was sorry and this was the last, the very last time I would risk my life for either IC or the company. She quieted and simply lay, face against my neck, kissing me now and again.

"Admiral Hays..." A nurse bustled in and came to an abrupt stop. Kaley managed to push herself off me, wiped her face with her hands.

"He woke up," she announced .

"So, I see. We have visitors to see you and inquire about him. Let me see." She came around the bed and took my hand, checking my pulse and blood pressure.

"You look much better . The Ganymede emergency surgeon insisted we keep you under until we could get you here and run some tests. Those blood transfusions really helped. How do you feel?"

"When can I leave?" I asked.

She snickered. "Don't rush it. Doctor Carter will check you over tomorrow morning. It's up to him. You've responded well."

She turned toward the door. "The visitors. Would you like to see them?"

I felt weak, but good too, all things considered. "Sure. The more the merrier."

She returned with Bobby, Bets, Virgil, Wendy, and Ray. "Five minutes, then everybody out."

They crowded in and Wendy, bless her, said just what I would have expected. "Hey Lazy Bones, when are you going to quit flaking off and get back to work?"

I managed what I considered a decent comeback. "Why bother? Virgil can run the show and you two are making all the cool discoveries with Bobby. I'll just take it easy with Kaley and watch old movies."

Everybody laughed. It occurred to me to ask, "What about the Bug site? Did we clobber it?"

Bobby grinned. "Got it. McKissack said he'll come by in an hour or so with good news."

I assumed Bobby meant a full report. His words relaxed me. It had been a close call. Bobby's worry about the relative size of the portals hadn't been an issue, but no one expected the ferocity of the counterattack when we connected our portal to theirs. I assumed they had learned from the destruction of their portals earlier and had been prepared for just about anything.

"Seriously," he told me, " Take it easy, maybe a couple of weeks. Kaley's taking you to her house for plenty of TLC. Go rest, relax, and let the pros handle the workload at S-Cubed."

"For sure," Bets chimed in. "I've been looking to impress Virgil so I can get a big raise. This is the perfect excuse to keep Kaley out of my way."

"Yeah, good luck with that," Kaley shot back. "If he gives you that raise, you'll never have any time to spend it, just like me." Which got another laugh.

We had a good-natured few minutes, then Bobby said, "Buddy, you're fading. Time for a nap. We need to get out of here."

The rest muttered in agreement. "Nonsense," I told them. "I'm fine and I don't need any more rest. What I need is to get out of this bed and walk around."

"Oh no," Virgil chided me. "I bribed the doc. You're staying where you are for now."

They began to edge out, with plenty of "get well's" and "take care's" as they left. Kaley and I were alone.

"How about another kiss?" I asked.

"Sure, just let me run down to the restroom, and then you can have my undivided attention."

I didn't realize it, but her move was a ruse. By the time she returned, I had drifted off, just as I am sure she planned.

I roused to find McKissack in the room. He and Kaley were whispering, but I said distinctly, "You guys cut it out. I need to stay awake, not doze the day away. To my astonishment, the sun had set outside our windows and dusk spread across the base. Kaley looked a bit guilty, but McKissack smiled and came alongside the bed.

"So, Admiral, how do you feel?"

"Fine and will you cut out the 'Admiral' stuff? I know it was just a courtesy appointment."

"Baloney. I reactivated you before you went off-world. You are a member in good standing of IC, and as one of my direct reports, I hereby order you to take it easy for two weeks. You are to return here via portal one week after being released for an additional medical examination, and again for a final one in three weeks. As you are a full member of the military, wounded in an enemy engagement, all expenses will be covered by IC insurance. Not that you don't have pretty good insurance on your own."

I was back in IC a third time. "And when," I asked, "Do I get sprung back to civilian life?"

"As soon as you are medically cleared. Cheer up, Admiral. Take it easy on the government's dime for the next couple weeks."

I suspected he was enjoying himself, being my boss for the time being, and nothing I could do about it. Nothing but let him have his fun.

I changed the subject. "Bobby said you have good news ."

"I do indeed. I'm glad he didn't spoil my surprise." He looked satisfied. "Two things. First, not only did we pacify the China Bug Portal site, but a second one too, only a few kilometers away. In addition, the Russians clobbered the last site in their county an hour later. So far as we can determine, after two full days of satellite surveillance world-wide, there are no indications of any Bug activity on the globe.

"Further, with the destruction of the two bug bases on Mars, it is cleared, and we have found no other Bug activity on the out-worlds. The solar system, I am happy to tell you, is Bug-free."

I breathed out a large sigh. "Thank God."

"Yeah. I think the Russians learned a big lesson. Russia and China have agreed, with enthusiasm, to fully participate in the worldwide governance of the World Portal Authority, meaning one hundred percent of all portal activity is regulated. Our portals just became a lot safer."

He beamed at me. "The second item. I requested a specific decoration of valor for your heroic action on Ganymede."

"Now wait a minute," I put in. "I've been out of IC for years and you only made me an Admiral so you could boss me around."

He stopped me. "Bullshit. You performed heroically in two battles already. I got tired of telling you there were no civilian awards for valor. The next time I pushed you in to dangerous duty, I made sure you were covered. I refuse to let your outstanding actions go unnoticed again. You're a Goddam admiral and shut up about it. I wanted to put you up for the Medal of Honor. You retrieved the launch control. You had help from your pal, but you did the heavy lifting .

"The CNO agreed up to a point, but he observed that since you were someone out of service, brought back under special circumstances, the award might cause some concern." He sighed and looked out the window for a moment. He suggested the Silver Star, but I'd done that for you and Overton, given your service on Mars. We compromised on the IC Cross. You get it whether you want it or not. No arguments. That's an order."

We stared at each other.

I more or less mentally shrugged and told him, "Of course, I'll accept it and be damn proud of it. I'm just not sure I deserve it."

"Comment noted but ignored. As the IC Cross is a high award, it will be presented at a formal service, to be scheduled when you're back on your feet. Maybe a month or two. I've been following that business with Kaley and your ex-wife. I know you want to get that cleared up first." He swung a gaze to her. She had been quiet as a mouse the entire time, but now she hugged him.

"You a pretty nice guy, Admiral. I thought all you top brass were stuffed shirts."

He grinned. "Some of us are tolerable. And it's Kinsey, by the way. None of that title crap between you and me."

She kissed his cheek. Kaley has always been a hugger and kisser, but the admiral was caught off guard and turned a becoming shade of pink.

"Gotta get back," he said. "Got a pile of work before I leave for the day."

To my eternal bewilderment, he stood at attention and saluted me. "My congratulations and best wishes, Admiral. It has been, and will continue to be, my pleasure to serve our nation with you." He did an about-face and exited, stage right.

Kaley and I exchanged wondering glances. "I meant what I said," she murmured. "I like him a lot."

"Me too. Now give me a kiss. I think I might take another nap."

"When you're up and around, and this Glynnis load is off my back, we're getting hitched, boss. Squirm all you want, I got you where I want you."

I grinned back as she stood. "You've had me where you wanted me for quite a while. We don't even have to wait to clear things up if you want."

"No. I want my life free and clear when we start ours together."

I yawned. "Have it your way. Now I think I'll..."

I lost my train of thought, drifting away.

CHAPTER 39 FINALLY, VINDICATION

After a week at Kaley's home, I felt ready to face the world. I walked into the doctor's office at IC headquarters, submitted to a full examination, and heard him give the opinion I was well on the way to a full recovery.

I nodded, smiled, shook his hand, took Kaley's, and we boarded the headquarters portal for the SSS lab. There, we stopped just long enough to say "hi" to everyone, and went home.

Home. I was surprised to find Kaley's house now felt like my own. Guy had notified me that we had a potential buyer for mine and when did I want move out? I told him immediately, and that all I wanted was a desk, my computer, books, and a few mementoes. Other than that, he could sell it "as-is."

We settled in, read a lot and watched my favorite entertainment, old black and white movies . I relived the glories of *The Big Sleep*, *The Maltese Falcon*, *Lady in the Lake*, and other noire favorites. We marveled over the music of *Oklahoma!*, *South Pacific*, *Mama Mia*, and *Phantom of the Opera*. True, the last couple were only maybe fifty years old, but they were still favorites.

Another week went by, and I started to get restless. You can only sit on a sofa so many hours a day, even when you're healing, before you get antsy. And that's especially if you're a couple like us who travel the solar system regularly. I suspected Kaley felt the same way. On Sunday, April 14th, sixteen days after I awakened in the IC hospital, I accompanied Kaley to church, took her out to eat at a fancy French restaurant in the evening, and announced as we each took our side of the bed, "Tomorrow, we start a regular routine."

"You mean back to S-Cubed?"

"No, I'd love to, and I know you would too, but we have unfinished business. Let's talk about it over coffee in the morning."

"I don't know what we can do that the authorities haven't," Kaley told me. "We checked with Guy and his staff every day last week, and nothing new."

I had pored over the situation in my mind for days now. I am not, and will never be, the fanatical analyst Bobby is, but I mimicked his grinding process, going over and over all the facts. I treated each issue like an onion, peeling back distinctive layers trying to uncover any new salient information. I had a few ideas to go over in detail with Kaley, and maybe Bobby.

Sitting at the breakfast table with unfinished eggs, coffee and sausage that had gotten cold, I called Guy. He was on a call, but I waited impatiently until he was free, which took seventeen minutes and forty-two seconds, according to my feverish count.

"You got any time today?" I asked.

"For you, spending so outlandishly that my retirement is guaranteed, of course."

"I'm happy to be providing for your old and feeble age. I want to talk to the detective, the operative who is directing the Kaley operation."

"Rather than him, you need to talk to the senior PI. I'll have to check their schedule. When are you available?"

"At your summons. The earlier the better."

"I'll get back to you." He hung up.

He got back in only ten minutes. "Ten-thirty. Can you make it?"

It was already nine, as we had slept in. "Of course. Bye."

I stood. "We gotta leave in thirty minutes."

"Jesus, I haven't even done my hair, let alone my face."

She fled. I picked up the plates, stuffed leftovers in her huge fridge, and went to dress. I had relocated a lot of my clothing and stashed it in a guest room closet, so fresh clothing was no problem. I had only a small bandage on my upper left shoulder, and my movement, with a few twinges, had returned to an almost normal range.

I could finally dress myself, had been able to for the last couple of days. Donning Chinos, a nice Pima cotton shirt, and my normal suede loafers, I was ready far sooner than Kaley, who had to do all those girl things. Without makeup, she looked ravishing to me, but she aimed to satisfy herself.

It took her forty minutes, but as they say, who's counting? Five-sixths of an hour would be plenty to get across town, since rush hour had played out. We took her car, a five-year-old Lexus mini-SUV that still had plenty of comfort and style, and to be honest a better auto-drive system than my car.

On the way in, I called Bobby, who was pounding out revised code for the experimental unit our project team had put together. "How're you doing?" he asked.

"Great. I need a favor. Could you be free early this afternoon?"

He considered in silence. "I was going to run to Mars to help Bets with a minor problem."

"Send Thuan. I need you."

No hesitation. "You got it. Who do I have to kill?"

"Hah. Meet me at my old house, the one I'm selling."

"You're selling the house?" He thought about that. "I guess it makes sense. Too many bad memories, right?"

"Right. See you there at three. Then food's on me at Billie Lou's."

"Can't miss that." We hung up.

Guy was prepared for us. One of the detective agency's senior operatives, a tall, gray-haired female who topped Kaley by two inches, appeared more like a corporate CEO than a PI, sat in a chair in front of Guy's desk.

Guy introduced us. "Madeleine Middleton, Carol Sellers and Charles Hays. They go my Kaley and Scotty."

She nodded, shook hands. "Kaley, Scotty. Call me Maddy. Guy said you had serious issues to discuss."

We sat, settling back, and Claire arrived with coffee and pastries. After a bit of fuddling with plates and coffee, I said, "I do have a thing or two to discuss. First, I'd like to get a status update."

She complied, in a strong alto voice that was, unfortunately, a bit reminiscent of Glynnis, though more steely. Fundamentally, there had been no more progress. The DeSoto Police and the county DA's office seemed loathe to move, given the oddities of the case, and Kaley's record as a solid citizen. Maddy did say the police spent hundreds of hours on Kaley's background. Not a single item had been found in Kaley's background to show motive or intent.

Kaley and I digested that for a moment when she finished.

"Okay," I started out. "First of all, my thanks for your exceptional work, especially finding the credit card. Second, I do not want to sound like I'm complaining or dissatisfied with your results but I need to ask. After you found the card in Glynnis's car, did you search further?"

I had to give her credit. She didn't seem upset or insulted. "I sent two operatives who I trust. After they found the credit card, they poked and pried around more, but they agreed going any further at that point wouldn't yield additional results."

Certainly reasonable. Today, however, I did not want to be the slightest bit reasonable. "Could you get access to the car again?"

"I think so. Far as I know, it's still in the impound lot. Your former wife had no close relatives, and if a will has been discovered, we haven't been notified. A search was made of her home, and a safety deposit box, quite a large one, was opened. A collection of expensive jewelry was found, but no will."

"Have you talked to her lawyers, the ones she used for our divorce ?"

The senior PI thought. "No, not so far as I know."

"Okay," I turned to Guy, "That's something you might follow up on."

I turned back to Middleton. "There is something else I want you and your crew to do, as soon as possible. Get access to the car again. Send your best operatives, as many as you want, but I want you to go too. Take that car apart. Take out all the carpeting, don't just poke around the edges. Remove the trunk carpet and padding, check in the spare tire wheel well, remove the inner door coverings. I mean, I want you to do everything but take the car down to its component parts, and maybe that too. It's an electric, so check the motor compartment, even the battery access. Okay?"

Her brows rose slightly, Kaley's too. Guy's face showed he was intrigued. After a moment, she nodded. Nothing seemed to surprise her very much and I could understand. As a PI with extensive experience, little would surprise her.

"You got it," she said. She addressed both Guy and me. "Do I report to you or Guy?"

"In this case, because I have a hunch and want to pursue it, call me first. Then call Guy." I cast a glance at my friend and legal eagle. "Okay with you?"

"Sure." He shifted his gaze to her. "But let me know ASAP after you inform Scotty."

Maddy gave me another inquiring look. "What are we looking for?"

I grinned. "You'll know it when you see it."

We discussed tactics and overall manpower. She didn't want to add resources without an okay but asked for a free hand in doing the search. "The more bodies in a treasure hunt," she remarked, "The faster and more thoroughly the job is done."

"Hell, turn your whole agency loose on it if you wish. I take that back. Use as many guys as you can who are top-notch and can contribute. Tell the boss, what's his name, Abernathy. I want every available body who can help."

"Got it." She looked at Guy. "I've got all I need. The sooner I start, the faster we're through."

He made a brush-off gesture with his right hand. "What the hell are you waiting for?"

She stood, nodded to the two of us in the client chairs, and slipped away.

"She looks competent," I said.

"Yeah, and a lot more." He elevated himself. "You guys get out of here. You've screwed up today's entire schedule."

"I feel certain your invoice will reflect that," I told him.

"Nah. I've billed you so many hours the last three weeks, I feel guilty adding to the total."

"Don't let your partners know. They'll petition to have you declared incompetent."

He waved us off with a smile.

As Triple-S was on the way home, we stopped off to say hi to the gang and got lots of hugs from everyone. Mary even kissed me on the cheek. We made our way to the joint Bobby-Scotty office. He was pounding his keyboard into submission with an attitude of fierce concentration. I suspected he was grinding as well although I could only guess at the possible problem.

"We got done early," I said. "So instead of at three, follow us over to my house now, okay?"

"I haven't had lunch."

"Do my errand, and then we can hit Billie Lou's early. You can have two giant chili burgers and a triple order of jalapeno poppers."

He frowned. "Okay, if I must. Let me grab a candy bar from the vending machine."

He took his own car, the Porsche SUV he'd modified to accommodate his outlandish long legs. My house wasn't more than fifteen minutes from the office. We parked in front, as I refused to enter the garage ever again. I let us in. Without stopping I led the way to the room where Glynnis had breathed her last.

The room, still empty, seemed sinister to me, and I thought I still detected a sharp tang of vomit in the stale air.

"This is the death room?" Bobby asked.

"Yeah," came from Kaley.

He sized it up a second time. "No wonder you want to sell," He shivered. "Place gives me the creeps."

It did me too. I shoved those thoughts aside. "So, here's what we're going to do. We're going to take this room apart, top to bottom, stem to stern, inside and out. We're looking for anything that could shed light on Glynnis's death.

"I do not believe Glynnis committed suicide. Such a thing was simply not in her character. I think she meant it to *appear* to be attempted murder, taking only enough of the medication to induce some serious symptoms. Somehow or other, she managed to kill herself in the process, but she never meant to, I'm positive. I think we can prove it."

Bobby nodded once. "Okay, let's do it."

We took the dresser apart, turned it upside-down and searched both the back and the mirror. I had a tool box in the garage, so I sent Bobby for them. I couldn't make myself go in there. Yes, no actual violence had taken place there, but I would forever have the picture in my mind of the DeSoto PD removing boxes of evidence from its interior. We the drawers from the body of the dresser cabinet, all empty, looking under the bottom of each. Result: nothing.

We repeated the disassembly exercise on the bedside table. Two chairs, a straight one, and a rocker, got the same treatment, even to pulling off the padding from the chair seats. We tried to pull up the carpet edges all along the walls, but they seemed well-attached with no sign of an attempt to hide anything. Result: still nothing.

That left the bed. "We take it apart," I directed. "Everything."

We did. Mattress and box springs removed, we went over them inch by inch. Any small slit in the coverings? Anything taped to the bottoms? No. We disassembled the bed itself, taking apart the headboard and footboard, searching for anything. No soap.

Finally came the steel underpinnings of the box springs, examining the undersides.

"Odd." Bobby was staring at one of the bed side rails.

"What?"

He pointed. "Look here. Not paper, but there's a piece of clear tape pasted on the underside of this rail."

I examined it, taking a minute to return to the den for a magnifying glass I kept in a drawer. Clear plastic tape, all right. I took another look.

"Give me a minute."

I also kept a jeweler's loupe in my old office. I got it, returned, put it on, and toggled the light. Fortunately, the batteries were still usable and the bright LED's gave a good light. I took a close look. Could that be...?

"Call the DeSoto police," I directed.

It took three hours. The officers wasted no time getting to the house, retrieved the rail, and took it with them. I mentioned what I found. The three of us said we would testify to finding and not touching the tape at all.

We left the house with the police, having extracted a promise from them to call as soon as they had results. Kaley, Bobby and I then proceeded to Billie Lou's where we celebrated Bobby's find, still not knowing how meaningful it might be, although I had a strong feeling it would break the case.

Bobby outdid himself with two chili burgers, double poppers, large fries, and a malt, with two cokes to top it off. Too tense to eat very much, I forced a burger down while Kaley nibbled a grilled chicken sandwich. We took bobby back to work, as it was only about six, and he normally worked much later.

We had just gotten to Kaley's when my personal sounded, a call from DeSoto PD. I answered to find Lieutenant Grissom on the other end. "Doctor Hays?"

"Yes. I hope you've got good news."

"Very good news. Our lab identified several fingerprints on the outer, non-adhesive side of the tape. A total of six prints, some overlapping, but very identifiable as your ex-wife's. It took some careful work, but we were able to remove it safely from the bed rail.

"There was a single, partial print on the underside. It's a partial print identified as Kaley's, and it matches the partial on the medicine bottle."

"Thank God."

"It's clear proof your ex-wife planted Ms. Sellers' print on the bottle. This will be enough to clear your fiancé."

We hung up, I grabbed Kaley, told her, and hugged her tight. We'd only had enough time to sit on the den sofa when PI Middleton called.

"Scotty? Great news. Under the padding in the trunk, we found a treasure trove. I guarantee you Kaley is free and clear."

She told me a little, reserving the rest until later, saying they took photos of the entire set of papers and she would make sure the police cleared our getting copies soon. I hugged and kissed Kaley again and told her, "They found what I suspected. With the discovery, plus the tape ono the bed rail, you are cleared, I guarantee."

She hugged me back and began to cry. I held her for a long time.

CHAPTER 40 FINALLY, MARRIED

"Enough is enough," I declared. "We're getting married. Now."

A week had passed, Kaley had been exonerated, and the MD's at IC cleared me to return to work, not that I hadn't done as I pleased for the last two weeks. The transparent tape, with Glynnis's fingerprints on the outer surface, and Kaley's one semi-complete partial on the adhesive surface, had pretty much cinched the deal. I think the DA would have dropped all charges based on that one piece of evidence.

The papers found cleverly hidden beneath the rear pads in the trunk of Glynnis's car, had been so much icing on the cake. They spelled out the following:

Glynnis' speculation how to worm her way into Kaley's confidence.

Specific plans to fake an attempted murder, while at my house, using the new drug she had identified.

Notes on stealing Kaley's credit card to buy the medicine.

A description of how she captured the partial from Kaley, planted it on the medicine bottle, and put it in my garage.

And finally, careful calculations of the medicine required to cause illness but not death. Showing, clearly, her miscalculations of the amount.

She had used a "standard" amount for a healthy man weighing one hundred sixty pounds. Not a female who tipped the scales at about one-ten.

It had been a close thing, and Glynnis might still have survived. Unfortunately for her, she had more than likely taken the medicine, waited to feel bodily distress, and then called the police. She had been gone by the time they arrived.

So dear psychopath Glynnis had finally vacated my life. I tried to feel a bit of sympathy for my departed ex-partner, but found it difficult.

Kaley didn't put up much of a fight this time. One thing she insisted on. "I want a church wedding. I don't want to get married in some justice of the peace office."

I whined. "That could take months to arrange."

"No it won't. Cut me loose, don't spare the horses, and I'll take care of it."

We were seated in her family room, after breakfast, where I had thrown my demand down.

"We don't have any horses. If you mean money, fine. How soon can it happen?"

"The bride's family pays."

"That's in a first marriage. I can spare some change to get hitched."

"Baloney. I'm paying. I know you'd pay for everything, given the chance. But it's my wedding, and I want to do it my way and pay for it."

I gave up. Arguing with Kaley was strenuous. I wanted to be able to pick my fights, and this one could never be won. "Fine. I insist on paying for the dinner after the wedding."

"Deal. I want it to be in my church's social hall, catered by Billie Lou's."

"You're kidding."

"Does this face look like I'm kidding? I want their great burgers, sweet potato fries, and those amazing fried pies his wife makes instead of a wedding cake."

"Somebody else makes them now, but they're still spectacular. Okay."

" One more thing. I want lots of really great beer, wine, and expensive champagne. Alex knows about wine and champagne. Tell him I want the best."

Alex liked good booze and had a surprisingly large beer and ale collection for a diner. He catered events, so he'd access to a variety of products of the grape. I started to add I needed my whiskey too, but decided this was Kaley's bash, We'd go with her choice of booze this time.

"So, when is the day?"

"Not sure. I can get it together faster than you think. Alex has to be available to cater."

She shocked me by reserving her church sanctuary for the following Thursday. Alex and his crew could make it, though he'd have to add extra help. No time for fancy invitations, but we got some quite nice, engraved-looking ones made up, and put together an outlandish list of nearly four hundred attendees.

Alex was excited when I gave him free rein with the alcohol budget, telling him Kaley wanted "the best and only the best." I wondered if she had any idea what a monster we'd created.

Kaley left it up to me to distribute the invites. I did. There was a general invitation at work. Virgil promised anyone who wanted to attend could have Thursday and Friday as paid days off. Word went out to all SSS sites, warning of our inability to service calls for 36 hours, barring a life-and-death situation. I delivered invitations to McKissack and Overton personally, running over to IC headquarters via porta, telling them I wasn't sure they had time, but they were welcome. I was glad to see Overton's leg seemed to be well healed. Maybe he'd dance with my bride.

The two were in a meeting when I arrived. McKissack grunted and said he'd be there unless another world war was declared. Overton declared loudly that there was no effing way he'd miss it, so I took my leave. They took care of delivering invitations to any number of other IC personnel we knew, including Mars site commander Captain Alford, Captain Martinez from Ganymede, and Captain McCall from Rhea battle, plus the medical folks who had attended me.

I dropped by Kaley's church with a general invitation to the congregation, as Kaley had many friends among them. A printed invitation went into their church paper on Sunday before the wedding. All in all, we ended up with closer to five hundred than four hundred invited, given the blanket invitations at church and office, including plus-ones. I figured we'd be lucky if even half of them showed up.

Came the day, and the church sanctuary, which easily held eight hundred, was SRO. Where everyone came from, I don't know. They seemed to creep out of the woodwork like cockroaches. Or, given my recently-developed aversion to expressions involving insects, like so many mice.

My mom passed away years ago, but Dad, who lived near Columbia, attended, to my surprise and pleasure. Kaley's parents came up from Florida, and a sister as well, plus her two kids from the coasts. Bobby stood up for me looking very striking but uncomfortable in his X-X-X-Tall formal wear, and to my surprise, Bets had the role of Maid of Honor in a lush pink chiffon.

Kaley stood out in a simple, cream silk wedding dress, with a high collar and very little embroidery. On her it made a stunning impression, and I made a bet with myself that a lot of twenty-year-old's in the crowd wished that they could look that lavish and beautiful on their wedding day.

Kaley's minister offered a simple service. After exchanging old-fashioned "love, honor, and cherish" vows, we were pronounced fully legal. I kissed my bride, who had tears in her eyes but a smile on her face.

We laughed, ate, and drank the night away. Alex chartered a small combo that played "old people music," as he put it, so we danced as well. The wine and champagne were nonpareil, the beer and a pair of ales fantastic. I was sure my bill would be astronomical. I was right. The champagne alone ran to forty-five thousand dollars. What the hell, I hadn't spent anything much since I bought the house. With it sold for more than seven million, I could take the booze bill out of my profits.

At last, we found ourselves down to family, which of course, included Bets, Bobby and Virgil, who were dating, plus my dad and Kaley's folks, who were getting along quite well. I spent some time with Kaley's parents. After half an hour talking to her mother, I had a much better understanding of where Kaley got her personality. The apple doesn't fall far from the tree. In Kaley's case, that was a good thing.

We had decided that we would spend the night at the Ritz, paying for rooms for everyone. Bobby and Virgil declined, and Bets had an early trip to Mars, so soon after they left, we departed for downtown Dallas.

The Ritz made check in easy. In the bridal suite, we sat on the sofa, with the room lights out and our window curtains open, to stare at the brilliantly illuminated downtown buildings.

"Finally," I observed. "It took a helluva lot of work to get you down the aisle."

"I'm worth it."

"True. I hope you're well rested."

" I slept extra the last two nights. I'm holding you to that promise you made. Let's see if you can keep up with me when I'm rarin' to go."

"Hah."

"I've read most men can't perform but once or twice a night. I hope you can do better than that."

"Listen, you. I know about 'having sex,' and I know about 'making love.' Tonight, I am going to make love to the woman who taught me what real, honest love is. You worry about your stamina. I'll worry about mine."

For answer, she kissed me. "What a wonderful, carefree night to love and be loved. With the Bug menace over, the world quiet, and no worries for us at all."

"Yeah, until the next emergency. Don't worry, my dear, our life is never, ever gonna be humdrum."

"Oh, I know. For now, for a little, teeny slot of time, the world is at rest, we are at peace, and there isn't an emergency we have to attend to. For tonight, neither of us has to save the world."

I took her hand, kissed it. She had soft, slender fingers for someone who used wrenches, screwdrivers, and test equipment as often as she did. " I'm about through saving the world. For good. It's a lot of trouble, and the medal they give you afterward isn't worth a hell of a lot if you get dead."

"I hope you mean that."

"Cross my heart."

"Good. I'm tired of having a near heart attack when you rush off to Ganymede or someplace at McKissack's beck and call."

"Hey, I'm an admiral now. We admirals sit behind a desk."

She made a rude noise. "You hate every instant behind a desk."

I kissed her fingers, then her cheek. "Keep me busy in the bedroom and I'll be too tired to go anywhere."

She returned the kiss, made it longer. "When are we going to get this show on the road, Bucko? Do I have to patrol the hall looking for lovers or do you begin to put out?"

I stood, took her hand and led her to the bed.

I kept my promise, though I must say Kaley's ferocious response was a revelation. We slept very little.

I awoke to full sunshine streaming in the southeast window of our suite. Kaley slept on. Looking at her face in repose, an odd thought struck me. After a night with Glynnis, I had awakened to no particular feeling at all except boredom. After the night with Kaley, I felt an enormous rush of love and thanksgiving that our life together was only starting. She stirred a level of emotion and affection which I had never imagined.

I lay quietly beside her, memorizing the curves and contours of her face, until she woke.

CHAPTER 41 THE BIG "WOW"

We'd only been back in the office for a couple of days when Bobby told me, "You have to come out to the university. Wendy, Ray, and I had a couple of great ideas. I promise you it's going to be a game changer in terms of space exploration."

He'd blown into the office, fresh from exercise and a shower, and was uncharacteristically talkative. His seeing Virgil, and I still felt too timid to ask how serious a romance was in the works, had given him more confidence. He seemed less timid, more settled, and his low moods were less frequent.

"When?" I asked.

"Early this afternoon. Kaley gets back tonight, right?"

Kaley was on an outer-loop round trip, first Io, then Rhea and back to moon Delta, our original portal installation. She assured me none of the problems were major, and she thought all could be attended to in one shift. Bets was on her own trip, and so Kaley had taken Kyle along.

"Far as I know. Let's take an early lunch, then head over to the university. Did you get a specific time?"

"No, but Wendy and Ray both have three o'clock classes. Ray has a night class as well, so I'd say one-thirty. We can be done before three. By the way, I feel like Mexican food."

We took off at eleven fifteen, hit Ojeda's for lunch, and were across town by twelve-thirty.

Wendy met us in the lab, beautiful, red-haired, and full of energy. She kissed us both but held on to me extra-long. "Last time I saw you, you were not in the best shape," she said.

"You saw me at the wedding."

"Yeah, but we kept our distance, except for the receiving line. You had so many Triple-S folks there, plus your families, and the people from Kaley's church. It was quite a crowd."

I gave her my most confident grin. "With respect to the Ganymede incident, I'm fine, fully healed. Martinez tells me Ganymede Beta is fully operational, and the jumbo's running fine. He said he's not volunteering Ganymede as the site for any more attacks, it's time Io took a turn."

Ray joined us, saying hi, "I had a couple of our grad students work most of the night. The new controls appear to be fully activated and the accuracy—well, you be the judge."

He turned on the power supplies, readied controls, and prepared to initiate the field sequence.

"Bring up the fields," Wendy told Bobby.

As he headed toward the control panel, I said, "Whoa. This thing's supposed to be in a vacuum bottle, right? If you open a wormhole to vacuum, it'll suck us all through."

Ray grinned. "Tell him, Bobby, it's your baby."

I turned toward my tall friend. His grin was wider than Ray's. "New invention. Don't need to worry anymore. Look at the near portal."

I stared at the inner ring. It had changed, oddly the same and yet different. It was thicker but that wasn't it. There appeared to be two rings, separated by no more than a millimeter or two, with separate controls and power lines.

I asked the question with my eyes. Bobby laughed. "I know what you're thinking. What the heck's the second ring for? It's not really a second ring. I call it a compound ring, one that completes the wormhole, but extends a shading field over the end of the tunnel, a membrane, very strong but somewhat flexible, that shuts off the vacuum completely."

"What if it fails, for God's sake?"

"That's the beauty of it. The only way it fails is for the wormhole to die. Then the vacuum disappears. It's foolproof."

I wasn't sure I believed "foolproof," but Bobby seemed convinced, and he *is* the genius.

"It eliminates the need to fire up the portal in a vacuum," Wendy said. "It turns the end of the wormhole in upon itself. Only Bobby could possibly figure it out. The math is both complex and subtle."

I believed it. I understood portal theory on a fundamental level, but there were tricky ins and outs to the basic equations. Bobby could explain them and I'd understand. Tackling them on my own? Forget it.

"Ready," he announced.

I watched as he set the cross field levels, adjusted the FlucGen, and initiated the portal. Sure enough, the interior fogged, faded, and revealed a dark star scene. I had to bend forward to stare down the small tunnel. Bigger than the previous arrangement, the portals were barely a meter in diameter, still a test bed rather than a full travel portal, although almost double the size of our original test device.

Bobby joined me, an odd remote control in his hand. Two chairs were arranged so we could sit and stare into the tunnel. Wendy and Ray stood beside us.

"There are things we know and things we're still trying to work out," Bobby said. "For example, I have no idea of the exact location of the other end of the portal. I am able to get hints about the location. In this case, that's beside the point. Now to the new things we can do."

He grabbed the rotary control on the remote. "This dial controls the amplitude of the FlucGen power via the control computer. Watch as I increase it slightly."

He adjusted the dial. The scene rotated slowly to the right, starboard, if you will. We had not changed the location, that is, the point of perspective, but it now focused on an adjacent view.

"That's amazing. You can remain in place while you examine the view from a fixed point."

"Yeah." He sounded satisfied and proud. "But wait, there's more, as they say in the TV ads."

He changed to a linear control he moved up and down. As he moved it up, the scene before us began to rush forward. We still looked in the same direction, but the scene came to us, rather like using the zoom lens on a camera. One giant blue star, which had been centered in the background, came toward us as other celestial sights rushed past .

Gradually, the star became more than a point of light, a small disk still centered. Bobby pointed to it and to its left. "Do you see the areas of dust and condensate? Planets are forming. We could explore them with this portal.

"Something else. As I said, I've no idea, yet, where that star lies. I can tell you, from experiments so far, it's in our Milky Way, about ten thousand light years away. We're not done yet. I've noted the exact readings to show this star, at this viewpoint. If I set those exact values tomorrow, we'll see this same viewpoint."

I breathed out. "It's repeatable."

"Very. We learn more about adjustments every time we use fine-grained control. Within a short time, a couple years at most or less than a year if we're lucky, we'll be able to dial up any place and go there with a single portal. Another thing, although it has to be initiated when no other portal is starting up, Once established, it's as stable and immune from interruption as a two-portal wormhole. It's solid as a rock"

I sat back, taking the revelation in. Bobby, Wendy, Ray, Thuan, and the rest of the team had taken a giant leap in wormhole travel, one as big or bigger than when Bobby and I had made the first portal-to-portal tunnel.

The three of them watched for my reaction. "I'm awed," I said.

"It's your discovery as much as ours," Ray declared. "You insisted we set up this project team when Bobby and the rest of us were doubtful. It would never have happened if you hadn't pounded the table and insisted."

"I never pounded the table. Not once."

Wendy punched my shoulder from behind, fortunately not the injured one. "You did. You knew something was there, something we didn't understand, and you were determined to figure it out. That led to today."

Bobby patted the good shoulder too. "He'll never take credit. He tried to tell the military it was all my doing when he found the missile remote control and nearly got his ass shot off. Yeah, I got to push the button but he had it in hand. It's just his way."

I continued to marvel. Ray said, "We're about to be late to class." I hadn't realized so much time had passed.

We said goodbyes and headed across town in thickening traffic as the afternoon rush hour came on. The day, sunny and bright, felt buoyant and full of promise. Bobby continued to discuss the discovery. I understood ten percent of it but let him talk. I wondered how soon we could begin to explore new worlds, feeling it would be sooner rather than later.

I attended to office chores for a couple of hours as Bobby pounded the keys. Having received a call Kaley would be home, but a bit late, I left for the house near dusk.

I had the lights on, table set, and delivery pizza in the oven, a nice Rosé chilled in the refrigerator when she walked in the door. She rushed over to give me a long hug and a kiss.

She stared . "You seem excited. I know you're glad to see me, but it's something else."

She knew me well.

"Bobby showed me something amazing today. While we eat, let me tell you about it."

Made in the USA
Columbia, SC
03 November 2021